THE
GHOUL OF
WINDYDOWN
VALE

THE GHOUL of WINDYDOWN VALE

JAKE BURT

FEIWEL AND FRIENDS
New York

For Theo and Ruthann

A Feiwel and Friends Book
An imprint of Macmillan Publishing Group, LLC
120 Broadway, New York, NY 10271 • mackids.com

Text copyright © 2021 by Jake Burt. Title page illustration copyright © 2021
by Brian Miller. All rights reserved.

Our books may be purchased in bulk for promotional, educational, or business
use. Please contact your local bookseller or the Macmillan Corporate and
Premium Sales Department at (800) 221-7945 ext. 5442 or by email at
MacmillanSpecialMarkets@macmillan.com.

Library of Congress Control Number: 2021906601

First edition, 2021
Book design by Aurora Parlagreco
Feiwel and Friends logo designed by Filomena Tuosto
Printed in the United States of America by LSC Communications,
Harrisonburg, Virginia

ISBN 978-1-250-23657-9 (hardcover)
10 9 8 7 6 5 4 3 2 1

The Rhyme of the Ghoul

The Ghoul of Windydown Vale, some say
Is a nightmare invented to frighten away
The children from places they oughtn't to be
Like boglands and quicksands as deep as the sea.

But if it's not real, then how do they know
Of its terrible wail? The way its eyes glow?
Or the curve of its teeth, jutting out of the jaw,
All bloody and dripping as it eats your flesh raw?

And how to explain the bones that we find?
The corpses of animals, ones left behind
With wounds made by claws, sharp as new knives . . .
Are all of these false? The tales of old wives?

We suppose, in the end, there's just one place to learn;
We'll remember you kindly when you don't return.

Chapter One

I couldn't be prouder to call Windydown Vale home. I mean, sure, we've got the Ghoul, and that's upsetting to some. So are the bog adders, eye leeches, mirror mud, rat plague, groundbriar, choker vines, and sinkholes. All have claimed their fair share of folk, and we'll own that. But credit where it's due: Not a soul in the Vale has ever been trampled to death by a terrified horse.

Course, it's early still.

• • •

The morning mist is just slithering in from the swamps, and I'm already arms-full, fixing to topple over in a heap of turnips, fresh-plucked chickens, and bottles of fancy wine. The inn's close, but that doesn't mean much when there's an army of tradefolk 'tween me and our front porch.

Their carts line the Long Walk, hung with everything from strings of garlic to sheets of silk. Like a flock of preening peacocks, they caw at anyone who gets close, including me.

"Boy! Need a pan for that chicken? Cast iron! Pre-oiled in pig fat and mutton tallow!"

"Copper! Hey, Copper, lad! Tell your pa we've got new quilts! All sizes, hand knit! Corners won't fray no matter how many times you tuck 'em!"

"Wards! Amulets! Talismans! Only fools venture into the swamps without Ghoul protection!"

I pull up, dodging a wheelbarrow full of salted fish as its owner hustles past. Peering over the mound of Mother's groceries, I spot Granny Erskine, who's reaching up to rattle a rusty horseshoe at anyone close. In the middle of the shoe is a bird's skull, tethered by bits of brightly colored yarn. Don't know how well it drives off evil, but its power against customers seems clear.

"Granny," I call. "Hey! Didn't we—"

"Copper! Tell these people! Ghoul'll get 'em for sure without an amulet!"

I juggle my parcels until I can see her square. She's tiny, with a whiskery chin and whispery hair. I lean down to eye level. "Mayors yelled at you yet today, Granny?" I ask.

She spits into the mud behind her, then hangs the horseshoe carefully from one of the hooks that line her stall. There are dozens more of the cobbled totems, not one alike, save that they all resemble the less cozy parts of a rat's nest. A stiff breeze sets her knickknackery to spinning, and

4

Granny pulls a quilt around her shoulders—one of the same red-and-green ones for sale farther up the Walk. "Reeves 'n' his lot got nothin' to say to me that I want to hear," she grumbles.

"Listen to me, then?" I plead. "You know you can't be selling these . . ."

"Genuine enchantments against all threats, magic and mystic?"

". . . things."

"But the Ghoul! Folk need *protection!*" she cries, words aimed at everyone but me.

"And that's a noble cause," I offer. "But there ain't a lick your bird bones and old horsecloppers are gonna do to save folks from the mud. Or anything else, for that matter. We start sending tradefolk out there thinkin' they're protected, we're gonna lose more of 'em than the Ghoul ever took."

She sniffles, sucking softly on the inside of her cheek. Then she starts closing up shop.

"Thank you, Granny."

"For *you*, Copper. Not for no one else. Gonna be a hard day, what with this storm comin'. Was fixin' to get a little dry wood, maybe build a fire to keep my—"

My sigh cuts her off. She smiles, revealing eight evenly spaced and equally yellow teeth. I navigate a bottle of wine to my other arm, freeing a few fingers to dip into the pouch at my belt. I wrangle out a couple coins, at which Granny clicks her tongue.

"Er . . . my eyes, Copper. Gettin' hard for me to see

which coins're which these days. Mightn't you have a slug or two of the sweet stuff?"

I stare her down. She gives me more of that gappy grin. Hiding beneath the jinglin' money in my pouch are two pea-sized lumps of gold. I dig them free and drop them into Granny Erskine's cupped palms. Catching my eye, she brings one to her lips, clacking the nugget against the gnarliest of her teeth. I grumble, and she cackles.

"Just foolin' with you, boy. Everyone knows Inskeep gold is good. Always has been."

I heft Mother's groceries and turn toward home. "Stay out of trouble, Granny," I mutter.

She snorts. "That's what the amulets are for!"

. . .

The mayors are camped on our porch like usual, rocking in chairs, sipping tea from well-stained cups, and grousing over a game of cards. Together, they have four good eyes, and two of 'em belong to Mayor Reeves. No surprise he spots me first.

"Copper? Is that our Copper?" he calls, leaning over the railing and swishing his hand through the fog.

"Yessir!" I shout back.

"Need help with all that nonsense?"

A gangly, top-hatted shape looms behind Reeves. "He means help with the wine!"

That'd be Mayor Parsons. He's got the squeakiest voice,

the cleanest shave, and the least to do among 'em. He used to be our preacher, but he gave it up in an official capacity when the old church sank. Now he sermonizes from our front stoop, glass eye roving over half his flock while the good one judges the other.

"I *meant* to be charitable, is all," snaps Reeves.

"Boys, boys . . . I believe that's enough. Young Mr. Copper may be the most affable among us, but he has responsibilities," says a third voice, deep and slow. Mayor Doc Bunder slips his cane 'twixt the other two, resting it crossways along the railing. His limp white hair covers most of what his eye patch doesn't, but I can still see him wink through the strands. "Granny give you any trouble this morning?"

I shrug, nearly losing a turnip for it. "Same as always."

Doc Bunder grins, patting his hands along the pockets of a brass-buttoned vest. "Think I've got a coin or two; I can reimburse whatever she fleeced you for."

"No worries," I respond. "Mother knows; she always weighs down the morning list with a few extra slugs. *For the charity of the Vale*, she says."

Doc winces. "Charity indeed." He sighs. Then he points his cane at my arms. "Sure you don't need help with that?"

"Thanks," I declare, "I think I'm good."

Or not.

Before I can put a foot on the steps up to the inn, I hear a scream. It's followed by a half-dozen more, all from the direction I just came. Peering into the gloom, I can make out the gray planks of the Walk for about fifty paces before the mist swallows them. There's nothing worth wailing about that I can see, so I venture up a bit, hoping to get a better view.

The horse explodes out of the fog a second later.

The animal is mad with fear—that's plain. And astride the poor creature, slumped forward and getting battered for it, is a girl. She's tangled in the reins, and even though she's bouncing about, I can still see her face.

It's covered in blood.

I'm so startled that I drop everything, turnips and chickens and bottles of wine tumbling off the Walk. Most land in the mud, which begins to claim them in its slow, undeniable way. I start to scuttle up the steps, but Mayor Parsons screeches, "Somebody! Somebody help her!"

I know it's stupid. Every bone in my body is telling me it's stupid. But when you're the errand boy for your mother and father's inn, a few things happen: You get strong. You get fast. You get affable—whatever that means. And you learn to take orders.

So I try to leap on the horse.

First thing it does is blast the wind out of me. I catch a knee in the gut, and I can't breathe. But I grab the bridle with my right hand, and my left snarls up in the horse's mane. For a split second, I think I've got it.

Turns out horses don't work that way.

Like I'm nothing, it drags me. My boots rattle along every plank of the Long Walk, the horse's sweaty shoulder

8

thumping against my face. I think to jam my feet down, maybe try to grab the reins, but its hooves churn so hard that they'd grind me up like sausage meat if I fell.

So I hold on for dear life.

People along the Walk are shouting, and I'm whisked past before I can hear more than a few words at a time. "My God!" they scream, and "Make way!" and "Save them!" and "Leggo the horse, you idiot!"

And someone says, "The mud!"

I growl through the pain and dare to look over my shoulder. The edge of the Long Walk is right there, and beyond it, the sticky, stinking pools of the mire. Teeth gnashing, I curl my whole body, putting my knees against the horse's flank. Then I jerk its head as hard as I can.

With a desperate whinny, the horse veers rightward, hooves splintering the wood at the edge of the Walk. The mud's waiting for us; the poor horse goes from stride to stuck in a single step. I'm thrown off, and my head clips the edge of the Walk, making me see white with pain. I blink it away.

No time for agony when you're sinking.

The horse thrashes, legs kicking high as it tries to scramble back to the Walk. A couple men have already fetched ropes, and they sling loops around the horse's body, getting ready to help it out. It's clear they can't see the girl; she's been hurled another ten feet past me, body barely visible in the mist.

Grimacing away a gurgle of panic, I grab the Walk and

pull myself up. I'm already knee-deep, and I can feel the cold of it oozing into my boots, sure as the dread dragging on my heart. As fast as I can, I jam my hands into the mud and feel for my laces. When I've got 'em loose enough, I shimmy free; far as mud is concerned, barefoot is the only way out, and even then you only get one burst before your legs start shaking, your arms quit, and you lose the strength to fight. After that, you've got a couple minutes left to breathe and think about your mistakes—less if you land facedown.

And the girl?

She's facedown.

I'm flinging fistfuls of mud behind me, sort of swimming in the stuff. Someone hollers for more rope. Three different lines get tossed ahead of me. I grab the first one I can, slinging it quick around my waist before I forge onward. By the time I get to the girl, her hair and the back of her dress are the only things left to grab. I guide her head up, and it comes free with a sickly *fwupp*. A bubble of mud blooms out of her nose.

Good.

Means she's still breathing.

"Reel us in!" I shout, and the rope bites into my waist. It hurts, but with four helpful souls tugging from the Walk, we're clear of the mud in no time. They've gotten the horse out, too, and a couple of stable hands are hard at work calming it. I fall to my back, looking up at the clouds.

Right on cue, it starts to rain.

"Get 'em both inside!" Doc calls. Strong hands lift me

by the shoulders. I try to move on my own, but my head is spinning all of a sudden, so I let them sort of drag me along, mud dripping from my feet onto the boards below.

Mr. Greaves, the wagoner's assistant, scoops up the girl, leaning over her to keep the rain off as best he can. Her head's turned toward me, eyes closed. It's nearly impossible to tell how old she is, though she's about the same height as me and my friend Liza, so I'm guessing she's our age, or near enough. There's still too much blood and grime on her face to make out her features, but even tangled and caked as it is, I can tell her hair is fine. It dangles like tree moss, so long it's sweeping the Walk. Part's been braided—not simple like my cousins do, but artlike. Citylike. Her limbs bounce oddly as Mr. Greaves carries her, and breath bubbles aside, she looks to be dead.

That just makes it all the more unsettling when she screams.

"Where!" she rages, her whole body twisting and bucking. "Daddy? Where's my daddy?"

Mr. Greaves has to put her down. She tries to stand, but she doesn't have the legs for it yet and she crumples, knees hitting the Walk hard. I shake free and creep closer.

"I . . . I know you're scared," I begin, lowering myself to her level. "But this is Windydown Vale. Trust me—safest place in all the mountains. You know that, right?"

She wails and slaps me across the cheek.

So that's a no, then.

As I'm covering up, lest her other hand possess an

opinion on the matter, she bolts . . . or at least she tries to. After three steps, she swoons. Mr. Greaves catches her before she eats plank, and he holds her arms tight. Still thrashing, she screams, "That demon! That . . . that *ghoul*! It attacked us! Took my daddy! Please! Please . . ."

Slowly, she slumps against Mr. Greaves, the fight leaving her like smoke from a dying fire. I sit back, stupefied. Blood mixes with rain, rolling down my nose and dripping from my chin. I don't even have the wits to wipe it away.

She says she was attacked. Her father taken by the Ghoul. She seems so sure, and so frightened.

But it's not possible.

I haven't haunted in days.

And I am the Ghoul of Windydown Vale.

Chapter Two

Broken windows.

That's what Father calls 'em: the messy, dangerous parts of life, full of noise and sharpness and pain. Terrible to endure, but once you do, you see the world a little clearer, like looking through a window with no glass. Getting dragged down the Long Walk, then hearing that girl say she was attacked by the Ghoul? It counts, and plenty. Makes it my third broken window.

The second was becoming the Ghoul, of course.

But the first?

That'd have to be when I died.

It was six years ago, just after I turned eight. One minute I was tucked in bed, blanket to chin. The next, I crashed into the far wall, along with everything else in the room. I tried to get free, but my blankets squeezed me like choker vines, and something had landed on my legs—it might have been my bed. So, trapped, I screamed for my mother. I screamed for my father.

Mostly, though, I just screamed.

Especially when the mud broke through.

It oozed up beneath me, soaking cold against my skin. It bled through every tiny crack in the wall, widening them and making the whole inn shiver. The furniture, most of it splintered, flowed toward me like thousands of spears—when the mud reached me, I could feel the slivers cutting into my shoulders. And still, I was trapped.

I grabbed at everything within reach. I raked the mud from my face over and over, and when I went under completely, I held my breath until my body decided two lungfuls of mud were better than nothing at all.

I'm pretty sure I died a little. I don't remember how I got out, though Mother says Father used an ax to get through the roof. I don't remember Doc Bunder sweeping the mud out of my mouth, or Mother breathing the life back into me. In fact, the first thing I *can* recall is sitting on a wet, grassy hill, a heavy blanket wrapped around me, my mother rubbing my back as we stared at what was left of the Windydown Inn. Half of it stood there, stately as always. The other half—my half, I suppose—was nothing but a pile of slowly sinking lumber. The whole place had split in two, neat down the middle.

I didn't know buildings could do that.

Mayor Doc Bunder said there was probably a sinkhole—like an underground cave that the mud and water ate into until its ceiling collapsed beneath our home. I wondered if every building in Windydown had a sinkhole, because the inn was the first of many to be lost as the mud continued to rise. The church was next. Then the general store, and the smithy.

Then the whole town.

It happened slow enough that we were able to move. Some people tried to rip up their entire house, using mules and horses to tug it along the slippery ground. Others, like us, salvaged what they could and rebuilt on higher ground. The rest left, including most of the families with kids. Can't say I blame 'em. Those of us that stayed knew we'd changed.

Like seeing ourselves through a broken window.

It was definitely that way with the mud. I'd never been afraid of it before, no matter how many times Mother and Father and the mayors used to go on about the danger. Liza and I would get into the most hellacious mudball fights, ending up so grimy that all the human you could see of us was our eyes. That stopped straightway; even a glance at the mud made my heart pound and my throat close, like I was drownin' a second time. I resolved never to go outside again.

Tough thing, though, with your whole town swallowed up by swamps.

Mother tried to coax me from the tents we put up on high ground, but I'd have none of it. Even Liza couldn't tug me out, so instead she sat with me, hours and hours, telling me about how hard my parents were working to build the new inn, and how the mayors, with their creaky backs and potbellies and skinny legs, went back to the place where we'd lost it all, dredging that muck with nets and grapples, looking for anything they could recover. Parsons even took a fishing rod, she said, casting over and over in the direction of the church steeple. Normally, that'd be worth a look, but I didn't budge. In fact, I stayed cooped up for nearly two years.

Took the Ghoul to pull me out of that mess.

Now I'm wondering what kind it's landed me in.

Chapter Three

Even though it's still pouring, our strange caravan is surrounded by a swarm of folk. Some hold satchels or coats up as shields. A few sensible ones have found parasols; they attract others like bees on roses, a half-dozen heads huddled where one's meant to be. And all of 'em are abuzz with questions.

"Did she say the *Ghoul*?" A skittish, soaked-through trademan gasps.

"It took her father?" another whispers.

A third, wearing a floppy green hat and a bow tie, sniffles, "What's all this about a demon? Sounds preposterous to me!"

In response, the wizened face of Granny Erskine pops from the wall of arms and umbrellas, and in a screech-owl voice she retorts, "Only thing preposterous in these parts is your hat!"

That sets off a fair squabble, one interrupted by the

thump-thump-thump of Mayor Reeves's old musket rapping against the wood of the Walk. Using the gun like a cane, he shuffles his way through. "For hell's sake, give the doc some space!" he growls, and the Valers among us do their best to widen the ring. When Reeves sees me, he hunkers down and squints. His gray eyes are asking a question of their own, and I know just what it is. I shake my head ever so slightly.

Grimly, Reeves nods. Then he shouts, "Doc! You take a look at Copper yet?"

Doc barks a few instructions to Mr. Greaves, who picks up the unconscious girl and starts toward the inn. When Doc's satisfied that the crowd won't meddle, he shuffles to me, squatting next to Reeves and putting his good eye in line with mine. I can smell the spitting tobacco on his lips and see where it's stained his teeth. He reaches up with warm fingers and pries one of my eyes open wide. I stare back at him.

"Pupils are all right. You didn't black out, did you?"

"Not that I can recall," I begin, my brow furrowing. "Then again, I probably wouldn't."

"Black out?"

"Recall."

Doc smiles, and he hands me an old cloth from his pocket. "Keep that along your hairline. It'll quell the bleeding. Gonna have a scar up there, but your hair should hide it."

I shrug, looking at the map of scrapes and scabs along my arms. Top of my head is about the only place not marked up, so the idea of another memento doesn't bother me overmuch.

"Told Greaves to take the girl to the inn. Figured your daddy would have a spare room."

"He does."

"That's a good start. There's more I'll need, though. Tincture of cordmint for sure. A clean set of bandages, maybe my sewing kit if any of those cuts run deep. I hate to ask it, Copper, but . . ."

"Sorry, Doc. I don't know cordmint from cow's milk."

"Hmm. Right," he says, and he rummages in his pocket, producing a key. He presses it into my palm, and I grip it tight. "Liza's ma, then. Take this to her. She'll know what to get. And while you're there, maybe see if Liza has some spare clothes. That girl was soaked through." I nod, and then he's gone, swallowed up by the mist and the masses.

I slip the key and Doc's cloth into a pocket and drag myself to an empty cart dock—the one Granny Erskine vacated two gold nuggets ago. More folk, Valers and visitors alike, press in. I try to wave them off, but they won't budge. Since I don't have a bone to toss 'em by way of answers, I give up, pulling myself into a ball. The noise of the crowd blends in with the pounding of the rain, lulling me into a bit of a think.

What could scare a girl like that? Or drag a grown man off his horse? A pack of wolves, maybe; we've got some, but they mostly keep to the firmer ground of the forests and mountains, since that's where the deer and rabbits are. Not likely to mistake a wolf for a ghoul, in any case. A mangy bear? I caught up with a bear once, but it was too busy wuffling berries off a bush to take note of me, and it didn't seem the leaping type. Another human? Cutthroats? Possible, but why attack like some beast?

Or leave the girl to run, for that matter . . .

It's Liza herself who stirs me. She bursts through the crowd, shouldering people out of the way, and she kneels in front of me. Her wide cheeks, tight lips, and dark eyebrows are streaked with the usual soot and ash, but rivulets of rain have washed her up some. The long, thin burn scar along the left side of her face is visible, and the pink of her skin shows through. Her mom must be running the forge hot today.

"Copper! Copper, you're bleeding!"

"I know it, Liza," I say, reaching up to poke at my forehead. It still hurts.

"Well, yeah, there too, but I meant your foot."

She's right. A nasty splinter, probably from where the horse's hoof busted up the Walk, is sticking out of my heel. I wince as she reaches forward, grabbing my foot and setting it against her lap. I'd argue, but she's even stronger than me, and her blacksmith's apron is so old that a bit of blood won't make much difference.

"Ow!" I whine as she fiddles with the wound. For having such thick calluses on her fingers, she's pretty fine with her grip, and she works the splinter free in a matter of moments, flicking it into the mud with a satisfied "Hmm." Then she takes the kerchief out of her hair, which is brown as cattails in high summer and darker still as it soaks up the damp of the day. She ties the cloth around my foot, good and tight. As she does, the others crowd in, thick as ticks on a slow moose.

"What happened, Copper?" Mayor Parsons demands. "Is the girl okay?"

Liza stands up, my foot slipping from her lap to bounce on the boards beneath me. I stifle a whimper.

"What's that? Not a word for Copper? You can see he's hurt!"

Mayor Parsons is no small man, but Liza matches him inch for inch; she's nearly as tall as me. And her arms are just as thick as mine, maybe thicker—what I've got comes from hefting flour bags and wine casks, and from climbing trees while on the haunt. Liza swings a hammer all day. So when she crosses those arms, he scoots back, offering a toothy smile and a tip of his rain-soaked hat.

"Of course, Ms. Smith. But I can see Copper's all right, can't I?"

"Yeah, I'm fine," I murmur. "I think."

"So—"

A sharp rapping noise cuts him off. Liza helps me up, and we turn toward the inn, where Doc Bunder is using his cane to get everyone's attention.

"The girl will be okay!" Doc announces, which sets off a chain of whispers. Then, locking eyes with me, he says, "Provided Copper can manage to get the help I requested . . ."

"I'm on it, Doc," I call.

"Help?" Liza asks. "You don't look to be in much condition to help anyone."

"Doc wants me to give your mother his key."

"Then we're for the forge," she declares.

"One second," I say, tilting my head toward Doc.

"She's resting now," he continues. "But she's skittish. Had a fright. I'd ask that you go about your day, not nose in. When we know more, you'll know more."

"Was it the Ghoul?" someone shouts. Mr. Villers, maybe? It doesn't really matter, because as soon as he says it, the whispers turn into thunder again. Liza shoots me a look and I shake my head quickly, rain dripping from my nose and chin. Together, we hurry away from the crowd, Liza half dragging me as I hop on one foot.

I don't realize how cold I am until we're in the smithy and the heat hits me. Most of the downstairs is dominated by the hearth, a fireplace every bit as big as the one in our taproom at the inn. Only where ours has a grating and a fox-fur rug in front of it, theirs juts right into the room, like a big old stony underbite. Mounds of glowing coals are heaped inside, and several metal pokers stick out like red-hot toothpicks. Furniture crowds against the outer walls—a little table, a few chairs and a bench, and various cabinets, chests, and dressers. A ladder in the corner leads up to a sleeping platform, a meager rail around its lip all that keeps Liza from sleepily rolling off the edge and into the waiting mouth of the hearth. Scary, sure, but so is drowning in your sleep if the Vale ever decides to just give in to the rain and flood all at once.

For that, the Smiths have set up a clever-for-now solution. Instead of patching the roof with supplies they don't have, Liza and her mom rigged up a bunch of funnels and chutes. They run in zigzags from the ceiling down to the first floor, and all of them end above a huge barrel. I asked once what it was for, and Liza picked up a hot poker, grinned, and shoved it into the water, her face disappearing in a cloud of steam.

Doubt we'll have time for such games now, though.

Liza's mom is at the hearth, her forehead glistening with sweat. A few strands of gray and white hair have escaped her short ponytail. She's got heavy gloves on, and she's handling a horseshoe with a pair of tongs. We watch as she carefully wiggles it in the coals, then transfers it to the anvil. That's when she spots us. Putting down the tongs, she spits into the hearth, wipes the back of her arm across her brow, and tosses her gloves on the floor.

"Good morning, Copper! Raining hard out there?"

I nod. I'm expecting Liza to jump in and tell her mom the entire story, but she's already rummaging in an old chest near the far wall, bringing out stacks of shirts, old books, and a mothy blanket or two.

"Ach! Liza! Get out of your father's things! What have I told you about—"

"Copper's foot is bleeding. He needs a bandage, and dry socks, and new boots."

Liza's mother peers at me. The rain must've washed away most of the blood on my head, but the fact that I'm sitting on her bench, dripping and shoeless, must convince her that something's the matter. Still, for Liza to be in her father's things?

Without looking at her mother, Liza kneels in front of me. "Foot," she demands, and I stick my injured heel toward her. She takes off the kerchief, tosses the sodden thing into the corner, then starts wrapping my foot in strips of clean cloth.

"Liza, you can't just—"

"It's not like he's coming back to get them, Ma," Liza huffs. Mrs. Smith scowls furiously. With the soot lining her cheeks, she looks positively monstrous. I clear my throat and earn two angry stares for the effort.

"Doc Bunder says he needs you to get some things for him, Mrs. Smith," I begin sheepishly. "There was a girl on a horse, but I jumped it and got them in the mud. The horse is fine. We're not so sure about the girl. Doc's got her at the inn," I ramble. "Oh, and she needs clothes."

"A girl? No one we know?"

I shake my head. "Tradefolk, most likely."

"What happened to her?"

Liza breathes sharply, and I shrug. We both know better than to mention the Ghoul around Liza's mom.

"Well," she says, shooting one more bitter glance at her daughter. "Sounds like Doc has his hands full. I trained with him a bit before . . . well, before I took over the smithy. Tell me what he needs, and I'll grab it."

"Cordmint. Bandages. A sewing kit."

Mrs. Smith nods. "Feel free to stay here and get dry,

Copper. Liza, keep the fire fed. Can't afford to lose a day, 'specially not now."

We both watch as Mrs. Smith grabs a pair of Liza's britches and a shirt, along with one of her nightgowns from a dresser. I wince, thinking Liza's going to protest, but I guess she's decided the silent treatment is the way to go; she's already fiddling with the tongs. Mrs. Smith opens the door, grumbles at the sheets of rain coming down, and stomps out. Once we're alone, Liza stands up. "So?"

"So . . . what?" I ask, making a show of testing my foot. The boots are loose, but the socks are warm, and I can barely feel where the splinter stabbed me.

"The Ghoul?"

Mother and Father know. The mayors know. And as far as *I* know, that's it. Or was, before Liza. I couldn't bear keeping the secret from her—not with how much her father meant to her. I keep waiting for her to tell her mom, too, likely in the middle of a fight to end all fights. But Liza's kept my secret, which means she's had to hide more than a few of her own.

"It wasn't me," I whisper, wringing the hem of my shirt.

Liza sniffles, and she turns to grab another log to throw into the hearth. It kicks up a plume of embers, many of which land on Liza's arms and hands. She brushes them off like a pesky cloud of swamp gnats.

"Something scared her, though," I admit. "Her face was all cut, like she'd been riding hard through bramble and low trees. And her horse was so riled it was frothing."

I skip the girl's fears for her father. That's a fire I'd rather not stoke any hotter at the moment.

"Well, you're not gonna be able to let it go."

I cross my arms. "Can't. It's my sworn duty to scout the swamps, report back to my parents and the mayors if—"

"Listen to your airs, Copper Inskeep! Sworn duty . . . *pssh*."

"Well, it is!"

Liza slides forward, putting a finger right where my heart beats. "And none of this is you desperate to impress folks? Copper Inskeep, hero of Windydown Vale?"

"It ain't like that," I snap.

"If you say so."

I step away, huffy and blushing. "I say so."

"S'pose you mean to go out?"

I grab an ingot of iron from a crate, then drop it back with a heavy clang. "Don't see any way around it. If I'm gonna find anything . . ."

Like her dad . . .

". . . I'm gonna need to be out there."

"Now?"

I shake my head. "Dusk, when I've got the dark to cover me. Last thing we need is someone on the trail spotting the actual Ghoul."

"Good. Means I might get to see you again before you set off. Never have gotten used to the notion of you being out there alone at night. It worries me."

I smile, then slip out. On Liza's stoop, I murmur, "Me too."

Chapter Four

Seems like Doc's announcement cleared most of the crowd away—they're probably already huddled around tables at the inn, whispering a thousand and one wrong ideas about what happened this morning.

And in a way? That gossip? It's my fault. Mother says the cure for rumors is a good meal, since the one will stuff the mouth so full it doesn't have room for the other. She had a proper feast planned, too—her famous turnip and chicken stew . . .

The ingredients for which I dumped in the mud an hour back.

Fortunately, the inn's credit is good with just about everyone in Windydown, and I've done more than my share of favors for folks. When Celia and Montrose at the farm wagons see me coming, they wave me in under their awning. As always, I'm greeted by colors even the drizzle can't dampen. Melons, pumpkins, and peppers glisten like gemstones, their skins wet with dew. They've got armies of apples in every shade of red I can name, and about a dozen I can't. Flowers, both dried and fresh, hang from the ceiling of their stall, and I breathe deep.

"Welcome back, Copper!" Celia says brightly, and she gives me a little cup of cider, fresh pressed and steaming. I hold it tight in both hands even though it's too hot, and even though I don't really have time to sit and chat.

"Heard about your spill," Montrose murmurs, a tiny pair of spectacles perched at the end of his nose. He's picking through a basket of mushrooms, tossing the wrinklier ones into the mud.

"Downright courageous, you are," Celia adds, reaching up to shimmy a hand through my wet-again hair. I blush.

"Where's your girlfriend? She know about your rescue?" I blush harder.

"Montrose! Leave the boy alone!" Celia scolds, but she turns back to me with a wink. "Liza'll find out about it soon enough. And trust me—girls like that sort of thing."

"She knows," I manage, my voice cracking. I grimace and take a sip of cider, quick. It burns my tongue.

Still grinning, Celia hands me a burlap bag. "Plenty more turnips in there, and carrots besides. You cleared us out of chickens this morning, unfortunately, but I know your ma. She'll make do."

"Yes, ma'am," I say quickly, and I turn heel, limping back into the rain.

I should be used to it by now; practically everyone in Windydown teases us, and it's near constant. I suppose it makes sense: Liza's my best friend. Has been since we were tiny. Any free time we got, we're together, though there seems to be less and less of that these days.

Oh, and we're the only two folk our age in Windydown Vale. Next closest are my cousins, and they're nine. In the other direction, it's Nestor, Mayor Reeves's grandson. He's twenty-two. There were hopes he'd meet a nice girl in a caravan of tradefolk, maybe convince her to stay, but he took sickly a couple years back and has been abed ever since. That leaves most of Windydown pinning their romantic hopes on poor Liza and me.

It's all kinds of unfair, but that's the way it is when half your town up and sinks. And I can't say I blame 'em. Still, it'd be nice to have a few friends, if only to give the waggy fingers and clicky tongues of Windydown's would-be matchmakers something else to fix on from time to time.

• • •

The mayors are already settled in their rocking chairs when I reach the Sunken Inn. The name was my idea, I'm proud to say. Mother thought it was gloomy, but Father laughed and said it was proof I'd recovered from my ordeal. I assured him I had, which was all kinds of untrue. But I didn't want them worrying, so I begged Father to let me help paint the sign quick before Mother could stop us. That's where I am now, slouching beneath that sign, wiping my new boots on the bristly mat.

"Welcome back, Copper," Mayor Reeves says amiably.

"Quite the morning, eh?" Parsons adds.

I nod. Doc has his hands crossed beneath his chin, and he's staring at his own belly.

"How is she?" I ask. He blinks a bit, then sits up.

"Oh, yes, Copper. Ahem. How . . . is she? Well, she's cut up some, but not bad. I do believe you saved her life."

I make a show of shrugging, but Parsons claps a hand on my shoulder and squeezes fondly.

"Thank you for sending Mrs. Smith, too," Doc continues. "She was most helpful, and we got the lass sleeping. She hasn't taken food yet, but she sipped some water and kept it down. Good sign for making sure she's not hurting anywhere we can't see."

"Shouldn't you be there with her?"

Doc smiles. "We're taking shifts. Liza's mother will be with her until the afternoon. Then I'll head in. It was most important that I talk to the gentlemen here. There are decisions that need making."

"You mean naps that need taking," Reeves murmurs.

"I said I was thinking, didn't I?"

"You always snore when you're thinking?"

I roll my eyes as the mayors bicker. Parsons shoots me a wink and waves me inside. "Reckon they're already talking about you in there, boy," he quips.

As I swing open the door and the commotion of a stuffed-full taproom assails me, I take a bit of comfort in being home. At least there's probably a hundred people inside that can vouch for me when I let Mother know what happened to her chickens.

Chapter Five

"Copper! Tell this fool the Ghoul does so exist!"

I hide behind my bag as I squeeze through the tables in the taproom. There's not an empty chair to be seen, and more folk are huddled around the fireplace, their wet clothes steaming. I'm already feeling dizzy from the press of bodies. The last thing I need is to be dragged into an argument about the Ghoul.

Seems I don't have a choice, though.

"Hey, Copper! Did you hear me?" Mr. Greaves calls. He jostles over, wrapping a big arm around me. His sleeves are rolled up, and his arm teems with hair, dense and prickly as pine needles. I wriggle free, but not before he's guided me in front of a man. I recognize him: the fancy-as-you-please trademan from outside, the one gussied up in a fine green hat and a bow tie.

"Go on!" Mr. Greaves demands. "Tell him!"

"Uh, the Ghoul does so exist?" I murmur.

"See!" Mr. Greaves barks proudly.

"Like I'll believe the word of a boy," the trademan snarls. "Is that all you've got to support your ghost story?"

"This ain't no boy!" Greaves huffs. I arch an eyebrow. "He's *the* boy. Son of all Windydown, and finest stock we've got!"

I set my jaw and lift my chin a little higher, trying to fit the picture Greaves just painted. The hatted man taps his foot and twists his lips. I glance at Greaves and shrug.

"Fine," Greaves grumbles, sitting on the edge of the table. The whole thing tilts, forcing a half-dozen patrons to grab their glasses before there's a spill. "Then *you* explain what happened to that girl today."

"Well, clearly she—"

He's interrupted by the din of dozens of chairs scooting at the same time, everyone leaving their own tables to get a front-row seat for the fussing. It lets me slither through, and I shift, duck, and dodge my way toward the kitchen. It'd be easier if the tables were arranged in orderly rows, but it's hard to set a room neatwise when you've got huge trees shooting up through the floor.

Four of them, in fact.

When Father suggested it, some folks laughed, but now most of the buildings in Windydown rely on the trees. The inn had always been the jewel of the Vale, so after the old town sank, we got first pick of where to build. We chose this spot—the earth seemed a bit drier, it was about in the middle of the Walk, and it had four stately, thick-bodied oaks. It took half the town to lay the trestles around the trees and to secure the crossbeams to their boughs, but when they were done, we had as sturdy a structure as you can make in a swamp. Mother hoped it would help put my mind at ease, maybe keep me from getting so twitchy when I was near the mud. Nothing doing, but at least the inn is safe for now, and the taproom is quite a sight with all the lanterns swinging between the trunks, benches built from branches, and everyone's initials carved into the bark.

"Copper! That you behind the bag?"

Aunt Abigail is standing at the bar, cleaning tankards and watching the room. She's got her red hair up, a big pile that no amount of pins can contain. When she lets it down, it reaches her waist.

"Yes'm," I say sheepishly. As our barkeep, she'll be wanting to know where her bottles of wine are . . . Instead of nagging me, though, she comes around and gives me a hug. It's all lumpy and kind of painful on account of the turnips between us, but she doesn't seem to mind.

"Heard you got run over by a horse! Glad you're okay!"

"I didn't get run over so much as dragged beside," I explain, and my gaze drifts to the kitchen door. "Are . . ."

"My sister was halfway down the Walk before Doc Bunder caught her, explained that you were running an errand for him. She knows you're okay, but she'll still want you to check in."

I nod. "I will. And I'm . . . well, I'm sorry about the wine. I know we're low, so—"

Aunt Abigail smiles and scurries behind the bar. She rummages for a second, then lifts up two mud-encrusted bottles.

"Had the girls fish 'em out when I heard what happened. We should be good for . . ." She pauses, head bobbing as she counts customers. "Well, the next hour or so, at any rate. Maybe this'll encourage folk to try some of the top-shelf stuff."

"There were five bottles," I admit.

"Yeah, Stacy—bless her little heart—picked up the broken pieces, brought them to me on a plate. She asked me if I could wring the drippings out of 'em into a new bottle. Can you believe that kid? Sweetest thing, not a lick of common sense."

I scan the room, spotting my cousins near the farthest cross branch. Like usual, they're dressed identically—blue dresses, red pigtails for days. And like always, they're together. Most folks can't tell them apart just by looking, and that includes me. Even their freckles are in the same places. The only way I ever get their names right is by what they're doing.

Right now, Fran is sitting on the branch reading a book. Stacy is hanging off the same bough, her fingers laced above it as she dangles. Laila's trying to climb Stacy; she's got a foot shoved into her sister's belly and an elbow digging in right between poor Stacy's pigtails. Stacy, for her part, doesn't complain.

Bless her heart, indeed.

Stacy spots me first, and her grimace turns into a grin. "Heya, Copper!" she shouts.

I wave. "Thanks for getting the wine!"

"No problem. It was fun!" she manages to say, despite the fact that Laila's muddy feet are now perched on her shoulders.

I think about going over and giving Laila a boost, just to spare Stacy's face from being the next foothold, but Laila hoists herself up soon enough, and then Laila and Fran help Stacy reach the branch. I smile and head into the kitchen. Before the door closes behind me, I hear Laila whine, "This is boring. Can we get down now?"

The kitchen is huge, but it's easy to spot Mother. She's at the oven, singing loudly as she bends to stoke the fire. Up top, a big pot burbles, its heavy cast-iron lid dancing. Father is nowhere to be seen, which must mean he's tending to some of the rooms upstairs. I dump the turnips and carrots onto the scarred and stained wooden table at the center of the room. The noise warns Mother I'm there, and she doesn't even bother to close the oven grate before she's on me, hugging and pinching and inspecting my head. Like Aunt Abigail, she's got her hair up, too, but Mother's curls are dark brown like mine and cut nearly as short. She tells folk it's because long hair and stoves don't mix, but she and I know the real reason she's always favored a close cut.

When she's made sure I'm okay, Mother's gaze turns steely. "Copper Inskeep . . . tell me these stories I'm hearing are utter nonsense, and that my son didn't lose my chickens while trying to headbutt a horse," she says, licking her thumb and using it to scuff at some lingering mud near my bandage.

"I wouldn't call it a headbutt," I mutter.

"Oh, so you *did* throw yourself in front of a horse?"

"Yes?"

"Did you lose the gold, too?"

I untie my pouch from my belt and set it on the table. The coins, muddy but safe, clink softly. Mother whistles with relief, but then she sees my blushy cheeks. "Gold is gone," I admit. "But not to the mud."

Mother sighs. "Granny Erskine?"

I nod.

"Maybe a little less charity for that one. She's gotten plenty of our gold over the years. Wasn't a problem when we were flush. Now?" Mother waves the tip of her knife about, indicating our magnificently rebuilt, and magnificently costly, inn. Then she stomps past to attack the turnips. I slink toward the door.

"Is the girl okay?"

I turn. Mother's hacking the turnips like bloody murder, but she's got a little smile at the corner of her lips, the kind she wears when she's got her pride up. I exhale with relief.

"I think so? Liza's ma is with her."

"That's good," Mother replies, and she sets the knife

down. "Heard some chatter from the taproom. Folk're saying it was the Ghoul?"

"Girl said it herself."

Mother's eyebrows rise and she whispers, "But you weren't out last night."

I shake my head.

Mother draws her lips in as she thinks. "It's a mystery, and that's for certain. Worse, it's one we don't have much time to solve. Can't have a man out there in the swamps, stumbling around. No tellin' what he'll find."

"Or what's found him," I add.

"Just so. And in any case, if that girl's daddy is out there, his chances . . ."

"Are fading fast," I murmur.

"Too right. Copper, if you're up for it . . ."

"I'm gonna," I say.

Mother nods, then returns to her pot. I reach out and grab a cube of raw turnip, popping it into my mouth and regretting it immediately. As I look for the dustbin, Mother says, "Before you go out, talk to the girl. I'll have this stew done quick; it'll make a good peace offering. Maybe get her to tell you where to start looking. And once you're haunting?"

I run my starchy tongue along my teeth. "I know, I know. I'm naught but eyes and ears."

"That's right. Don't you dare engage with anyone, even if they look tradelike. Just observe, then report back. We need to know if we're dealing with the imagination of a scared girl," she says grimly, scraping scraps of carrot into the pot, "or a threat."

I nod. If anyone knows the dangers of the swamps, it's Mother.

She's the one who made me the Ghoul, after all.

Chapter Six

Two years.

That's how long I stayed scared of the mud.

Well, okay, I'm still scared—any healthy-minded soul would be. But it got to be so bad that I'd get belly-sick at the mere thought of venturing outside the inn. It was like I could taste myself dying all over again, feel the mud settling in my sinuses and creeping throatwise into my lungs. And Mother and Father? They were patient with me. Tried coaxing me out. Promised me treats. Even gave me a fistful of gold and told me I could have my pick of anything on the Walk.

None of it worked.

On my tenth birthday, my parents set up a to-do on our porch. Fuse-lanterns, cracklers, and a pudding cake that took up an entire table. Liza spent what must've been a month at the forge making me a present: a metal model of the inn itself, complete with windows and a coppery canopy. Even had little figures of us to play with. And what did I do?

Clung to a tree trunk.

Refused to come out.

Mother and Father fretted. Liza got steamin' mad. She marched right up to me and told me that I might as well have died on a permanent basis, way I was carrying on. It was a cruelty, and Mrs. Smith dragged her off, apologizing with one side of her mouth while the other let Liza know just how much trouble she'd brought on herself. I cried, and I stewed, and I told my parents I was sick of being so scared.

That's when Mother decided it was time.

She finished thanking the mayors and the other guests, and then she tapped Father on the shoulder. There must have been something in her look, because he sighed deep, glanced longways at me, and nodded.

"Follow us, Copper," he said.

I did.

Together, they brought me to the storage room on the third floor. Mother lit an oil lamp while my father pulled dustcloths off a few chairs. He sat, wincing as his bad knee clicked. Then he patted the chair next to him, his bushy eyebrows lifting in a kindly fashion.

When I'd settled, Father began. "I know you've heard the mayors goin' on about you—how you're the future of Windydown Vale, how one day you're gonna own this inn, this town, and the whole dang valley."

I blushed. "Mother says they're just bloviatin'."

She smiled. "Maybe a little, but they're not wrong. They see the heart of you, Copper, and they know you're destined. This inn? It *will* be yours, and folk *will* look to you. Part of bein' an Inskeep, and a Valer, born and raised."

"I know," I muttered, my chin falling. Cleavin' to a tree and weeping was hardly mayoral material. Still, I didn't want to disappoint Mother and Father, so I forced my gaze up, took a deep breath, and added, "I'll be ready."

"We've no doubt, son," Father said. "And that's why we brought you up here."

I looked about, thinkin' the mayors might pop out with a sword to knight me or some such. Instead, Mother set the lamp down on the floor and asked, "How much do you know about the Ghoul of Windydown Vale?"

I shivered like the devil just walked his fingers up my spine. "It's got huge claws, sharp teeth, and eats the flesh of humans," I whispered, recalling the poem my little cousins were always singing. "'Specially bad boys and girls who stray off the Long Walk or don't mind their chores."

Then, even quieter, I said, "It got Cutty. And Liza's daddy."

Mother sighed, a soft smile on her lips. She took the third seat, smoothing her apron before reaching out to grasp my hands. "Legends, Copper."

"Stories," Father added.

"*True* stories, right?" I asked.

"Most legends are seasoned with a bit of truth," Father said. "This one more than most. And a good thing, too."

My face scrunched.

"Think about this, Copper," Mother said. "What'd happen if tradefolk decided to pass us by? Just head through the swamps on their way north or south?"

"They couldn't, nohow! Their wagons'd get stuck, and they . . . they could *drown!*" I said, eyes wide.

Mother nodded.

"And what if a weary traveler made camp near the trail, 'stead of comin' to the inn?" Father asked.

"They'd be swarmed by biteflies, for starters," I replied, my neck feeling itchy all of a sudden.

Mother squeezed my hands. "And what would happen if highwaymen or cutthroats tried to set up in the swamps? Prey on folk?"

My brow knotted. "We'd be ruined, I guess?"

"Or near enough," Mother said. "But they don't. And travelers and tradefolk—they stay out of the swamps, too."

"Well, of course," I replied. "Nobody's fool enough to try it. Not with the Ghoul out there."

Father patted my arm and leaned in. "Seems to me you're onto something, son."

After a long spell, during which Mother and Father glanced at each other near a dozen times, I said, "So . . . the Ghoul kind of . . . helps us? Keeps bandits away? Scares folks from the swamps?"

Mother took a big, deep breath. Father rubbed the back of his neck and grinned. I did too, but my smile faded when I realized I still hadn't a clue what they were talking about.

"It's time we showed you something," Mother said. She walked over to the locked cabinet at the back of the room, past the barrels and extra bedding and old curtains. She reached into a pocket and pulled out her key ring, flipping through until she found a little brass one. I thought she meant to unlock the cabinet, maybe show me our earnings ledger or some secret treasure.

I didn't expect her to move furniture.

With a grunt, she yanked the heavy thing away from the wall. Behind it, hidden until now, was a little door, set square in the middle and no bigger than the page of a book. Mother stuck the key in its lock, twisted, and tugged the door open. Inside was too dark for me to see, but she reached in and pulled out a bundle.

"Is that a present?" I asked.

"Of a sort," Mother replied, and she handed it to Father. He set it in his lap and crooked his finger so I'd come close. Then he untied the worn, rough rope that cinched the whole thing together.

"Are those tools?" I whispered as I looked at the metal poles wrapped in the cloth. They had rakelike heads, or maybe claws—long, curved hooks spread out like a mountain buzzard's talons. Next to those was a mask. I couldn't see the front of it, but it had holes for eyes and a bit of twine connecting one side to the other. Father set the poles on the floor and turned up the mask.

I covered my mouth and screamed.

Staring at me was the most hideous face I'd ever seen. It was sickly white, the color you'd expect to glisten at the edge of a maggoty piece of meat. Dark circles had been charcoaled in around the eyeholes, and at the mouth clung two rows of curved nails, hammered in close. They looked like vicious teeth.

"This is the Ghoul, Copper," Father said. His voice was low.

"But—"

"It's true," Mother added. She brought the lamp closer, and the shadows shifted across the horrible thing. "This mask . . . these claws . . . they've been in our family for three generations now. When rumors of the Ghoul start dying down, an Inskeep'll put these on, then head out into the mudflats and the borders of the forest."

My mouth hung open like a fresh-hooked fish's.

"Not to harm anyone, mind," Father continued. "Nor even to get close. But prowl around the edge of the trail? Rustle the leaves and stare from the bushes at a lonely trademan in the gloom?"

"Guarantee he won't risk the swamps after that," Mother said somberly.

"That's right. He'll hightail it into town, safe and sound. Any luck, he'll tell everyone he meets what he saw, maybe build the story up so that he doesn't seem the coward. *I barely escaped!* or *It was twice my size!* It all helps our cause."

I only half heard what my parents were saying. My eyes were still on that mask.

"But what about the real Ghoul?" I asked after a few moments.

"Maybe, once upon a time? I've been going out like this for years now, and I've never seen hide nor hair of a real ghoul," Mother replied.

"You?" I gasped.

"Yes. Your father's knee won't handle the mud. Never could. And now that Cutty's gone, I'm needed in the tap-room more than ever. That leaves ghouling to you. You're big. You're strong. And you're more than ready."

I stood and backed up, knocking over a stack of stored chairs. "But Cutty was *eaten* by the Ghoul!"

Mother shook her head. "I don't think so. Remember how often she talked of going south? Making something of those dreams of hers?"

I did; even back when she was babysitting me, Cutty would go on and on about how she was meant for more than barkeeping and nannying. She was born to be onstage, performing in huge dresses of satin and lace and "kissin' the cheeks of the high-and-mighties."

"Expect to be getting a playbill from her any day," Father said.

I still couldn't make sense of it, like my mind was filled with mud. No matter how much I tried to clear away, more questions kept oozing in. My face must have gotten real dark just then, because Mother knew what I was about to ask.

"We think the same thing happened to Liza's dad."

"Like as not, they ran off together."

Mother reached back and swatted Father. "What a thing to say!"

Father rubbed at where she hit him and shrugged. "Timing lines up, is all."

"A gross rumor, *is all*. Emeline Smith is our friend, and poor Liza . . ."

I shuddered. But then another notion hit me, so powerful I stood straight up. "Liza's mom told her the Ghoul got her daddy! And you said it was the Ghoul who took Cutty!"

Mother took my hands, and she sighed. "The Ghoul might not be real, Copper . . ."

"But the risks out there are," Father said. "If stories of the Ghoul keep folk—keep *children*—from wandering in the swamps, so much the better."

"Liza's mom knows?"

"Not about this," Mother asserted, running her fingernails, *click-click-click*, along the toothy nails of the mask. "But she knows her husband left. She knows it hurts. And she knows how much it would wound Liza to think of her daddy abandoning them."

"I . . . I've gotta tell Liza," I murmured. Mother's eyes got wide.

"No! Promise you won't tell a soul. We'd all be in danger."

"How?"

Father glanced at Mother. She cleared her throat and set the candle aside, her hands suddenly atremble.

"There are folk who wouldn't take kindly to finding out the Ghoul ain't real."

"And more who'd be delighted to learn it . . ."

I whispered, "Like the bandits?"

"Yes, for instance," Mother replied, and she clasped her hands around mine again. Her fingertips were clammy. "We hope the stories are powerful enough so that you won't have to put this mask on much. But the threats aren't going to disappear. That's why we need the Ghoul, and why we need you to swear to us you won't tell, Copper. Windydown's reputation, maybe even livelihood, depends on it . . ."

This felt momentous. I swelled with the importance of it. Me. Copper Inskeep—the Ghoul of Windydown Vale! Braving the swamps and the mud and all else, protecting the people that had protected me.

I promised, and hard.

Swore on my own life.

It's the only promise I've ever broken.

Chapter Seven

Back out in the taproom, things have reached a proper boil. All the commotion brought the mayors in from the porch, and they've joined the shouting, like a sky full of starlings fighting over the last worm. The triplets perch above it all, feet swinging and fingers pointing at the reddest faces and the waggliest beards.

"Doc! Did the girl say she was attacked by the Ghoul, or didn't she?" Greaves demands.

"Well, now . . . I'm not sure . . ."

"It had to have been the Ghoul! What else could it be?" Wendell Fishmonger cries, slamming his tin mug on the table. That earns him a withering glare from Aunt Abigail, who's keeping track of cups and cutlery behind the bar.

The green-hatted trademan sneers. "Something that actually *exists*?"

"Are you calling me a liar?"

"I have yet to see a shred of proof that—"

"Ask Emeline Smith if the Ghoul exists!" Mayor Reeves shouts. All of the Valers go quiet, and the tradefolk glance nervously at one another, especially the ones who've traveled through Windydown before. When the only noises left in the taproom are a discomfited cough and the grinding of chair legs on the floor, Mayor Reeves continues. "Or Cutty Villers's father! Or Widow Poole!"

"I saw it myself once! Damned thing was lurking round my provisions, scraping at the bags with those claws!" a trademan yells.

Yup. That was me.

"That's nothing! Try waking up with the fiend tearing at your tent flaps!"

Me again.

"Old mate of mine says he was set on from behind, fought the creature off with his knife! Where he cut it, it bled black bile. The drops scorched the ground and smelled of sulfur!"

That one's a lie.

"And I," Mayor Parsons adds, "personally witnessed the creature skulking at the edge of town. I feared for my life, but when I brandished my cross, it hissed and disappeared. A true sign that we are haunted by the kin of the devil! Only the good hearts and faith of the people of Windydown are enough to keep it at bay. You're lucky you made it to this fine inn! The girl's father, I fear, was not as fortunate."

Parsons shoots me a quick look, and I wince. About two

50

years ago, before I got really good at haunting, I made the mistake of coming too close to Windydown with the mask on. Mayor Parsons saw me, since he's always among the last to leave the inn each night. I know this is just his way of testing me, though the "kin of the devil" bit stings, and it makes me uncomfortable all over again. I don't hear much of what anyone else says after that.

At least, not until Mr. Fancy Hat takes that piece of green frippery off his head.

"My apologies, all," he offers, his chin dropping to his chest. He covers his heart with the hat. "I am persuaded. It's just . . . I have traveled some . . ."

A few other tradefolk nod.

"And in those travels, I've heard my fair share of stories. I don't put much stock in them, 'specially not when they come from frightened little girls . . ."

I glance upward. The triplets are frowning something fierce.

"But this runs deep. I can see it."

"As deep as Windydown's history is long, friend," Mayor Reeves says gravely. Several other Valers murmur agreement and cross their arms.

Including me.

"In that case, I am moved!" the man cries, and he stands up full. More than that—he clambers onto the table. Aunt Abigail's jaw drops. Fran gasps, Stacy covers her eyes, and Laila giggles.

"I set out tomorrow, bound southward!" Mr. Fancy Hat

announces. "On my route there is a man, one possessed of unique skill and experience. I shall let him know of your plight, and it may be that he can help. Indeed, it may be that there is no one else who can! Windydown Vale—you've suffered enough."

With that, he leaps off the table, stumbling a bit at the end. Mr. Greaves catches him and sets him on his feet. They don't exchange words, but Mr. Greaves's arched eyebrows say plenty. Some of the tradesmen set to clapping, and Laila joins in.

She's the only Valer who does, though.

"Good sir, I didn't catch your name," Mayor Reeves says, wrapping an arm around the man's shoulders.

"Reynard Finch, at your service."

"Well, Reynard. Come—I'd learn more of your offer and the man of whom you speak. I'd also like you to meet a few other people in town . . ."

"Certainly! And if my acquaintance can indeed be of service, might there be a reward for the helpful intermediary? I've heard tell of the prosperity of the Vale—trade and coin and the gold of the mountains. Judging by the beauty of this establishment and the bustle of the town, I'd say those rumors were well founded, no?"

Reeves squeezes Finch closer. "We can discuss that, too."

Reynard seems quite pleased, and together the two tromp out of the inn. They brush past Liza, who's just coming in, a bundle of freshly burnished forks in her hands. She narrowly avoids stabbing Mayor Reeves.

"What was that all about?" she asks when we find each other. "I heard . . . clapping?"

"You did."

"For?"

"I don't rightly know," I admit. "But I think that man just promised to help us solve our problem."

"Our problem?"

I swallow nervously, my gaze flickering from person to person.

"Our Ghoul problem," I whisper, and Liza's eyes widen.

"Are those our forks, Liza dear?" my mother asks sweetly. She's just emerged from the kitchen, a cloth-covered tray in her hands.

"What? Oh, yes, Mrs. Inskeep," Liza replies, and she hurries over to set them on the bar.

"I told you, it's Nettie." Mother smiles as she hands me the tray. Little wisps of steam sneak through the cloth where it's draped over a bowl of stew. Beneath the cloth I can see other shapes—a small loaf of bread, a block of cheese, and what looks to be an apple. The smell makes my stomach rumble a bit, but I push the thought away.

"Nettie. Right," Liza says, scratching her cheek with a sooty hand.

Mother grins as she looks at the two of us. I peek at Liza, then away. She's staring at the floor.

"Stew for our new guest. She's in room three, first floor. Maybe a lad round her age could deliver it?"

I know when Mother's telling, rather than asking.

"I'll come with you," Liza adds.

"A good idea," Mother says. "And Copper? What we talked about?"

"Yes, ma'am," I say, and together we slip out of the tap-room to find the girl.

Chapter Eight

I n the hall, Liza's mother sits crisscross on the floor, pulling briars off a raggedy dress—the same one the girl was wearing when I rescued her. Mrs. Smith holds a finger to her lips when she sees us. "Girl's sleeping, I think. I figured I'd try my best to salvage her frock, but it's in sorry shape."

"Did the girl say anything 'fore she drifted off?" I ask.

"'Where's my father?' and 'Don't touch me' were recurring themes. Poor thing was frantic, but when I helped her change, she didn't bite me, which I gather is an upgrade."

Liza leans in. "What's that about her father?"

I wince as Mrs. Smith explains. Liza's gaze shifts from me to her mom and back, and it feels for the world like the air just got thicker. I swallow slowly and hoist the stew. "Maybe once she's eaten a good—"

"Who's there?" we hear from the back, the voice trembling.

So, not asleep.

"It's my daughter and Copper, the boy who saved you!" Liza's mom calls. "Brought you some food, dearie! I'll send them in now!"

"What? Mom, no," Liza whispers. "Tell me what happened to her daddy."

"I can handle it," I say. "Liza can go back to the forge and—"

"Liza, please. She's a girl your age, and if I've ever seen anyone needing a friend, it's her. Get in there."

A proper stare-off ensues, only broken when the girl calls out again. With an eye roll heavy as a sermon, Liza grabs the tray. "C'mon, Copper," she says gruffly, and she makes her mom scoot aside. I shuffle along behind, murmuring "Excuse us" as we pass.

The room is only half lit. Drizzle darkens the windowpane, and it takes me a moment to see the girl. She's huddled as far against the headboard of the bed as can be, arms wrapped around her knees. It looks like Doc Bunder and Mrs. Smith managed to get her cleaned up a little, because most of the mud is gone, except what's nearly dry in her hair. Her face is creased with welts and little cuts, but now that the blood's been washed away, they don't look nearly so bad. Her eyes are red, and when they're open as wide as now, it makes her look all manner of eerie. She glances at me. I wave from the door.

Liza marches right up to the bed.

"We brought you food. Or, you know, Copper did . . ."

Liza's face scrunches for a second. "Well, Copper's mom made it. But still ... um ... I made the forks."

She tugs the cloth off the bowl. The fabric had sagged some, so it comes away dripping, leaving Liza to dab at the bed while the girl regards the stew.

"That's a turnip," I note helpfully, pointing at a lump floating in the bowl.

And that's the last thing anyone says for a while.

Liza sits on the edge of the bed. The girl flinches, drawing up even tighter. Liza busies herself arranging and rearranging the food on the tray, as if moving the apple closer, or the bread farther away, will make a difference. I set to cracking my knuckles, but that only makes both girls stare, so I hide my hands behind my back and run my tongue along my teeth instead, trying to figure how long it's proper to wait before asking a girl about the monster she thinks ate her father. Eventually, I decide to try a gentle approach.

"We can leave you be," I murmur. "Wait outside while you—"

"You saved me."

I shut my mouth so quick I nearly bite my tongue. Liza reaches down and breaks off a chunk of the bread. "Talking's good, honey! Have some food?" she coos, and she holds out the piece. The girl ignores it.

"You saved me from the mud," the girl says again, bloodshot eyes looking past Liza and right at me.

I run a hand through my hair. It's still damp.

"I don't know if you could say it was *me* . . . lots of folk were there with ropes and—"

"I hit you."

I rub my cheek. "Yeah, that was definitely me."

"I'm sorry," she mutters. "Please don't go."

I force myself to take a deep breath. Then I slide over to the bed and sit next to Liza. She moves the tray to make room.

"I'm Copper," I say. "And this is Liza."

"I'm Annabelle," the girl replies. Her accent is hard to place. Definitely from the southern cities, but it's neither fancy nor quick. More like quiet music. I have to lean in a little to hear her.

"You know where you are, Annabelle?" Liza asks. *Her* accent is all Windydown, same as mine: heavy on the *o*s and *r*s, dark on the *e*s. *Like we've mud on our tongues*, some say.

"A hostelry?" Annabelle wonders.

I shrug. "Near enough. My folks own this place."

"Not to push, Annabelle," Liza continues, "but I meant *do you know what town you're in*? The Vale?"

"No place safer," I add. "Not in the whole world."

Annabelle glances at Liza for just a moment, then locks eyes with me again. "Yes. The nice man with the eye patch said," she whispers. I notice she's tugging at the hem of her nightgown—or, rather, Liza's. She's already got a thread loose, and she's wrapping it around her fingers. The tips are turning purple. "I'm afraid I threw a terrible fit before. I still don't feel myself."

"Some food, maybe?" I ask. Liza picks up the bread again and holds it out. Annabelle takes it but doesn't eat. Instead, she holds it close, like Stacy with her stuffin' bear.

"Please," she says after a few moments. "Has my father come?"

"Not that I know of," I reply. "Could you maybe tell us what he looks like? Or a name? Even, you know, something about the spot that he . . . that you last saw him?"

"No signs of him at all? He would be asking for me. I know he would!"

Liza shrugs sympathetically. "Without a doubt. But if he was, we'd have heard by now. Like they say, the only thing that passes through Windydown faster than a breeze is gossip."

"Were you and he riding alone?" I ask.

"Yes. He was bringing me north to see my mother."

Liza blinks. "Your mother?"

Annabelle ignores her, instead untangling her fingers and pulling a bit of crust off the bread. She slips the tiny wafer between her lips and chews. Liza and I share a glance. After a few more bites, Annabelle sits up, brushing crumbs from her lap. She hands the bread back to Liza, who looks at it like she's just been given a dead rat. "Um, does this mean you're finished, or—"

"Are you sweethearts?" Annabelle says suddenly.

Liza coughs, and she clenches the bread so hard it crumbles to bits. I leap off the bed like she's just caught fire. "I'll get a dustpan!" I offer as I run out of the room, hoping my own face isn't as beet-red as Liza's.

I've made it less than three steps down the hall when Mrs. Smith stops me. Doc Bunder is right beside her.

"How is our patient?" he asks. "Thought I heard some chatting back here. Good sign?"

"There are crumbs!" I blurt.

"Generally a symptom of eating," Doc says with a smile. "A very good sign."

As Doc and Mrs. Smith brush past me, I stumble down the hall until I find a quiet corner. Then I slump against the wall. Getting asked about Liza 'n' me is nothing new, but having it come from this strange girl? It's got my chest tight in a way I haven't felt since . . .

. . . well, since the night I told Liza my secret.

As her closest friend, I was honor bound to do it. At least, that's what I tell myself. And it beats the truth by a fair shot: I had been fixing to kiss her. It felt like all year I was building to it, too, trying to suss out if what folks said we should be was, well, what we were.

The problem with that? I had no clue how *I* felt. But I told myself that if I could only kiss her—nothing fancy, just a quick peck like Mother and Father when they pass each other in the kitchen—well, then I'd have a better idea of whether we were as inevitable as everyone claimed.

I waited until there was a clear night. It was pretty out,

too: fireflies to match the stars. We walked some, stopping every so often to look down into a still pool, the kind that makes the sky seem double and the night glow bright. She had just finished laughing at something I said. I don't even remember what it was, but Liza's got the kind of laugh that gets you saying a thousand stupid somethings, just to find the one that'll make her giggle. When it got real quiet again, I slid up behind her, close as I could get. Then I whispered in her ear, "Liza, could I—"

The words *kiss you* never made it out of my mouth. I scared her so bad she whipped around and socked me in the chest. I stumbled, my feet twisting and arms wheeling.

Then I fell.

The mud caught me—it'll always catch you. And Liza was there in a heartbeat to hoist me free. I wasn't hurt, but I looked like a chicken half-dipped in fry batter. She fell to laughing again as I slumped down on the Walk, and she held my hand as I shivered there. I could've tried for the kiss, but with my hindquarters all drippy I felt the moment for romance had passed. And when she pressed me? Demanding to know what I got all whispery for in the first place?

I panicked. Told her about the Ghoul, right then and there. Her face went from shocked to deathly grim in a snap, and by the time I finished walking her the rest of the way home, she was fuming. Been at loggerheads with her ma ever since, and a little colder to me.

Or I've been more bashful with her.

Or something.

And regardless, I haven't tried to kiss her again.

"Copper? C'mere!" I hear Doc Bunder call. I take one more look up at the ceiling to calm myself, then slip back into the room.

Seems I missed a to-do.

The tray of Mother's stew is toppled, bits of turnip and carrot in a murky puddle near the upturned bowl on the floor. The cheese sits in the middle of the mess like a lonely island. Annabelle is doubled over on the bed, hands to belly. She's groaning and heaving, but nothing's coming up.

Maybe because most of it's already on Liza's apron.

Mrs. Smith rubs at Annabelle's back, and Doc holds a little bowl with a cloth crumpled in it. He snaps his fingers at me and says, "In my bag, Copper. The cordmint!"

I spot his black leather bag on the floor and rush to pop the clasp. Inside is a jumble of bottles, bandages, and tiny metal tools, along with a few cloth pouches of gold nuggets like the ones Mother keeps stowed behind the cutlery. I start digging through and reading labels, but Doc has tiny handwriting, so I'm left squinting and wondering what someone might use "limb salt" or "peptic treacle" for. I'm about to grab a dozen bottles and hope for the best when Doc says, "Orange bottle, blue label!"

It's right there, clear as anything. When I grab it, Doc holds up his hands and I toss it to him. Popping the cork off with his teeth, he pours a little onto the cloth, then more into the bowl. Approaching slowly, he holds the bowl beneath Annabelle's head. Almost immediately, she stops retching.

"Bad stew?" I ask Liza.

"She didn't even take a bite! I put the tray in her lap, she looked down at it, and then . . ."

"She erupted?" I offer.

Liza scowls at me, but nods.

"Not everyone likes turnips," I mutter.

"I daresay there's nothing wrong with your mother's stew, Copper," Mrs. Smith explains. "Girl's just had a rough go of it."

Doc Bunder agrees. "She needs to rest. Best leave her be for now."

"Liza," Mrs. Smith says, "you can go get cleaned up. Make sure the hearth is fueled. We'll be behind today, but might be that we can make a little progress before dinner."

"Fine," Liza says, and she grabs my hand, tugging me away. I stumble behind her as we storm through the hall, burst into the taproom, then cut to the front door. When we're out on the porch, Liza stops to untie her apron. She growls as she holds it over the edge, shaking it and letting the slimy bits drip into the mud.

"Liza, what's—"

"Wrong?" she snaps without looking at me. "I just got puked on."

"Um . . . at least it happened before she ate the stew?" I say as cheerfully as I can.

"And you didn't tell me she was *pretty*."

I take a step back. "What?"

"You heard me."

I frown. Liza and I might be best friends, but there's nobody in the wide world that has the power to vex me quite like she can. "Sorry," I drawl. "Must have slipped my mind, somewhere between my head wound and her *horse trying to run me over.*"

"They do that when you *jump in front of them, Copper.*"

"Why does it matter if the girl is pretty?"

"So you *do* think she's pretty?"

I can't think of an answer that won't get me flung off my own porch, so I just shrug. Liza growls, but then she crosses her arms over the railing and leans into the rain, letting it cool her. "Sorry, Copper," she murmurs. "I'm just having a weird day."

"Me . . . too?" I respond, joining her at the rail. "But hopefully things'll come a bit clearer soon."

"Depends on what you find out there tonight."

I sigh, squinting through the fog. I can see the shadows of the deeper swamp.

"It surely does," I say.

Chapter Nine

There's a bit of high ground just behind our inn; the only way to get to it is through the kitchen, since the mud has risen so much in the last few years. It used to be that I could walk around the entire building, even underneath— just slip in next to the support beams and the trunks of the trees. I tried it once, but when I looked up and saw the floorboards of the inn, I imagined them creaking, then cracking, then collapsing on top of me. I never went below again. Of course, now I'd need to be able to breathe mud to do it.

A little shed casts its shadow in the moonlight, just past the meager garden Father's planted. I tiptoe through the herbs and sneak inside.

Then I take my clothes off.

I'm not nakifying, though I'm sure the biteflies, mosquitoes, and leeches would love that. I prop Liza's daddy's boots in the corner, wiggling my free toes in the dirt. The cut on my heel pains me some, so I leave the bandage on, even though it'll be utterly ruined before I'm halfway to anywhere.

My pants are the next to go, and I fold them up neat atop the boots. Tucked at the back of one of the shelves is a bundle of old rags and work gloves. I dig through the pile until I find the britches I hid there. When they got so old the knees blew out, I went ahead and tore the bottom halves of the legs off. It's the same with the shirt I button on—I ripped the sleeves off at the shoulders. I look like I've been savaged by wolves, but it's worth it. Means I'll be able to move quickly. And quietly. And carefully.

Which is exactly what I do.

I could find the Ghoul's hiding spot with my eyes closed at midnight on a starless night if I had to. Not that I would—for all the progress the mud has made, there are still big patches of tangly vines, thorny bushes, and knotted tree limbs to dodge, and by the time I've reached my destination, my arms are itchy with tiny cuts. Only a few are bleeding, which means it was a good run. I can't stop to savor the victory, though, because as soon as I do, the mosquitoes are on me. I flick my hands around to ward them off, then sprint again, right up to my hiding place.

My nightmare place.

There are only a few remnants of Old Windydown left standing, and those stick out from the mist and mud like lonely gravestones. To my right, a couple rooftops are connected by rotting planks, bridges forgotten once we'd salvaged everything we could from below. Past those is the worst of the swamps. It's pure, glistening mud, far as I can see, with one grim exception: the church spire. It juts up like an angry finger shaming the sky, the cross a great *X* to warn folk away.

On my left, I can make out the skeleton of the stable, blackened beams reminding me of the fire that took it. That was the same night the Windydown Inn cracked in two; the noise was so terrible it frightened the horses, who knocked a lantern over and set the whole structure ablaze. I didn't learn about it until later, and my first question for Father was whether they got all the horses out in time.

He still hasn't answered me.

I find a tiny little tuffet of grass and rest for a second, slapping at my arms and legs to keep the bugs off. Then I launch myself forward again, hopping from high spot to high spot, working my way along the path until I'm there.

Home.

The place I died.

And where the Ghoul lives.

Only the left half of the Windydown Inn remains, and even that's overgrown. The moonlight coming through the mountain peaks bounces off swirls of mist, casting strange shadows along the splintered timber and torn-open rooms; I can see a bed hanging precariously off the edge, like a strong breeze would be enough to send it spinning into the slime below. I conjure a few good thoughts—Mother's sweet pies, games of rollyskims with the triplets, the way my hand felt when Liza took it. And then I leap.

It's always much easier with the claw-poles, but my fingers and feet are strong. I manage to catch a windowsill and hoist myself up. The room I'm in is tilted so badly that I slide immediately to the corner, but I let it happen. A bundle of moldering linens and ripped pillows softens my landing, and I mutter an apology to all the mice whose nests I probably disturbed.

As I crawl my way forward, I keep whispering. "Don't look at the ceilings, Copper. It won't sink on you, Copper. You've done this hundreds of times now, Copper." I'm not sure it helps, because I'm sweating so bad it's getting into my eyes, and it's hard for me to take a deep breath. But I keep moving, because I know if I stop, the memories will suck me down, sure as mud. And that's just the way I like it—reminds me that haunting is dangerous business.

And keeps me from taking the Ghoul for granted.

At the end of a short, warped hallway sits an old chest of drawers. I figure it must have been thrown out of one of the rooms when the building split, because it's missing its top drawer and all four legs are broken. Bracing my feet against the edges of the chest, I dig my fingers underneath the lip of the bottommost drawer. I wriggle it enough to get a good grip, and then I wrench it free. The drawer is empty, save for a few irate moths that flutter in my face.

Behind it, though?

I reach into the dark, rummaging until my fingertips

touch the bundle. I pull it out and turn until I can stand properly, one foot on the left-hand wall and the other on what used to pass as the floor. Balanced like that, I'm able to use both hands to unwrap the kit. My heart is thumping, and I hold my breath as I take stock.

A plain overshirt, draped with flaps of pale cloth.

A pair of muddy, torn pants.

Two spindly claw-poles.

And the face of Windydown's Ghoul.

Chapter Ten

As soon as I'd sworn to be the Ghoul, Mother took me out. I whimpered, and I trembled, and I had to hold her hand, but she got me all the way down the Long Walk, to where the planks stopped and the dirt road to the south started. She made sure no one else was about, and then she snuck us behind a few big oaks. "Watch," she whispered.

I did, with wide eyes and a belly full of knots.

She started with the mask, pressing the grim thing to her face and tying the twine tight. The suit wasn't more than a cinched bit of streaky canvas with some shredded cloth sewn on, made to look like hanging scraps of skin. The weirdest part was the claws. They had leather straps near the bottoms. Mother looped them around her wrists, even using her teeth to tug the straps. When they were secure, she grabbed the poles and shimmied the arms of the suit down over them. Then she hunched forward, kind of like an old man, and she started to sway. I couldn't see her eyes—just those inky black holes. And when she hocked up some wetness, holding it in her throat to gurgle and choke on?

It was terrifying.

"Stop!" I mewled.

She swallowed, and from behind all that creepy, my mother's soft voice emerged. "Can't, Copper. You need to learn."

My teeth chattering, I nodded.

"Now it's your turn," she said, and she carefully transferred the costume to me a piece at a time. I was no help; Mother might as well have been dressing a sack of beans. But she got me Ghouled up, by and by. Even the mask. I could hear my breath whispering past the nails.

"One more thing," Mother murmured as I hefted the claw-poles. She had brought a coil of rope, and she looped it around my waist.

"What's that for?" I asked.

"I love you, Copper. Be strong," she replied.

And then she shoved me into the mud.

Anyone daring the swamps that night would've thought the Ghoul was eatin' well, way I carried on. I thrashed and hollered, raking at the mud with the poles. I begged Mother to save me, cursed her for betraying me, and sobbed so hard I snotted all over the inside of the mask. She watched from the high ground, a hand on her heart and the other pointing above me. "The trees, Copper," she begged, voice breaking.

Overhanging the pit of muck was a thick bough, draped in moss and forked like the devil's tongue. I threw my hands up, but the branch was way too high.

Or would've been, if I hadn't been wearing the claws.

To my shock, I snagged the bough. Pulling up, I dragged my legs from their bog-cold prison. Then, by swinging myself forward, I was able to launch onto the firmament. I collapsed at Mother's feet, flipped onto my back, and stared up at the night sky.

I had done it. I had survived the mud.

Turns out that was just the first test. Wrenching free from the mud was a last-resort sort of deal. The goal, Mother explained, was to avoid the mud entirely.

That meant learning to fly.

After we cleaned the mask out, Mother showed me the incredible way she was able to use the claws to vault, swing, and grapple her way over the mud. She took us back into the swamps, running parallel to the Long Walk but never getting close enough to be seen. I scrambled to keep up, glad she stuck to a stretch where I could leap from high patch to high patch. Every so often, she'd give me the claws and force me to try. Where she was graceful, I was gangly. Where she was lightning-fast, I was molasses-slow.

But I stayed out of the mud. And little by little, my fear shrank.

At least until she showed me the bugs.

Just before dawn, we stopped. Ahead in the gloom, Mother crouched atop a massive old log. She looked so creepy that I stumbled back a bit. Water pooled in my foot-prints, slowly erasing them. She sank a claw deep into the wood, and she used her other hand to beckon me close.

"What?" I whispered.

"Last part of the Ghoul. Look."

My skin prickled cold, but I obeyed. With a sharp talon, she pointed me to the other side of the log.

What I saw was one of the strangest things I'd ever encountered in the Vale.

"It's glowing!" I exclaimed. An eerie, greenish light illu-minated my mother's mask as she leaned over the patch. Waving a claw, she bade me to come closer.

The patch wasn't just glowing. It was *moving*.

"Gnat larvae," Mother said. "Just hatched."

"What? Why?" I asked. I had meant *Why are they glow-ing?* But Mother answered a different question.

"For this," she said, and she rolled up a sleeve. The claw-pole was still attached to her forearm, but she could let go and use her fingers, leaving the claw to wobble and wave in the air. Without so much as a tremble, she shoved her hand into the squirming mass, using her first two fingers to crush a wide line of the little creatures. When she pulled her fin-gers away, they were covered in glowing bug bits. I watched, mouth agape, as she brought her fingers up to the mask.

And shoved them into the eye sockets.

I slapped a hand over my mouth, but Mother seemed calm. Her fingers rooted around in the holes for a few sec-onds.

Then she grabbed me by the collar.

"Look at me, Copper," she said. I tried my best, but couldn't bring myself to peer into those black empties.

"I said look!"

"Okay!" I squealed.

I still have nightmares about what I saw; probably fair, since I've been giving tradefolk the same for years now.

Mother had her eyes closed. I could see the bug guts smeared across her eyelids, flush and shining that sickly green. When she opened her eyes, the light went out—at least until she blinked.

"Stay here, but watch me," she commanded. I pulled myself up onto the log so I wouldn't sink, and I scooted as far from the patch of bugs as I could. Then I made myself into a little ball, caught my lower lip between my teeth to keep from crying, and watched.

Mother shot away twice as fast as she had in coming here. I got the briefest glimpse of how quick she could move with the claws, but then I lost her in the fog. Every part of me wanted to cry out for her, but I knew I shouldn't be screaming.

Five seconds later, I did anyway.

Off to my right, two floating pinpricks of light appeared, like a ghost or willy-wisp was coming for me. They bobbed and swayed, then vanished, replaced by a throaty, spit-laced gibbering and the sound of claws rending through the trees. A few moments later, the lights appeared again on my left.

The whole time, I knew it was Mother.

The whole time, I was scared out of my mind.

When she finally leapt back onto the stump, I was crying and begging to go home. She wouldn't hear of it, though. The rest of the day she trained me. Rest of that month, in fact. And there was much to learn—not just how to put on the costume and use the claws, or how to find where the gnats laid their eggs. There was how to sneak up on a wagon without spooking the horses, how to get into a camp and get out before a trademan could load a rifle, how to tell the difference between a bandit and a businessman, and what traces to leave so that a traveler would decide it was better to ride hard for Windydown Vale rather than risk a pitch-black midnight with a creature like me on the loose. Mother also made me find a hiding place for the costume— one far away from the inn, so nobody would see me coming or going with it.

That was four years ago. Not since, as I went from my parents' timid son to the swamp-haunting protector of Windydown Vale, did I ever see anything remotely resembling an actual ghoul, save my reflection in a patch of mirror mud on a moonish night. And there's not been a fright reported, or a horror witnessed, that wasn't my doing.

Until now.

Chapter Eleven

Only when I reach the swamps do I stop sweating. Only then does my heart stop pounding, which is funny, since I'm running faster than I have in days. Branches and bugs slip past my mask like grain off a scythe. Ahead of me, a sticky stretch of mud, almost like a creek, extends across my path as far as I can see. Most folks would need to skirt around, maybe find a log to cross on or a few boulders to hop.

The Ghoul ain't most folk.

I sprint right to the edge, bare feet feeling the sudden sponginess of the ground. Before it gets too soft, I leap, reaching with the right pole and smiling as the claw catches an overhanging limb. I pull up, hard as I can, and let momentum carry me, left claw already slicing through the air to snag the next one. I manage to go about ten paces without my feet actually touching the ground, and when

I run out of branches, I hurl myself ahead. My legs stick in the mud like darts, but I don't give it a chance to cling. Instead, I rake forward, catching a bush on the opposite side and heaving myself upward. My toes come away sticky, and that's about it.

Annabelle gave me a fair bit of nothing to go on, so once I'm on the southern trail, I decide to strike out at random. The rain, which has started up again, makes tracks a lost cause, but if I can spot a few broken branches or some scraps of the dress Annabelle was wearing, maybe a bit of horsetail in a briar patch, it'll do.

But there's nothing. Not in any of the spots Annabelle might've been torn up ridin' through.

Proper stumped, I make my way deeper into the swamps. Only the tallest, oldest trees remain here, looming like lonely monuments to the valley that was. When I've found a good spot, I snag a big ol' branch and hoist myself up. Crouching in a thick nest of leaves, I slip the mask off and squint into the darkness.

That's when I see the lights.

At first I think it's just my eyes—a glint of moon off a raindrop, or maybe a firefly playing tricks with me. It's too bright to be gnats, for sure. After I blink a bunch and wipe the soaking strands of hair from my brow, I peer again.

Definitely lights.

Definitely bright.

And definitely not on the trail.

I didn't come out here to scare any tradefolk, but my

curiosity overcomes my caution. Sliding down the tree, I do a quick check, tightening all the bindings on my claws, making sure the mask is back on snug, and adjusting my shirt so that no clean skin shows.

Then I get to haunting.

Darting from tree to tree, bush to bush, I take the wide, looping approach that Mother taught me. "If you even think they've seen you before you're ready, you run, Copper. That's your job done," she warned. It's good advice, because it doesn't take that long to load a musket, and my aim is to finish my sneakin' before that ever happens.

About fifty paces out, I notice that the light is precise, like a lantern or two. I find a good rock to hop on, cocking my head to the side to listen.

At first, all I hear is the patter of the rain, which jumps to a roar every time a breeze shakes the droplets from the leaves above me. Still, I'm patient, and eventually I pick up other things: the reedy song of a few stubborn peeper frogs. The neigh of a horse. A wooden door slamming.

"A wagon?" I whisper. Annabelle certainly didn't mention traveling with any kind of carriage, and bandits don't generally ride about in something so conspicuous. I slink forward, wondering—just for a second—if I should shed my costume, walk up, and introduce myself. It's not likely to be Annabelle's dad, but maybe whoever they are saw something? It's a nice notion . . .

One I completely dismiss when I spy what's in that clearing.

A team of four horses, each one bigger than any I've seen, stands tethered to a nearby tree. Steam rises off their black bodies, and their heads are lowered into feedbags, eyes shielded by black leather blinders. They chuff and snort, sharp hooves digging furrows into the loamy ground. One of them nickers, a low, guttural chuckle like it knows I'm there. It sends a shiver through me, and I slip to the next tree, trying to see around them.

Wish I hadn't.

Hanging from the lowest branches are three shapes, oblong and strange. They dangle in the wind, twisting and bumping each other. The light's behind them, so I can't rightly make out much, but I can see enough to tell that each one of them is dripping.

And not just from the rain.

"Blood?" I whisper, and I look down. There's a pool of it, bright and crimson, beneath the things, and in its reflection I can see what's beyond.

Yup. It's a wagon all right.

If wagons were built in my nightmares.

A pair of lanterns—the lights I saw in the distance—sit atop the flat roof. They sputter and flicker in the wind, flanking and casting shadows 'cross one of the most unsettling things I've ever laid eyes on. It's a skull, completely fleshless. At first I think it belongs to a bull, for it has huge horns that curl out, gleaming white and sharp. But the shape is strange, especially the teeth.

Those look razor sharp.

And besides, no animal I know has a head that big. Not a cow, not a horse, and not anything I've read of in books, 'cept maybe them that tell fairy stories. The more I look at it, the more horrified I become. There's a wrongness to it, a twist of those fangs and jut of the snout that makes it seem leering and predatory and greedy.

Kind of like the mask I'm wearing now.

I swallow nervously and crouch down, peeking beneath the swaying, swinging, bleeding things. The wagon is about twenty paces away. It's huge, with great wheels that stand nearly as tall as one of the triplets. Light shines through the cracks around a door in the side of the wooden wagon, and a little window, its shade drawn, allows a dim glow to emanate. As I watch, that light is blocked.

Someone's moving around in there.

Someone big.

It's the sudden unlatching of the door that scares me to skittering. A towering form fills the frame. I can't make out any features, but I do catch a glint—the blade of a long knife, picking up the lanterns' glow and shining out into the mist. I stifle a scream and scramble away, claws hooking anything I can to pull myself along.

Forget Annabelle's father.

Forget haunting.

I need to be elsewhere.

Anywhere but here.

Chapter Twelve

t's near midnight by the time I'm done stowing the Ghoul and sprinting back to the inn. A single lamp flickers in the kitchen window; Mother leaves it lit whenever I'm out, so that I'll always have a bit of brightness to guide me home. I can barely see it through the mist, but I lock on that comfort and tear through the last few patches of briar. When I reach the shed, I'm covered in welts and bites, but that's normal.

What's not is my father waiting inside for me.

"What news?" he says as he puffs on his pipe. I slap a muddy hand over my mouth to keep from screaming.

Instantly, he puts the pipe down. "Sorry, Copper! Thought you saw me here! The smoke didn't give me away?"

"Too foggy," I pant, heart trying to jump up my throat with my words.

"Ahh," he says sheepishly. I wave through his sickly sweet smoke, my nose wrinkling. He apologizes again.

"I didn't know you'd be so long, so I fetched some leaf to pass the time. Gets a bit much in here, doesn't it?" he muses.

"A bit," I reply.

"Brought you some water," he says, pointing at an old bucket on the ground. I immediately plant my feet in it, sighing as the warmth helps peel the mud away. "And some water," he adds, giving me a cup. Swamp running is thirsty work, and I've gulped most of it in just a few seconds.

"Thanks," I say as I wipe my arm across my wet lips. I regret it as soon as I taste mud, and I kneel down to wash my hands and arms, too.

"So? Any sign of the girl's father?"

The way my face clouds gives him all the answer he needs.

"But you found something?"

"A wagon," I murmur, shuddering.

"Tradefolk?"

"Not unless they aim to barter night terrors."

Father cocks an eyebrow.

"Huge thing, with four giant horses to pull it. And a beastly skull for a hat."

"That's powerful odd. Bandits?"

I shrug. "Didn't seem it."

"Soldiers?" he says, frowning. "I've seen war wagons done up gruesome."

"I didn't see any army. Just one man, and only brief. I hightailed it before he could spot me."

Father's expression softens, and he rests a hand on my shoulder. "Wise, son. You did what you could. I'll let the mayors know what you saw. You can rest up."

"Yeah, maybe," I reply, glancing at the inn through the shed door. "But I still don't know if that wagon's connected to Annabelle."

"You think it might be?"

"Two oddities in one day? Not sure what to think," I admit. "And I'm not gonna get any answers until I can talk to her again. For all I know she's—"

"Still awake, last I checked, and chatty," Father says. "Well, actually, Mayor Parsons is talking, but she's asking enough questions of her own to keep him going well into next week."

"About what?" I ask, standing up and peeling off my sweaty swamp-running gear.

"You. Or, rather, the Ghoul."

"What's Mayor Parsons saying?"

"Quoting scripture, mostly." Father holds up his pipe like a chalice of holy water and proclaims, "'For the demon shall prey upon the pilgrim and stall his progress to the promised land!' Or some such."

"He's gonna scare her worse than she already is."

Father nods. "I reckon so. And that's why I'd like you inside. She's mentioned you a couple times; seems to trust you. If anyone's going to ask her about that wagon, it should be you."

"I'm on it."

"Change clothes first. You're filthy."

"I surely am," I say, and I duck out of the shed, leaving Father with his pipe.

The kitchen smells of supper, which smells this evening like meat pie. Mother's left a bunch of dough trimmings in a sea of flour on her pastry board, and I cram a few in my mouth, letting them melt on my tongue. I know I'm not supposed to—Liza and I got into some cake batter once, made ourselves sick for near a week—but I swear, there is nothing on this earth more diabolically tempting than raw dough. I grab a pear and a piece of that crusty bread, too, and sneak up the back staircase to my room.

When the Sunken Inn was built, Mother and Father offered me my pick of all the guest rooms. I chose the smallest. That surprised them a bit. They'd been dealing with my fretful whimpering every night they tried to put me to bed; since I died, I couldn't stand to sleep in a closed-in room, not even for one night. But this room? I knew it'd do for me. It's at the very back corner of the top floor, which makes it almost the highest spot in all of Windydown. In fact, the only spot higher is the roof above my room.

So, naturally, that's where my bed is.

After I wash up and get changed, I climb atop the little wardrobe in the corner. I've done this so many times that I don't even need to look where I'm putting my hands and feet. I push on the loose ceiling board Father helped me hinge. It swings upward, and I clamber onto the roof. Then it's only a short scramble to the awning that covers my sleeping mat, tucked right against the chimney. I sweep the cheesecloth aside, leaving just enough open for me to look out over the Vale, and I flump down, careful not to crush the pear or bread. The cloth keeps the sparrows and flies away, but I'd rather not tempt fate with leftover crumbs. I eat while staring off into the night.

The Long Walk extends into the distance, lazily winding but staying generally on the same line. It reminds me of a tree branch, kind of like the ones in the canopies just above me, with boughs and leaves sticking off every so often. The inn is a flower, big and bright and beautiful. The shops, like Liza's mom's smithy and Doc's apothecary, or the stables, are smaller blossoms. And the little platforms that shoot off to either side, the ones that tradefolk park their wagons on? Those are leaves, their little lanterns glowing in the dark like dewdrops. It's both comforting and mesmerizing, and part of me wishes I could curl up and go to bed.

But I can't. Not with that wagon out there.

Shivering, I take the last bite of my pear and chuck the core off the roof. After a second or so, I hear it splat sharply in the mud. Licking my fingers, I get ready to make the climb down.

It's time to talk to Annabelle again.

Chapter Thirteen

The taproom's mostly empty, though there are a couple of Valers nursing mugs of stout, and Father's at a back table with Mayor Reeves and Doc Bunder. They're leaned close over a plate of browned apples and crumbly cheese, whispering. Father catches my eye and offers me a nod. I return it and slip into the hall.

There's only one open door, and it's Annabelle's. Light spills from the room, as does the drone of Mayor Parsons's voice.

"Windydown Vale's the betweenest place in the world!" he declares, "Right smack in the middle of everything. To the east and west? Those are the Teeth. Can't have a valley without mountains, and the Teeth are ours. Or we're theirs, crammed between those spindly spires like a wad of gristle that just won't chew. South are the cities—as you likely know, young lady—and north are the harbors and the wide, wide sea."

I roll my eyes, imagining Parsons's hands moving as he talks, long fingers snapping, pointing, and wagging. Sure enough, when I peek in, his arms are twisting every which way. He's seated in a stiff wooden chair, the oil lamp on the table turned to cast his skinny shadow along the wall. Annabelle is in bed, her own hands folded over the quilt and her back propped by a half-dozen pillows. At first I think it's just those two, but then I notice Fran squished into the corner between the bed and the wall, a book propped on her knees. Coming up the hall with a glass of water is Stacy, and I smile at her. She gives me a little wave and heads in, handing Annabelle the glass. That leaves me wondering about Laila.

I spot a pair of feet sticking out from underneath the bed a second later, toes wiggling, and I have my answer.

"Copper? Is that Copper?" Mayor Parsons asks, and I slip in. I think about sitting on the edge of the bed, since there's not much else to the room, but something unnerves me about the tightly tucked white bedspread, perfectly smooth and flat except for the little lumps made by Annabelle's feet. I stand next to Stacy instead.

"Hello again, Annabelle," I say.

She lifts a hand to wave. I offer her a tight-lipped smile.

"I was just telling Annabelle that there's more to Windydown Vale than the Ghoul. Jewel of the Mountains, they call us!"

"Because of your wealth?"

Parsons's left eye goes as glassy as his right, the mist of memory clouding his vision. "Once upon a time," he sighs, "there was gold to be had in the Vale, and plenty. A young panner and his mates could amass a tidy trove—not to rival the queens of the south or builder-barons of the north, mind you, but enough to lay down roots. Now? Well, we're a center of commerce, but I like to think the real treasure is the hearts of the people of the Vale. Tough as diamonds, fierce as rubies, 'n' good as any gold. Have been from the founding. And I should know. I was there!"

"You were one of those panners?"

Patting his heart humbly, the former preacher says, "Well, not I alone. Had a good measure of help, I did, including from this lad's grandfather!"

Annabelle turns those big, dark eyes on me, and I nod. "Mother says we were a mining family before we were inn-keeps. Kind of where I got my name."

"And was your grandfather a mayor like him?" Annabelle asks.

Before I can answer, Laila's freckled face shoots from under the bedskirt, and she points at Parsons. "He ain't the mayor," she declares. Then she ducks out of sight again.

"Laila!" Stacy snaps.

"That's what Mama says," Laila calls from underneath. "Ain't none of them mayoral on account of nobody voted."

Even Fran looks up. Parsons blinks a few times, the

lid over his fake eye moving slightly slower than the other. Then he grins.

"From the mouths of babes," he chuckles. "It's true. Not a one of us is duly elected."

"So *mayor* is . . ."

"Because we're old and think we know better than everyone else," Doc Bunder says, stepping into the already-crowded room. Parsons stands up and offers his chair, but Doc waves him off. "Just here to check on my patient."

Parsons nods. "And Reeves?"

Doc sits down next to Annabelle, a few loose pillows tumbling his way as the mattress sinks. "Back now. He made sure Finch got off all right."

I bite the inside of my cheek to keep from saying something. Parsons, though, does it for me.

"We really think this gentleman is going to procure help for our . . . our 'problem'?"

Doc shrugs as he leans forward, his fingertips finding Annabelle's wrist. "Doubt it," he responds slowly, checking her pulse. "'Twouldn't be the first trademan vowing to be the savior of Windydown Vale. More than likely he was just trying to take the heat off, what with his grandstanding in the taproom."

Suddenly Annabelle grabs Doc's arm. He pulls away quickly. "I didn't hurt you, did I, dear?"

"This man," she says, her voice intense. "He could stop the Ghoul? Find my father?"

Doc glances back at me, then at Parsons. The preacher approaches the bed.

"Now, don't fret, miss. You leave that to us Valers. We'll help."

"When?" Annabelle demands, and she starts to stir, her feet kicking the blankets down a bit.

"Soon!" Parsons promises. "As soon as you're ready to tell us what happened . . ."

More than happy to have Parsons do my job for me, I lean in.

"We were on the trail; it was dark; we were attacked! My father made me flee, and that thing dragged him into the swamps! It was horrible . . ." She trails off, gaze going to the rain-streaked window as she shudders. Stacy reaches out to take Annabelle's hand.

"Oh, don't worry! You're safe here. Mama says the Ghoul doesn't come near Windydown on account of the Mighty Ruckus!"

Annabelle's head tilts, and she looks at me. "Mighty . . . Ruckus?"

I nod. "Every full moon, everyone in Windydown lines up on the Walk. Mayor Reeves'll load up his muskets; Mother and Father grab pots and pans. Liza and her mom . . . well, Liza's mom . . . brings out her smithing hammers."

Stacy claps. "Then we all start shooting, banging, and hollering! It's tradition. Scares the Ghoul away."

Annabelle sits forward.

Parsons smiles. "After that, we celebrate. There's wine for the elders. Sugar knots for the kids."

"And what does it look like?"

"Like the world's raggediest band is hittin' the high note, I reckon," I say. "Buncha people millin' around with cookware, all—"

"Not the Ruckus. The Ghoul."

"Oh. Oh, yeah . . . ," I mutter, thinking of the mask's vacant eyes. "Well . . . I guess it's . . . Wait . . . didn't you see it?"

She lowers her head, fingers twining. "I . . . I'm not rightly sure what I saw. Maybe if you told me . . ."

"It's got glowy eyes, like this!" Laila proclaims, popping up like a pouncing polecat. She pulls her cheeks down while she rolls her eyes back, just the whites flashing at Annabelle and me.

Stacy joins her. "Folks say it's all tall and gangly, but you couldn't tell 'cause of its hunchy back," she says as she stoops, curling her fingers into claws and sweeping her knuckles along the bedspread. Then she makes a terrible face, twisting her head to the side and letting her tongue loll out while she snarls.

I tap my foot impatiently. "That's not exactly—"

"And it drools a lot, on account of its teeth are so sharp and broke that it can't close its mouth. That's why it's so gibbersome—you can hear it all 'glargle graggle blaggle' when it's about to eat you. Did you hear any glarglin'?"

Annabelle looks at me. I pull my arms in tighter.

"I can't be sure . . . Maybe?"

"The smell is the worst, though!" Laila whispers glee-fully. "Folks say it's nastier than dead things . . . like, the burps of dead things! No, like the burps of somethin' that died from chokin' on old, squishy cheese!"

"What?" I scowl. "Laila Mott . . ."

"That's what I heard!" Laila insists. I know the smile she's wearing, though. She heard no such thing, 'cept when it came out of her mouth just now.

"The Ghoul doesn't smell," I mutter.

"And how would you know, Copper?" Laila retorts.

I clench my teeth, blinking as a bead of sweat catches the corner of my eye and stings me. Annabelle and Laila both stare, but before things can get much more uncomfort-able, Doc Bunder thumps his cane on the floor with finality. "It's late," he declares, "and this girl needs rest. Perhaps we should all retire for the night."

"But we shouldn't leave Annabelle alone!" Stacy exclaims.

"No," Doc agrees. "Best we keep watch, especially if our Miss Annabelle is still feeling peckish."

"I'll stay!" Laila offers, flopping belly-first onto the bed. "I can braid your hair and tell you all the cuss words I know."

Annabelle smiles. It makes her look much less ghostly.

"I don't think that's wise, little lady," Doc Bunder says. "We're well past your bedtime."

Laila pouts and slinks back down to the floor.

"I can do it," Parsons says. "I'm betting Annabelle has more questions about Windydown that I'd be happy to—"

"I think Copper's here for the night shift," Doc Bunder says quickly, giving Parsons a staredown. The old preacher's brow furrows for a moment, but then he smiles and winks.

"I am, yeah," I confirm. "That is, if it's okay with you, Annabelle?"

"I'd like that," she replies. Something about the way she says it puts a tickle in my cheeks. Doc nods. Parsons grins. Fran clutches her book to her chest, Stacy pouts, and Laila kicks at my leg.

"Out, you three," Doc Bunder says firmly. "Find your mother. Ask if she'll trade with Copper once she's tucked you."

"Ugh!" Laila pouts.

"Fine," Stacy grumbles.

Fran just glowers at him over the edge of her book, but she falls in line behind Stacy and shuffles out. Parsons takes them by the hands and says, "I could tell you all about the old church . . . Did you know we had pews made from the very first trees ever cut down in the Vale? Why, you could sit on one of those benches for at least five minutes before getting sore!"

Doc chuckles. "Probably not the bedtime story they were hoping for."

I manage a smile.

"Going to sit out in the taproom for a bit, Annabelle," Doc says. "Copper'll know where to find me if you need me. I'll leave the door open—helps the air circulate."

"Thank you," she says.

Doc grins, and he rests a hand on my back. Then he's

gone, and we're alone. Annabelle takes a deep breath, but says nothing. She's staring at me something fierce, though, curls of black hair framing her face and eclipsing the pillow. Feels like I'm a book she's trying to read, and she's skippin' right to the end. I clear my throat, preparing to ask her about the wagon.

"So, um, I—"

"Please forgive me," she whispers.

Okay, I wasn't prepared for that.

"For earlier," Annabelle adds.

"Earlier? You mean this?" I respond, rubbing at the spot on my cheek where she smacked me. "Doesn't even hurt. The cut on my head still throbs some, and I got all these scratches—"

"About the girl. Asking if you were sweethearts."

My mouth is still in half jabber, so I just say, "Oh."

"'Tweren't my place, and I don't know what came over me."

"It's all right," I manage, wincing as my voice cracks.

"I could tell anyhow, way she looks at—"

"We're not," I blurt. "More like good friends."

"You're not more like good friends?"

I shake my head. "No—I mean, um, yeah. We're good friends. Not, you know, more?"

"Ah," she says, and she takes a sip of water. I notice she holds the glass with just her fingertips, like a mandolin player fretting a chord. When she sets it down, she does so silently, and she uses the long sleeve of her nightgown to dab at her lips.

"Um, more water?" I offer, even though the glass is still three-quarters full.

"No, thank you. And I interrupted you before. Please—do go on."

I sit on the very edge of the bed, calloused and cut-up hands clasped before me. "Annabelle, on your way here, did you travel with a wagon? Or see one in the swamps?"

"A wagon?"

"Big. Strange-looking. Team of black horses."

Annabelle flinches. At first I think I've hurt her somehow, but the furrow etched in her brow tells an angrier tale. "No," she says. "There was no one. Not to hear my screams, not to help, nothing. I wish there *had* been a wagon. Maybe he'd be with me now if there was. Why do you ask?"

"I went out," I say softly.

"Out?"

"To look for your dad."

She gasps, and it's like her whole body swells with hope. Room seems to fill with it, in fact, which only makes the weight of it settle on my heart all the heavier. I have to glance away to deliver the bad news. "Annabelle, I'm dreadful sorry. There wasn't a trace of your father."

There's a moment. Then her tears begin to fall, coming so hard and hot that she can't get the breath to muster a sob. It's enough to make me mist up my own self, so I say as cheerfully as I can the only thing I can think of to comfort her.

"At least I didn't find his body!"

Yup. That brings the sobs. I stand and back away, hand casting behind me for a chair. When I find one, I collapse into it, eying the door nervously in case someone hears her wailing.

Nobody comes, though.

So I just sit there.

Watching her soak the bedsheet with her tears.

Watching her suffer.

Then, finally, watching her settle.

With a great, hollowy breath, she whispers my name.

"Yeah?" I say gently.

Annabelle points at the door. "Are they all gone?"

I follow her gaze. "Gone?"

"No one outside?"

"In the hall, you mean? I can check."

I'm already halfway to the door before I glance back. It isn't but a second, but in that time she's out of bed and near to falling. I bolt forward just in time to catch her, my arms wrapping full around. We stay that way for an awkward moment, and I have three thoughts.

The first? A person ought not to get so close to another's face. There's an unsettling mix of little hairs and veins and tiny holes—sort of like wet tree bark, only warmer.

Thought number two is *That's probably why folks close their eyes when they kiss.*

Three is "Oh, Lordy," and that's what I say when I hold Annabelle back at arm's length. Her expression is fierce.

"Help me get some shoes," she demands.

Me being all mystified, I actually look around the floor for footwear before I come to my senses. "What? No!" I exclaim. "You need to get back in bed!"

"They said you know the swamps. You can take me, show me how to be safe. You can help me find my dad."

"It's past midnight . . ."

"Which means he's been out there almost a day, Copper. With that monster . . ."

I grit my teeth. "No body, remember? I'm sure he's okay," I lie.

"Well, we'll find out then."

I stomp my foot. A little shot of pain reminds me that I haven't been treating that particular limb very well of late. "You can't. Even if I were to take you, in your condition you'd get swallowed up in five seconds flat."

She stares at me, eyes baleful and lower lip quivering, like a teapot on a too-hot stove.

Then she boils over, wailing and cursing and tearing at her hair.

So I panic.

"All right!" I sputter. "I'll make you a deal! Okay?"

Her shoulders relax just a little.

"Soon as you're able to walk, I'll take you out."

Annabelle lifts her head. Her cheeks are bright, like rain-touched roses. "Out? To . . . to find him?"

I nod.

To my surprise, Annabelle flings her arms around me, pulling me in tight. She smells like cordmint and lavender

97

soap. I manage to get my arms up before she can pin them, but then I've got no clue what to do with them, so I just hold 'em out all winglike. Her lips to my ear, she whispers, "You promise?"

I wince, pulling away. She blinks, two more tears finding their way down her cheeks. I rub the back of my neck and sigh.

Then I stick out my hand.

"Normally, there'd be mud," I say. Annabelle sniffles and stares at my palm.

"Mud?"

"For a pact," I explain. "We'd both get handfuls of mud, spit into 'em, then shake until it all squeezed out of our fingers and back down into the bog. That's how you swear. But this'll do for now."

"Oh," she says, and she takes my hand, fingertips soft along mine. I shake once, firm like my father taught me, and then let go. Or at least I try. She draws my hand to her, wrapping her fingers around it like a fresh-captured firefly.

"Try to get some rest," I say, and I gently free my hand. "I'll be just outside if you need me."

She watches as I dim the lamp, then drag the chair into the hall. As soon as I've settled, I hear her call, "Thank you, Copper."

I'm silent for a spell, until I hear her breathing hit the heavy pulse of sleep. Then I close my own eyes. There, looming, is that wagon. A shudder claims me, and in a tone to match, I whisper, "Don't thank me yet."

Chapter Fourteen

Annabelle is staring at me from across a particularly gooey patch of mud. She's got one hand tangled in the tree branch above her, and she's reaching out with her foot, dabbing at the mud with her toe while she cringes. It's a far cry from the warrior face she wore this morning; she'd marched right into the kitchen before the biscuits were even in the oven, declaring that she was done watching the world go by while she sat about and fretted. It had been five days with no news, so I understood her drive.

Of course, as they say, there's nothing like mud to slow a body down.

"It's cold," she whimpers.

"No turnin' back now, though," I say. That's not 'specially true; we could call it a day anytime. But much to my surprise, the mayors want us here, long as possible. I thought when I told them of the promise I'd made to

Annabelle, they'd get me out of it, tell her it was much too dangerous. And, at first, they did. But then she set up in the taproom, pestering every new trademan and -woman she saw. "Have you seen my father? This tall, a kindly face, gray eyes, spectacles? Please! You must help!" she'd cry. No one had the heart to tell her she was scaring away coin, looking all terrified and weepy as she did. And worse, several of the heartier tradefolk started talk of a rescue party. Even drew up search routes, gridified and codified and everything. When Mayor Reeves got wind of that, he changed his mind double-quick about gettin' Annabelle out and about. "Not near Old Windydown," he warned, "or any of the other quaggier spots. But if you can find a little wallow, wear her out a bit . . ."

"It'll keep us from having to rescue a rescue party, too?"

"Good lad," he said.

So here we are.

"Do I have to wear this?" Annabelle frowns, fidgeting with the rope around her waist.

"Do you want me to pull you out if you sink?"

"I surely do!"

"Then yeah?" I say.

She purses her lips skeptically.

"You know, we could just keep to the high ground, search for your dad near the Walk."

"We didn't get attacked near the Walk."

"Means we'd avoid the worst of the mud, though," I counter.

"No. I want to learn." She catches the corner of her lower lip between her teeth and tucks an errant curl behind her ear. "Could I see you run it again? Please? I'll rescue you if you sink!" she says, wiggling the rope between us playfully.

I can't help but smile, though grinnin' is a good way to get a mouthful of mud. So I take a deep breath, set my jaw, then dart forward. I make it four steps before I start to sink, and then I lean over, fingers slashing at the muck to either side as I will myself on. It's not a huge stretch, but it's one that I could've taken without getting so much as an ankle dirty if I was in costume. Without it, I'm wearing mud socks by the time I circle back to Annabelle.

"Fast is best," I say, steadying my breathing. "Can you . . ."

She takes off, heels kicking up grime before I can even close my mouth, dooming me to muddy teeth despite my earlier precautions. I'm spitting and sputtering, but not so bad that I don't see Annabelle make it halfway through the patch with no problem, almost like she's walking on air. Being lighter than me is a help, for sure, but even that can't save you if you stop.

Which Annabelle does.

"Copper!" she shouts, and I leap to. Tugging her back with the rope's no good right now, since she's not sunk deep enough; I'd just topple her over, and that'd be even more dangerous. So I rush in, legs churning through the drag. She's knee-deep by the time I get there.

"C'mon!" I say. "Legs straight up and down. Get your feet free. Don't try to move forward. Just up."

I show her, yanking my right foot free with a phlegmy *splorch*. "See? Like climbing stairs."

She's trembling, but she follows my lead, grabbing my arm and hefting herself up. Together, we wade our way to the far bank, then collapse into the grass. I look at her. She's staring at the branches above us, panting.

"You okay?" I ask.

"I was fine for a bit . . . didn't hardly feel like I was sinking at all. But then . . ."

I nod, wiping my filthy hands on the grass. "Then it grabbed you."

She pulls up, wrapping her arms around her shaky knees. "Yeah."

"That's the trickiest part. You've gotta fight through that."

"Feels like my legs are burning."

I point to the far end of the mud patch. "Achy legs are not bad. At least you got out. See that shiny spot over there?"

Annabelle follows the line of my finger. "I do."

"That's mirror mud. What we were just in is nothing compared. It'll swallow you in less than a minute. Quicker if you struggle."

"There are *different kinds* of killer mud?"

"For certain. And the Vale has 'em all," I say, sweeping my hand along the misty horizon.

She sighs. "So don't go in the mud if you don't have to?"

I nod. "Yup, and if you do . . ."

"Fight till you're elsewhere."

"Precisely," I say, and I'm relieved to see Annabelle smile a little. It quickly fades, though. "Something wrong? Is the rope chafing you? You can untie it, now we're safe."

"It's not that," she mutters, though she does start working at the knot around her waist. "I was just thinking—if my dad managed to escape the Ghoul, but found himself in this . . ."

"He'd not sink that far," I explain. A flutter of hope lifts her lashes, but I go on, grim as I can. "A body that doesn't struggle will kind of get suspended there, just below the surface. Trademan brought his old dog to town a few years back. It went missin', and when we dragged the mud around his wagon, we found that hound not more than a hand deep. Guy figured it must've rolled over in its sleep, swallowed its weight in mud, and . . ."

I trail off when I see that Annabelle's gone a bit green.

"Just wanted you to know the risks. Sorry if I scared you," I say.

"No," she manages. "It's another lesson."

"Still, probably not the best time for the old hound story."

"There's a best time for it?" she asks, messing with the muddy cuffs of her pants.

That's fair.

Blushing properly, I unhook the canteen off my belt and offer it to her. "You can pour some on your feet if you want. Helps with the sticky feeling."

"No, it's okay. I need to know what it's like if I'm going

to help you look for my father. I'm just not used to wearing pants, is all."

She's got a pair of Liza's britches rolled above her knees, just like I wear mine. She put them on this morning after I convinced her that a flowy dress wasn't the best kit for mud running.

"What's your family do?" I ask, taking a swig from the canteen.

"Do?"

"Yeah. What kind of work would let you get away with not wearing pants?"

That came out weird.

"I mean, like—innkeeping. I don't know what I'd do without pockets. And Liza's got dresses, but she doesn't hardly wear 'em, on account of swirly skirts and hot forges don't mix."

Annabelle gazes off, like she's trying to see straight through the trees and mountains.

"My father's a barrister. I've never known my mother to take up work."

"Barrister?"

She nods. "A lawyer. He argues cases in the high courts. I don't really understand it myself. Mostly he's busy."

"And you—"

Before I can finish, she turns abruptly.

"Copper . . . if you're out here so much, you *must've* seen the Ghoul, right? Why hasn't it attacked you?"

"I've never met a creature like that out here," I say quickly. "Not once. Never."

Annabelle squints. "You're saying there's no Ghoul?"

I make a show of plugging the cork back in the top of the canteen.

"Copper?"

"I'm not saying it doesn't exist. Just that I've never encountered it."

The color starts to get up in her face. It reminds me of Liza when she's fixing to fuss at her mom.

"Then what attacked my father and me?"

I hold out my hands. "A wildcat, maybe?"

"And how many of those have you seen out here?"

"I . . . well . . ."

None. The answer's none.

Annabelle stands and wipes her hands on the sides of her pants. Then she holds an arm out for me. I take her hand and let her help me up. Before she lets go, she leans in and kisses me on the cheek.

"Wha—"

"Thank you, Copper. For taking care of me these past few days. For showing me the swamps. For being out here with me. For trying."

I reach up to touch where her lips did. "Promise is a promise."

She nods. "Then if you haven't seen the Ghoul, you haven't seen it. And I'll take comfort in that."

"Thanks?"

She smiles, hitches up her pants, and takes a deep breath. Then she stares out at the swamps and says, "What's next?"

We spend the rest of the morning working our way around a big loop. Annabelle gets better at moving with every stretch of mud we clear, and when the inn is in sight, she even challenges me to a race back to the shed.

"I'm not sure," I say. "If I get too far ahead, and you get in trouble, I might—"

Aaaand she's off.

I dig my toes into the mud. Then I sprint. Takes me just a few seconds to match her, and we run side by side for a spell. I wave at her, but I don't think she sees—she's watching my feet. Feeling a mite show-offish, my cheek still tingling from that kiss, I shoot past, giving my heels a little shimmy every time I yank them free of the grippy earth. When I reach the shed, I turn and wait. Annabelle's panting as she reaches me, but she's laughing. I shake my head.

"What?" she says, leaning against the side of the shed.

"Nothing," I reply. "Just surprised, is all. What you've been through? Don't know that I'd be able to find it in me to laugh."

Her giggles die off, but she's still smiling as she plunges both feet into the bucket of water I drew before we left. As she wriggles her toes, she says, "It feels good to be doing *something*. And to move. Being bedridden while my dad's out there? Close to lunatic, I was."

"Nothing to be ashamed of," I offer, wiping my own feet in the grass.

Her smile changes, and she blinks a bit. "Father wouldn't

agree. He'd want me to be poised. It's very important to him."

"Must come in handy in court."

"Yeah," she whispers, and she sniffles.

"C'mon, before the flies find us," I say, holding the back door open.

"More tomorrow?" she asks.

I nod. "Every day, if we need to."

"Thank you, Copper. Will you take lunch with me? I think Parsons means to visit, and I enjoy his stories more when there's others to listen with."

"Less preachy that way," I say knowingly. She nods, and we share another laugh before heading our separate ways to get changed. I've got a few quick chores to take care of before I can join her in the taproom, so by the time I get there, I'm expecting to see her halfway through a plate of biscuits and fruit, or maybe asleep in a chair while Parsons waxes pontifical.

I don't expect to see her backed up against a tree trunk, Liza's finger wagging in her face.

"Whoa!" I call, and Liza spins. There's a Long Walk worth of veins popping out along her forehead. Annabelle skitters behind me.

"I don't know what I did to anger her so!" Annabelle says. She hasn't even changed out of her muddy clothes; Liza must've cornered her right as she came in. "I just told her we were in the swamps, and she . . . she . . ."

As Annabelle breaks into quiet sobs, I look sidelong at

Liza. She crosses her arms and tilts her head toward the inn door. I glance over.

There's an oblong box sitting on its side, lid all askew. Dumped before it are a bunch of heavy iron ingots . . . the ones that, I realize with a wince, I was supposed to help Liza carry this morning.

"Eight more where that came from, and a cart full of scrap, too," Liza says.

"That's my fault," I say, my hand to my chest. "But what were you laying into Annabelle for?"

"Go on," Liza says, pointing at Annabelle. "Tell him."

I look over my shoulder. Annabelle is cowering.

"Tell me what?"

"What she said when I asked where you were!"

I turn, holding up a hand at both girls. Not sure what I'm trying to accomplish, 'cept maybe to keep Liza from tackling Annabelle.

"Annabelle, you don't need to—"

"I said you were helping me learn!"

"After that!" Liza growls.

Annabelle wipes a hand across her nose and says, "I just asked her . . . if . . . if her father was missing, wouldn't she try anything she could to find him?"

Yep.

That'd do it.

I face Liza. She meets my gaze with ferocity, but I can see past the anger, right to the welling tears. I gesture toward the spilled box.

"I know," I say softly. "I know exactly. Let's go. I'll help you with—"

"Oh, you know? You *know*, do you?" she whispers through her teeth. Then she looks past me.

"Liza, don't . . ."

"Hey, Annabelle! You hear that? He *knows*," she snarls. "But did he tell you *what* he knows? That your dad's gone? Doesn't matter what took him. He's gone!"

Liza's tears are heavy on her cheeks now, and she storms away, grabbing the box and the bars, all in one great swoop. She kicks the door so hard the frame rattles, and on the porch I can see the mayors, wide-eyed and curious. Liza curses as she twists through the door. Before she's out, though, she turns to face us one more time.

"And he ain't coming back!"

I glance at Annabelle. She's got one hand over her mouth, and the other casts about like she's trying to find a chair before she faints. I grab one and slide it behind her.

"Here. Sit. I'll . . ."

I was going to say something helpful. Maybe *Get you a drink of water*, or *Take you out to look some more, right away*.

But that's not what comes out.

"I gotta go," I murmur, and I chase after Liza.

Chapter Fifteen

It takes me the rest of the afternoon to help Liza haul all the iron and scrap to her house, and she doesn't say a word the whole time. By the time we're done, I've got a blister garden growing on my palms, and Liza doesn't look any happier. In fact, when I drop the final box of scrap inside her front door, she strides over to the forge, shoves her hands in her heavy gloves, and says, "You can go."

Liza's mom, who was hammering on a horseshoe, puts her tools down. "Everything all right, darling? You sound . . ."

"I'm fine," Liza says. "And Copper's got other things to do."

"I do?"

Mrs. Smith eyeballs me. Then she winks. "I'm gonna see to the woodpile round back. Might need a few more logs to keep the heat up," she says cheerfully, and she hurries out, patting me on the shoulder as she passes. I glance at the side of the hearth; there's a neat stack of wood as high as my head. I sigh. Liza picks up her mother's hammer and starts at the horseshoe, hot embers flying with each ringing blow.

"I'm still here, Liza!" I shout.

"Why?" she replies.

"'Cause you're upset!"

"So's Annabelle, probably. Why don't you go comfort *her*?"

I try to wander around to see Liza's face, but she shuffles in a circle about the anvil, keeping her back to me. Even with her blocking, I can feel the heat. That, plus the back-swing of her hammer, means I'm not getting any closer.

"I already tried!" I yell.

Liza stops mid-swing. Her shoulders twitch—maybe it's a laugh, maybe a sob . . . or maybe she's trying to figure out if it's worth chucking her hammer at me to get me gone.

"Oh, you *have*, have you?" Liza spits, voice cold enough to snuff a forge.

"I . . . what? Yeah? I suppose? Mayors told me to look after her, on account of she's upset a lot . . ." I cut myself off before I can add *Kind of like you were when your dad disappeared.*

"And Copper Inskeep, the heart and soul of Windydown Vale, is right there to hold her hand."

"Maybe? I don't know! Mostly she just asks questions. Like, a *lot* of questions. How things work, how I get about in the swamps, about the Ghoul . . ."

Liza spins, her eyes wide. "You *told* her?"

I hold up my hands. "Well, of course I didn't tell her *that*. Nobody gets to know but them who need to know."

"And when you decide she *needs to know*?"

"She won't!"

"Oh, but I did?"

My mouth opens, but I find myself suddenly wordless.

"I wish you hadn't told me, Copper. It messed everything up. Everything," she whispers.

The forge fire crackles, and a trickle of soot spills from the lip of the hearth. Liza ignores it, waiting to see if I've got a response. I surely don't.

Liza knows it, too.

"Do you remember what it was like before?" she presses, leaning against the anvil and gazing at the fire.

"Yeah," I say, stepping forward.

"A few chores, a few lessons," she murmurs, "and then . . ."

"Then we got to live our day. I know. It was easier."

"Right?" she grumbles, dropping her hammer to the floor, heavy and hard. "No *The forge'll fall to you, now that your father's gone*, or *One day, Copper, you'll be mayor!* or *Someday soon, you two'll be . . .*"

She blushes. So do I. "Be nice to go back, yeah?" I say, trying to get a smile. She scowls instead.

"Don't know we can. Not with Annabelle here, anyways."

"Is it because she reminds you of your dad leaving?"

Her eyes widen, but then she snaps back to that scowl. Reaching down, she yanks her hammer off the floor and twists it in her hands. "Yeah, Copper. That *must* be it," she says.

I hear her, but something's telling me I've either hit the nail on the head too hard ... or I just smashed my own thumb, as it were.

"I ... I should probably go ... ," I murmur.

Liza clicks her tongue, then spins. She brings the hammer down on the horseshoe with a violent clang. I have to shield my eyes against the sudden surge of sparks.

"Best get on that, then," she yells over her shoulder. "Run off and find Annabelle's daddy! Be her hero! Make Windydown proud!"

"Liza, I—"

Clang.

"Why do you hate her so—"

Clang.

"Liza! Just—"

Clang.

"Damn it!" I shout. That puts a hitch in Liza's swing, and I make full use of it. "Maybe you're right! Maybe I'm looking to be a hero! Or maybe, Liza, the reason I'm trying to find Annabelle's daddy is because I've spent the last three years wishing I could do the same for you!"

She freezes, hammer held high. Before she can respond, I tromp out the door, making sure it slams nice and loud behind me. Mrs. Smith is carrying an armful of wood up the steps, and I nearly bowl her over as I trudge past. She calls after me, but I can't bring myself to stop.

At least not until the earthquake.

113

Chapter Sixteen

Okay, so it's not an earthquake. But I can hardly be blamed for mistaking one for the other, what with how the Long Walk is rumbling beneath me. I skid to a stop near the inn. Annabelle, clean and dolled up in a dress of green brocade, clutches the porch railing. The triplets join her, heads turned southward. Parsons, Reeves, and Bunder are staring, too. In fact, it seems like the whole of the inn has poured out.

Of course, I look as well.

Not that I need to.

I've already seen what's coming.

Four horses, night-black and tacked in red, are clopping up the Walk, driving their shoes into the wood like they're hammering nails. Behind them, that fortress of a wagon rolls, so wide it takes up all but a bit of the Walk, and so high its top is level with the inn door. A mountain of a man fills the driver's seat, lashing the horses and bellowing commands. When the wagon is even with the inn, he jerks sharp on the reins and the horses rear up, screeching and bringing their hooves down so hard splinters fly. I flinch, even though I'm two dozen planks away.

"What in the Lord's name is that?" I hear from behind me. Liza's come out, and she's staring past me at the wagon.

I guess we're still talking, at least.

"Nothing good," I whisper.

We watch as the man stares down a few tradefolk, who have the good sense to pack up their wares and pull out of the wagon dock they were squatting in. Once they're clear, the man barks another series of commands, emphasizing each harsh word with a flick of the reins. There are gasps as he manages to get those horses to maneuver his wagon into the dock, where it just barely fits sidelong.

"Whoa," Liza mutters.

"Yeah," I reply. At the back of my mind, I know there are apologies to make and tangles to unravel, but I guess Liza and I know now's not the time. Instead, we tiptoe forward, eyes never leaving the man and his wagon. We watch as he jumps down, boards rattling beneath his big black boots. He rubs the flank of each of his horses, whispering in their ears, and he wedges the wheels of his wagon, tossing heavy, cross-hewn logs down like they're matchsticks.

Then he turns to face the inn.

"Ladies and gentlemen! People of the Vale and those from without!" he booms, removing a broad-brimmed, purple velvet hat and swinging it low. "Your prayers have been answered. I am arrived!"

I don't know if he expected cheers or clapping; he's mighty disappointed if he did.

I suppose we're still taking in the sight of him.

That purple hat is the most sensible thing he wears. The rest is more spectacle than the Vale gets in a year. A curly golden wig, twisted slightly askew, crouches atop his head. His sideburns and mustache form a great, sweeping wave across his face, dividing his gleaming grin from the dark of his eyes. A yellowed, sweat-stained ruffle climbs up his neck to tickle his knobby chin, blooming from a gold-buttoned waistcoat of shiny blue. More ruffles burst from the cuffs of his sleeves, and leather boots travel the long road from his toes to his knees, the grommets shining silver as he bows. It'd be overmuch to take in were the man not half again as tall as me and thrice as wide.

But he is.

So we gawk.

Parsons and Reeves glance at one another. Liza puts a gentle hand on my shoulder and urges me forward a bit. Then she tilts her head toward the wagon. It's hard for me to wrench my gaze from the man, 'specially since it seems he's about to speechify, but Liza's gone pale, so I look, too.

I wish immediately that I hadn't.

That giant skull seems to stare back at me, and the daylight doesn't diminish its eerie visage one bit. If anything, it's worse—the eye sockets seem deeper, the horns broader, and the teeth sharper. But that's not what's got Liza spooked.

BARL SHUMPETER, it says, painted in scarlet and gold on the side of the wagon—the side I couldn't see in the swamps. DEMONOLOGIST, MONSTER HUNTER, DRAGON SLAYER, AND EXORCIST. Festooned around the letters, pinned up with iron nails or hanging from hooks, are skulls. Some are bigger than humans', some small as rats'. Most are unnatural: Horns where there shouldn't be. Ridges. Fangs. Extra eyeholes or none at all. They're joined by strings of bones and pitch-black feathers.

And that's just the beginning.

"Behold!" the man roars, reaching beneath the wagon. There must be a latch or a catch there, because he splits the entire side of the wagon in two, easy as opening a cabinet. The inside revealed, I make out a bed, desk, wardrobe, and chest toward the back, and an empty iron cage near the front. Shelf after shelf lines the revealed walls, each one heavy-laden with jars. It reminds me at first of Doc Bunder's apothecary or Mother's pantry, but then I get a better look.

The jars are filled with dead things.

"The three-headed serpents of Bakerston!" the man declares, pointing at the top shelf. Suspended in red liquid are scaly coils, wound so tight it's impossible to tell whether they belong to many creatures or just one. "Slain by Shumpeter! And here! The eye of the Olrich Cyclops!"

Yep.

It's an eyeball all right.

Big as my head.

He hops onto the back wheel next, hoisting himself up until he can slap at the top of the wagon. I don't want to look, but he makes it impossible not to. "The skull of Villithurm, the Plague-Dragon of the Western Reaches! Slain by Shumpeter!"

A trademan next to us whispers, "I heard of that dragon! One of the worst!"

More and more folk are gathering as the man—Shumpeter, I'm guessing—makes his presence and his conquests known. Each foul thing—or, more often, chunk of foul thing—he points out sends another dagger of distress stabbing through me until I'm casting around for Liza. She lets me lean on her as Shumpeter continues.

"Yes! Every one of these monsters, put down by my hand. Nobody does it cleaner. Nobody does it faster," he declares, slamming the wagon doors closed dramatically. "And nobody does it better. You can take that promise to the grave!"

There are a few gasps. One of 'em is mine. It seems to please Shumpeter, who whips his hat back onto his head and gives a deep bow. Then he rises up, grins the devil's smile, and says, "Now, what's this I hear about a ghoul?"

Chapter Seventeen

Mayor Reeves descends cautiously, aware that the eyes of Windydown are on him. Parsons and Bunder follow close behind.

"Mister . . ."

"Shumpeter! Like it says on the wagon!" the man says, waving a ring-heavy hand behind him.

"Shumpeter, yes . . . ," Reeves replies. His voice is unnatural—deep, almost like he's trying to match the other man grand for grand. "Welcome to Windydown Vale. I am—"

"In need of my assistance, way I hear it!" Shumpeter announces.

Reeves lifts a finger. Before he can say another word, though, Shumpeter drapes an arm over his shoulder and turns him toward the inn.

"I'm sure you're eager to talk details, as am I, but the

trail's been long and"—Shumpeter pauses, toe of his boot kicking at a board—"bumpy, which I'm sure you can appreciate. Let us palaver over the finest Windydown has to offer, and, being men of facile tongues and pragmatic minds, I've no doubt we'll arrive at a suitable way to thank me for my services."

Reeves is no small man, especially for one pushing eighty, but Shumpeter has him dwarfed. It's all Reeves can do to keep the other from picking him up bodily with just that one arm. And as Shumpeter strides toward the steps, the other two mayors fall apace behind, bushy eyebrows arched and fretful hands in pockets. We follow.

At the base of the steps, Shumpeter stops. He lets go of Reeves, who brushes off his shoulders and straightens his waistcoat. The bigger man reaches into one of the half-dozen pouches at his belt and pulls out a coin with a flourish. Stacy and Fran flinch. Annabelle folds her hands over her lap.

Laila hops to meet him.

"You look like a watchful sort," Shumpeter says. Then he falls to one knee, which puts his head in line with Laila's, even though she's two steps up. "See that wagon?"

Laila nods rapidly.

"Got all manner of dangerous in there. Beasts and oddities most of these good, simple folk can't comprehend. But you, my dear? You know their secrets well as I do, don't you?"

It's not clear what Laila's supposed to know, but the way she's grinning, it seems she's mighty proud to know it.

"Good girl!" Shumpeter says, and he presses the coin into Laila's palm, seeming not to care that her fingers are grimy. She brings it up, holding that coin in both hands.

Then she bites it, Granny Erskine–style.

"It's real!" she exclaims, holding the slightly bent and tooth-marked coin up to her sisters. Stacy and Fran just stare.

"See? A bright one, you are. That's why I'm trusting you with my wagon. You'll watch it for me, won't you?"

Laila gapes at him for a second. Then her face screws up, brow knit and lips pursed. It's as serious as I've ever seen her. She nods, and Shumpeter flips that massive hat from his nest of gold curls, setting it right atop Laila's head.

I swear, I've seen mushrooms with less audacious caps.

As Shumpeter climbs the steps, Laila marches across the Walk. She stands in front of the wagon, arms crossed and feet spread, shooting a prickly eye at anyone who dares glance her way.

Annabelle is Shumpeter's next stop. She tries to meet his gaze, but she gets a faceful of sun for the effort and she hurriedly looks away. It's uncomfortable seeing him so imposing, like she's a butterfly in a bear's cave. I step forward, but Liza catches my arm.

"Ahhh," Shumpeter says, "the flower of the Vale, I reckon! Let me guess . . . dress as pretty as yours . . . Why, your family owns this fine establishment!"

I hear Liza snort behind me. Annabelle blushes furiously, and before she can stammer an answer, Stacy responds. "No, sir. It's none of hers. Copper's mommy and daddy run the inn."

And then she points at me.

I back up a few steps, bumping into Liza. Shumpeter strides toward me, holding out a hand.

"Perhaps we should . . . Maybe inside . . . Just a boy . . . ," the mayors mumble, but the man ignores them.

"Pleasure to make your acquaintance . . . Cooper, was it?"

"Copper, sir," I say, grasping his hand. He squeezes hard enough to make my knuckles pop. My voice wants to squeak, but I don't let it. "Copper Inskeep."

"Inskeep?" Shumpeter echoes.

"Yes, sir."

A guffaw erupts from the depths of his barrel-like belly.

"Well, bless the practicality of the small-town mind! Of course it's Inskeep! And you'll be telling me your soot-stained and aproned friend is the stolid Miss Smith!"

"Um . . . yeah?" I say. "This is Liza."

Shumpeter reaches out to shake her hand, too.

"Mmm-hmm," Liza replies, staring at his palm like he's offering her something from one of his jars. Shumpeter keeps the hand out there for a muddy second, and when he gets the notion that Liza's not buying, he brings his other around and claps them together loudly. It startles Liza, who makes a face. I catch her gaze and shrug.

She mouths back, *Stolid?*

I shrug again, since I've no clue what it means, 'cept that it didn't endear Shumpeter to Liza one bit.

"Come, Copper Inskeep!" Shumpeter calls over his shoulder. "These wise gentlemen and I have business to discuss, and we mean to do so with full bellies and emptied cups!" Then he thrusts a hand at Annabelle—the same one he offered Liza. "And this enchanting young lady can attend us . . ."

Annabelle accepts his grip hesitantly, and he seems to hoist her up the steps with no more trouble than he might a just-plucked marsh rose. She glances back at me, eyes wide, and I hustle after the entourage. A twinge of something—nerves? Anger?—bedevils me, but I'm on the porch before I can figure out what's what.

"Wait," Liza says, snagging the back of my shirt just before I go in.

"Happy to," I respond, exhaling and shaking my head. We scuttle to the corner of the porch and lean together, just like when we'd conspire as little kids. Liza sneaks a peek at the wagon, where Laila is snapping at a few curious passersby and drawing lines around the wagon with her foot.

"This isn't good," Liza whispers.

"I know it," I respond. "He seems . . ."

"Loud?"

"Dangerous," I counter.

"For you more than anyone. He's a monster hunter!"

I'm having trouble coming up with a response that'll

make me look braver than I feel. After a few moments, I murmur, "Everyone needs a vocation, I guess?"

"Copper . . . *you're the monster!*"

I wrinkle my nose. "The thought had crossed my mind."

Liza glowers at me. "So what's your plan?"

"Plan? He's twice my size and has a wagon full of dead things. Think I'm gonna avoid him. Any luck, the mayors will get him to drive on out of here before nightfall."

Liza brings a hand to her brow and rubs. Her sooty fingers leave marks like double eyebrows, which only makes her look twice as fiery. "You heard him. He's here to hunt the Ghoul."

"Maybe he's a goodly sort?" I mutter. "Give him the benefit of the doubt?"

"Copper," Liza hisses, "some folk you give the benefit. The others you doubt. Like Annabelle."

I feel a bit of heat creeping up my collar. "What about Annabelle? Poor thing needs our help, and you get all bristly?"

On cue, she bristles.

"Maybe you *should* doubt her!"

"Why? Other than messing your apron and misplacing a few words, what's she done?"

Liza sets her jaw and turns heel. I reach out to stop her, but something tells me laying a finger on her now would be a good way to lose it. As she stomps down the stairs, she grumbles. It's hard to make out, but I think it's something like, "Head so full of mud he can't see what's plain."

I sigh and spit off the porch. It takes me a slow moment

to compose myself; I'm steaming, and that's no way to go into a crowded room. Still, half of me wishes I'd stay mad, because the longer I linger, the more that heat bakes into a crusty layer of worry, and it doesn't feel like it'll scrape off anytime soon. I rest my palms on the railing and stare at the wagon again. Somehow, it seems like it's gotten bigger.

"Hey! Copper Inskeep! No lookylooin'!" Laila shouts, and she wags a finger at me.

I stick out my tongue, and she fires off a two-handed gesture that'd get her a paddling if her ma saw it. Shaking my head, I turn about and slip through the inn doors, looking for the monster slayer.

Chapter Eighteen

Shumpeter has taken up court at the end of our longest
table. His fancy blue waistcoat is hanging from the
back of his chair, leaving him in the ruffly white shirt, the
cuffs of which whip about as he gestures. Even sitting, he's
as tall as Annabelle, who stands by his side, hands tucked
against her belly.

I slip in among the tradefolk. They huddle about the
edges of the taproom as though they're afraid to sit down.
The mayors are scattered around Shumpeter's table, and
my father has joined them. Stacy and Fran hide behind the
bar with their mother, who is slowly wiping out tankards
and hanging them from the tree branch above her. It's Doc
Bunder who speaks.

"Those are some colorful tales, Mr. Shumpeter," he says
respectfully. "And the Vale is as fond of a story as anywhere . . ."

"Ah!" Shumpeter shouts, slapping a hand on the table

so hard that the whole room jumps. "I can see I've sold myself quite enough. A man of business, you are! I respect that! And to business we shall attend . . . once we've broken bread. The journey has left me parched and hungry. Where is that Copper lad?"

The eyes of the room shift to me.

You're the pride of Windydown, I tell myself. *Act like it.*

"Yes, sir?" I say, grinning overbig and striding forward. Father gives me a little nod, and that calms me some.

"Your mother is the cook here, yes?"

"She owns the inn," my father states. "And yes, she's the cook. Won't let another soul touch her pans."

Shumpeter claps his hands. "A master craftsman guards his tools. I respect that! Son," he says, turning to me, "does this fine establishment have a menu?"

"It's midweek, sir," I explain. "That means lamb shank, barley bread, and apple tart."

"Excellent! Bring me a double portion of all three! And for the rest of the table?" Shumpeter points at each man in turn, all of whom shake their heads politely. "More for me, then!" Shumpeter laughs.

I give him a little bow and spin, weaving through folk to get to the kitchen door. Aunt Abigail slides over to put a hand on my shoulder, and she gives it a squeeze. Before I can make it all the way out, though, Shumpeter's voice booms across the taproom.

"Oh, and boy? For the bread? What types of butter do you have?"

I glance at Aunt Abigail. *Types?* I mouth, and she shrugs.

"I'll check!" I call, and then I disappear.

In the kitchen, Mother is already plating the lamb.

"I heard," she says.

"He wants . . ."

"Butter. Yes. I heard that, too. There's a crock in the larder."

"Mother?"

She pauses, turning around and smoothing her apron. I guess she read the quaver in my voice, because she comes over and puts her hands on the sides of my head, gently smoothing my hair. "It'll be okay, Copper. Your father and the mayors'll handle it."

"He's here to hunt the Ghoul . . ."

"Of which he'll find not a trace. We'll weather this storm, son, and in the meantime, we let the man spend his coins. Apparently, he'll pay good money for butter . . . ," she says, winking. I smile, and by the time she's got Shumpeter's tray ready, I'm hardly trembling.

Out in the taproom, Shumpeter is still talking. It makes me wonder if he's taken a breath yet.

". . . and that's when, right as I was about to accept the governor's invitation, our mutual acquaintance, Mr. Reynard Finch, found me."

Doc Bunder coughs. Reeves and Parsons share a glance.

"You have met Mr. Finch, yes?" Shumpeter presses.

"I did," Reeves says. "In fact, it was hard to miss him."

There are a few tradefolk in the crowd who were here

when Reynard did his tabletop proclamation, and they nod. One of them calls, "He said he'd get help!"

"And he did!" Shumpeter proclaims. "Not four days ago, Reynard scampered up my steps, face flushed and lungs a-heaving. 'Barl, my esteemed friend!' he tells me. 'I've just come from a place in dire need of your help! Quaint little town, salt-of-the-earth people—kindest and most gentle of folk. Windydown Vale, it's called.' I did what I could to calm the man, and then replied, 'Yes! The Vale! Their hospitality is legendary, as is the food at their inn!'"

Apparently he'd been watching the kitchen door like a marsh hawk, because Shumpeter beckons me forward. I put the tray down, and without even looking, his hand shoots forward and grabs my wrist. I stiffen, but before I can holler, tug away, or punch him, he flips my hand and slaps a gold coin into my palm, just like the one he gave Laila. I stare dumbly at it as his huge mitt curls around mine.

"A bit more than a copper for you there, Copper!" he chortles.

"Thanks, sir," I reply. "Never heard that one before."

Father casts me a look, and I shrug.

Shumpeter slathers butter on a hunk of bread as he continues. "So Reynard, our fine fellow, explains that this lovely little hamlet is beleaguered by a creature most foul—a ghoul. I assured him that I'm familiar with the species: the living dead, cursed to roam at night, ever hungry for the flesh of the pure ..."

The bite of bread he takes is so enormous that it leaves

a halo of butter above his mouth, waxing his mustache and the tip of his nose. As he chews, he turns to Annabelle. "They have a particular fondness for bone marrow . . . If a ghoul's about, you'll know by the cracking sound in the woods all around you. That's the ghoul enjoying its feast while it contemplates its next one . . ."

Annabelle seems to go a shade greener than her dress. I want to lean in and whisper to him about her father, but he's built up too much steam.

"Reynard was justifiably concerned, and his pleas struck a chord in my heart. I sent the governor my deepest regrets, readied my wagon, and came straightway! A good thing, too, by the look of it. This young lady seems positively terrified!"

Without even having to get up, Shumpeter reaches over and corrals Annabelle. He plunks her down in a chair next to him, sliding over his tray as if he means to share.

"Tell us, sweet girl. Are the stories true? Does Windy-down Vale suffer the predations of a ghoul?"

Annabelle lowers her gaze to her lap, hair tumbling to frame her face. The entire taproom has fallen silent, so her single, jagged sob tears through the space like an arrow to the hearts of all who listen.

"It . . . it took my father," she whispers. "And no one can find him."

Shumpeter's tongue roves out, collecting the butter from his mustache as he listens. Annabelle shivers through a few more quiet breaths and then looks up. When she does,

Shumpeter slams his fist on the table, causing his tray to hop, his tart to topple, and the whole of the room to gasp.

"A tragedy!" he roars. "That a flower such as she could be robbed of her doting daddy, just when she needs him most! And I'm sure these folk have done all they can to help you?"

Annabelle sniffles and nods.

Then she points at me.

"Copper's been wonderful, sir. He knows all about the Ghoul and the swamps, and he's been looking for my father for days," Annabelle says. As she goes on to describe the Ghoul, Shumpeter swings around, staring at me with a twinkle in his eye. I back up a step.

"A good, good lad! The best!" Shumpeter declares. "Where is this boy's guardian?"

"I'm Copper's father."

The way he says it makes me stand a little straighter, shoulders square.

"You've done a fantastic job, sir!" Shumpeter says, and he pushes away from the table, chair groaning and floor-boards creaking. My father barely has time to stand before Shumpeter's hand is swallowing his.

"Rule number one in hunting a dangerous beast?" Shumpeter announces. "Know the territory. And since I don't, I'd like to hire your boy here, Mr. Inskeep. Don't worry—I'll keep him safe, and he can teach me a thing or two about our quarry. What do you say?"

"You want me to send my son into the swamps with a stranger?"

Shumpeter laughs. "Are we strangers? Is that what we are? I know your name; you know mine. I know your trade; you know mine . . ."

"And yet I don't know you."

Father's tone is calm but sharp. Shumpeter might be the bear to my father's porcupine, but if he presses, he's gonna taste the quills.

Shumpeter pats one of the pouches at his belt. It jingles tellingly. "You will, of course, be compensated for your son's time."

"Douglas," a man from the crowd says. It's Barnabas Tucker, an old wine lugger that's stayed at the inn about as much as any trademan alive. "Maybe let the boy go? If it means gettin' rid of the Ghoul . . ."

"What better chance are we going to have?" another adds.

Several more tradefolk nod and murmur.

My father doesn't budge.

It's Reeves who finally breaks the staredown.

"Doug . . . ," he says, wary of the ring of tradefolk watching. "Tell you what. I'll go, too. Keep track of 'im for you."

Reeves and my father share a look, one that includes a quick sidelong glance at Shumpeter. It makes me wonder which of us Reeves means to keep an eye on: me, or the monster hunter?

"Here's a man who wants what's best for his people!"

Shumpeter tells the crowd, his big hand slapping Reeves's back in a friendly sort of way.

"Hear, hear!" a few folk respond.

Father turns to me. He puts both hands on my shoulders, leaning in to make it clear that no matter how many are watching us, it's just him and me.

"Choice is yours, Copper," Father whispers.

"Can I think on it a spell?" I reply, my forehead nearly touching his.

Out of the corner of my eye, I see Shumpeter sliding toward us, trying to be all casual-like. Reeves shuffles in front of him.

"Take your time, son."

I don't take long. Part of me is powerfully uncomfortable with the idea of heading out of town with the man who makes a living slaying the likes of me, even with Reeves along for the ride. On the other hand, I'm thinking that keeping tabs on Shumpeter might not be the worst idea. I look around the room. Bunch of the tradefolk are hopping foot to foot, craning to hear what I say. What's it going to look like if the innkeepers' son turns down a chance to help rid them of the monster that's been at their heels for years? Still, I'm unsure.

Until I look at Annabelle.

She's got her hands clasped like she's praying right at me, and there's an ache in her manner that tears at my heart. "*Please,*" she whispers, and that settles it.

"I'll do it," I say.

Father nods. Then he faces Shumpeter.

"Copper may go . . . One day and one night only, then you deliver him back here. Mayor Reeves is with him the whole time."

"Excellent!" Shumpeter exclaims, pouncing over to wrap an arm around both me and my father. "You won't regret it, Douglas. And as for you, Copper . . . why, when all the people of Windydown Vale hear how you helped me defeat the Ghoul, you'll be a hero! We'll set out tomorrow at dawn!"

"I . . . have chores," I mutter.

"I'll take care of them, Copper," my father says softly.

I smile as best as I can, but my skin is crawling. Somehow, Shumpeter's big arm draped across my shoulders feels more suffocating than any mud pit I've been in since I died. We watch as he eats the rest of his food.

Then orders seconds.

And thirds.

I'm awestruck; I've never seen a creature put so much food in its mouth all at once, and there's a strange way Shumpeter's chin bounces while he chews. Puts me in mind of a frog. The rest of the crowd is less enthralled, though, and they clear out, leaving just Annabelle, the mayors, my father, and me to witness the spectacle. After maybe the biggest belch ever to rattle the windows of the Sunken Inn, Shumpeter sits back, laces his fingers over his belly, and says, "I believe the time has come to discuss remuneration.

Children, you need not be present for the particulars. Why don't you run and play?"

Father nods, and I collect Annabelle, Stacy, and Fran. We retreat to Annabelle's room.

"What's *remuneration*?" Stacy asks.

"Means payment," Annabelle says. I stare at her, and she blushes. "Southern schooling."

"How much you think he charges for ghoul extermination?" I wonder as I head over to the window. As soon as I've got it open, I shove my head right out into the cool evening air. To my surprise, Annabelle joins me, wedging herself into the space until we're shoulder to shoulder, her long hair dangling from the window like a midnight waterfall.

"Whatever he asks, it's worth it," she responds.

I don't reply.

"Hey, Copper?" she says after a few moments.

"Yeah?"

"When you're out there with him . . . will you keep an eye open for—"

"I will," I say.

"Thank you," she whispers, and she kisses me on the cheek again. It startles me just as much as when she did it in the swamps, so much that I don't say another word. And even after she wriggles out of the window frame, I stay put, trying to keep my mind on tomorrow's expedition and my gaze on the curl of smoke wafting up from the blacksmith's chimney, its line jagged but unbroken against the horizon.

Chapter Nineteen

Mayor Reeves leans over his musket like a walking stick, fingers twined and foot tapping. I'm standing next to him, pitching pebbles into the mud. Reeves squints at the inn door.

"Shumpeter said he was just gonna . . ."

"Eat breakfast," I sigh.

"And that was . . ."

"Three breakfasts ago."

Reeves shields his eyes and peers at the sun. It's well over the mountains and shining hard on the face of the inn.

"He is paying for all this food, right?"

"Overpaying, yeah," I say, flicking a fly off my sleeve. Reeves chuckles. "What?" I ask.

"Did your pa tell you Shumpeter's asking price?"

"For killing the Ghoul? No."

"Ten thousand."

I drop the rest of my rocks. They clatter on the Long Walk and sneak through the slats, 'cept the few that roll backward and under Shumpeter's wagon.

Reeves shakes his head, long beard dusting his belly. "Durned fool."

"What did he do when you turned him down?"

A crooked grin exposes Reeves's haphazard teeth. "We didn't."

"You . . . We . . . *What?*"

"Could've promised him double that. Triple. All the coins in the southlands and every bit of gold we've got stashed. Don't matter."

"Huh?" I mutter, and then, "Oh!"

"Now you're gettin' it, boy. We only pay Shumpeter if he finds the Ghoul . . ." Reeves taps the tip of his musket on the boards twice. "Which he's not gonna do—not while he's got Copper Inskeep standing next to him and me lookin' out besides."

"And in the meantime," I say, "he keeps tossing coins around like they're . . ."

Reeves smirks. "Pebbles."

"Glad you're coming, Mayor Reeves," I say.

"Had to. It's my job to look out for all of Windydown Vale," he murmurs, putting a hand on my arm. "That includes its sons . . . and its Ghoul . . ."

I smile, and we settle back in. Reeves starts whistling "Ghoul's Britches." Liza's dad used to play it on the fiddle. He'd sit on our porch back in Old Windydown, plucking while Liza and I made up silly dances. Every time we got to the verse about those britches being cursed by the witches, we'd fall down laughing.

I'm kind of surprised I still remember the words.

Makes me wonder if Liza does, too.

It's just as Reeves hits the bridge that Shumpeter flings the inn door wide, stomping down the steps and adjusting his wig.

"Grand morning!" he says.

Reeves sucks his teeth and hefts his gun over his shoulder. "Has been for a while now."

Shumpeter laughs. "Isn't that just so?" he replies. "Copper, you got a good night's rest, I hope?"

"I slept," I reply.

"Marvelous!" Shumpeter declares, as if I told him we'd bagged the Ghoul while he was finishing his fried potatoes. I glance at Reeves. The furrow 'twixt his eyebrows is getting deeper by the moment.

"That fine young lass inside tells me you're in the know 'bout where we might find this creature, and when," Shumpeter says as he steps past me. A bristling, jangly key ring dangles from his belt, and he deftly flips it until he's holding a single heavy iron key. There's a padlock nearly as big as my head on the wagon, keeping those break-apart walls from, well, breaking apart. He unlocks it, reaches for the catch, and pries one of the walls open. I watch him rummage until he says, "You still there, Copper?"

"Oh, yeah," I reply. "Annabelle said that I—"

"Annabelle! Yes! That's her," Shumpeter says.

I clear my throat. "She said I knew all that stuff?"

"She surely did!" Shumpeter replies, pulling out of the wagon with an armload of gear. At the top of the heap is a gun, long and heavy and nothing like Mayor Reeves's. He holds it out to me.

"That's . . . that's okay," I murmur.

He turns to Reeves. "Musket is a fine weapon, but for my money . . . and I've made a lot . . . the blunderbuss is the way to hunt a creature like a ghoul. More stopping power up close—and we know how close our monster likes to get, eh, Copper?" Shumpeter lunges forward suddenly, teeth bared. I flinch, and he seems mighty pleased.

Reeves looks from the blunderbuss to his musket and back. I do the same. Shumpeter's weapon must weigh three times as much, and it's got a muzzle like a cave, wide and deep and yawning. "Never much for a blunder," Reeves says coolly. "Load time means you don't get more'n a shot off."

Shumpeter winks. "Doesn't matter when you only need one."

I grin like I know what he's talking about.

"Lock that back up for me, will you, Copper?" Shumpeter says, and he tosses me the padlock. I manage to snag it without fumbling, and I click it into place through the fat metal loops of the clasp.

"We're not taking the wagon?" I ask when I'm done.

"Wagon's a mite large for our work," Shumpeter notes, tapping the side of his nose. "Something that big could scare away our ghoul!"

Ain't that the truth.

"So we walk?" Reeves mutters.

"We ride," Shumpeter corrects. "I trust you both know your way around a horse?"

I nod. Reeves coughs. "Been a while, but I'll make do," he assures us.

It turns out that Shumpeter's horses are gentle and well-trained. I half expected mine to drag me to my doom like a muck kelpie, but instead it just snorts and nuzzles my neck until I laugh. Shumpeter presses a few coins into the stablemaster's hands, loads his gear on one horse, then hoists himself on the other. I worry for a second that he'll be too much for the creature, but it holds, and he reaches forward to rub a hand affectionately along its muzzle.

"That one is Courageous Nellie," Shumpeter says, pointing to Reeves's horse. Reeves seems unimpressed. "And Copper, you've the company of the High Duchess Magdalena. We call her Mags."

"Heya, Mags," I whisper, and she flicks her tail.

"These two are Brimstone and Perdition. Bree and Perdy for short. They're the youngest of the sisters."

"Nice to meet you," I say fondly. Shumpeter grins, flicks Perdy's reins, and gives Bree a light swat on the rump.

"All right, young ghoul hunter. Which way?"

"Sir?"

"You're the expert. Do we seek our quarry to the north, or south?"

Reeves catches my eye, a bit of his beard drawn between his lips. He gave me the same look before I took Annabelle out, and I know his meaning well enough: *not near Old Windydown*. I agree; last thing we need is Shumpeter finding my costume. So I point to the southern trail. Shumpeter grins, shouts, "Hya!" and eases Perdy into a trot.

Just like that, we're off.

It takes only a few minutes to put Windydown behind us, though it's a while yet before Mags's shoes touch soil. We don't talk much for that first stretch, since we'd have to shout over the clopping on the Long Walk. As soon as we step down onto the trail, though, Shumpeter sets to.

"So, Copper," he says amiably, "what's the word in Windydown?"

"Sir?"

"Chitchat, son. Picking your brain to pass the time. Truth be told, though, I've got other motivations."

"Maybe we should move more quietly?" Reeves suggests. "We are hunting, are we not?"

"Lower your musket, good man!" Shumpeter says. I guess he must be speaking metaphorical-like, because Reeves's gun is packed in his bundle behind him. "By all accounts, we'll not see the Ghoul until nightfall. Indeed, it might behoove us to make a bit of din. Perhaps the vile thing will grow curious and be more likely to favor our camp with a visit!"

Reeves twists his lips skeptically, but then shrugs.

"Anyway, Copper, it may surprise you to know that I'm not altogether unfamiliar with your little village."

"You've been to Windydown before?" I ask. Reeves shifts in his saddle, and I notice he's gripping his reins pretty tight.

"No, nothing like that. I'd've remembered your mother's cooking if I had," he says appreciatively, rubbing his belly. "Part of being a monster hunter is knowing your history, since evil collects legends like flies on rot. So before I tackle a beastie, I scour the city records. Talk to old folk. Read some tales. Yup. Windydown's got herself a reputation."

"Like what?"

Shumpeter clicks his tongue. Perdy swerves a little, but Shumpeter's sharp with the reins. "Good people. Safe passage. And gold."

That last word falls heavier than the others, like a stone hitting the water at the bottom of a deep, deep well. I think of Mother, and of Granny Erskine.

"Mines're gone," Reeves snaps. "Sluiceways, too. Nobody's panned so much as a nugget since the sinkholes took us and the valley flooded."

"But that beautiful inn . . . that wonderful and well-maintained Walk . . . surely you've got something squirreled away?"

I shrug. "Well, we've got a few slugs, but—"

"I think that's enough, Copper," Reeves warns.

"Yes!" Shumpeter says with a laugh. "Quite right. How uncouth of me, especially when we've more pressing matters to discuss. Tell me, how long has the Vale suffered the malevolence of the Ghoul? If it's been haunting this valley for millennia, it might have a deep and well-established lair. I wonder . . . have you known the creature to appear at random, or is there a migratory pattern to its prowl?"

My brain is playing catch-up to Shumpeter's words, so I look to Reeves. He locks eyes with the barrel-chested man, head bobbing in time with Nellie's gait, and something passes between them. It reminds me of the way Aunt Abigail sometimes gives the triplets a "wordless talkin'-to," 'cept with Reeves and Shumpeter, I can't tell who's doing the talking. Eventually, Reeves grumbles, "Well, if you're half as good a hunter as you say, there'll be no need for timelines, muskets, or even a third night in the Vale. You can be on your way . . ."

"With ten thousand coins in my pocket," Shumpeter says firmly.

"Aye," Reeves responds, and we fall silent again.

In the swampiest part of the Vale, where Old Windy-down sits, there aren't many trees left. Plenty of their skeletons, of course, and half-buried trunks crusted with mushrooms, but no big, leafy boughs. Certainly nothing to build an inn on. Out here on the trail, though, where the horse's hooves kick up honest-to-goodness dust, the trees are so thick I can hardly see through 'em. That's what makes it all the more shocking when Shumpeter reins in suddenly, points to the forest, and growls, "There."

I slow Mags, and Reeves brings Nellie around. We both

peer into the gloom, but I can't see anything, 'cept maybe more trees. There must be something, though, because Shumpeter slides off his horse, grabs his blunderbuss, and slips between two sycamores.

"Now wait just a . . . ," Reeves mumbles, and he bids Nellie go as close to the tree line as she can. There's no good way she's going to fit, though, so I hop down, handing Mags's reins to Reeves.

"I'm on it," I assure him, and I follow Shumpeter.

He hasn't gone far—maybe two dozen steps or so. He's at the base of a particularly knobby and scarred tree, and he's looking down at something. When I approach, he sticks his hand out to warn me, then curls his fingers.

Come on slowly, boy.

A few more cautious steps, and I see why. There's a swarm of biteflies churning and chewing on something. They're so thick I can't get but a glimpse of what's underneath, but I don't need to.

The blood-greased leg bone jutting up from the center tells me plenty.

I bury my nose in the crook of my elbow. Shumpeter touches my shoulder and looks at me, maybe to see whether or not I mean to puke. I shake my head, and he nods. Then he uses the bulby end of his blunderbuss to point at the shaft of bone. It's dark, but I can make out where the joint was broken off, leaving a spearlike tip. Just beneath, there are deep slashes. They look like jagged knife wounds.

Or claw marks.

A panicky part of me screams *Annabelle's daddy!* but the thought is quickly banished. The shape's all wrong to be human, and there're scraps of fur scattered around the thing. I breathe as big a sigh of relief as a body can near such an odor, and I blink at Shumpeter to tell him I've seen all I care to.

We head back to the trail, where Reeves has gathered the reins of all four horses. "They're a bit uneasy," he informs us. "Mind telling me why?"

Shumpeter wipes his brow with a kerchief from his pocket. "Well, Copper? Your report?" he says, encouraging me with a sweep of his hand.

I clear my throat and stand up straight. "Carcass," I say, trying my best to imitate Doc on the diagnosis. "Deer, from the look of it. Not long dead, but enough to reek and bring the flies to supper."

"And?" Shumpeter says expectantly.

"It's been chewed. Meat and bones."

Reeves is grim as he listens. After a few moments, he says, "And you think it was the Ghoul?"

Shumpeter replaces his blunderbuss atop the gear. "Can't be sure yet. What other beasts do you have around these parts that might be able to inflict such wounds?"

"Wolves, mostly," I say. Like bears, they don't much go for the mud, so I haven't seen one personally, but I've heard howls echo along the mountainsides before. Reeves mentions the bears, but Shumpeter shakes his head.

"I've seen more than my fair share of wolf and bear

kills. Plenty of pretty little towns just like yours have called upon Barl Shumpeter, desperate to find the horror that dragged off their favorite son or daughter in the middle of the night. More often than not, it's no supernatural threat. Doesn't make it any less heartbreaking, but it does speak to the rarity of monsters in these modern times, thank the Lord."

Reeves crosses his arms. "So in your expert opinion . . ."

"This wasn't wolves. They'd have stripped every scrap of flesh from that deer. Our killer was after a different kind of treat."

"Marrow?" I ask.

"Marrow," Shumpeter confirms.

"Hmph," Reeves says.

"We'll move on a little farther, find a place to camp. It may be that our dearly departed friend"—Shumpeter pauses, favoring himself with a chuckle that I can't fathom—"is a grim coincidence, but it also may mean we've stumbled upon our foe's hunting grounds." His eyes still locked on the trees, Shumpeter bids Perdy into a collected walk and we fall in line, Reeves leading Bree with the gear.

Ahead, the trail veers sharply to the right, a moss-covered boulder forcing the diversion. I know the spot well. It's a popular resting point for tradefolk; part of it juts out like a pouty lip, good for shelter on a rainy night. I've haunted more than a few travelers out of that hidey-hole, but now I'm peering into it like it's the first time I've seen it. There are shadows I've never noticed before, broken shards of stone littering the ground like cast-off teeth. I shiver and look away.

"Here," Shumpeter says, distracting me from my thoughts. He's found a big gap in the trees on our right, one all four of our horses can fit through at the same time. The undergrowth is crushed pretty flat, too.

"Deer run," Reeves declares quickly, almost like he's trying to fit it in before Shumpeter can.

"Good eye, grandpa!" Shumpeter responds. "That was my thought, too. We follow this, I bet we find a stream, clearing, or high patch we can use. Come!"

Shumpeter works the reins and guides Perdy into the woods. Fortunately for him, all of the lower branches seem to be bent or broken; he doesn't even have to hunch over to get through. Reeves and I have room to spare. It's a good thing, too.

Means we can avoid the second deer carcass in the middle of the path.

"Definitely not wolves," Shumpeter calls back solemnly as we pass. I try not to stare, but it's too gruesome to look away. Even when I close my eyes, I can see it, and it makes me crawl inside my head awhile, rolling about with those thoughts. Gets so bad, in fact, that I don't recognize where we're going till we're there.

It's a place I've been to before.

In the dark, and in the rain.

Shumpeter was there, too.

"See? A clearing!" he announces, jumping down and

guiding Perdy to the same tree I saw her tethered to before. It looks different in the light, but my arm hairs are still dancing, and the first place I look is in the branches.

Nothing.

"I suppose you'll be wanting a fire," Reeves says. He's already in his bag, rummaging for matches.

"Centerpiece of any campsite, in my opinion," Shumpeter replies with a wink. I try for a smile, but I guess it veers too far into grimace. Shumpeter strides over and tugs me to his side. He smells like sweat and sausage.

"If I know my demons, the Ghoul won't come into the clearing with a roaring fire. It'll be curious and hungry, but you don't build up a legend by taking chances. That girl . . . the poor one who lost her father . . ."

"Annabelle," I say.

"Right. When she was recounting her woeful tale, she mentioned that she and her father were attacked before they had a chance to set camp. Says you confirmed that's how it likes to hunt."

I nod. Shumpeter rubs a hand in my hair, and a tingle of pride spreads from the top of my head to my cheeks. It's not enough to dispel my misgivings, though. Can't be a coincidence, us being back here.

"How lucky are we, grandpa, to have the expert with us!" Shumpeter declares.

"I . . . I just know what everyone says."

"Boy hears a lot in the inn," Reeves adds.

"One could hardly imagine otherwise!" Shumpeter says,

and he spreads his hands. "Come! Let us gather wood for this magnificent fire. Copper can educate us as we do."

We don't have to go far. Windydown got its name for a reason; there isn't a dead branch that lasts long in the Vale. And it seems like every time I pick up a stick, Shumpeter's there with a new question about the Ghoul or Windydown. It reminds me of Annabelle herself, only Shumpeter's not kissin' my cheek for the favor.

I decide to count that blessing twice.

And anyway, it's Reeves that answers most of the questions, 'specially those on Windydown itself. He even explains about the inn: how long it's been in my family, and how owning the inn is such an important position—and my mother such an important woman—that my father took her last name when they married. That gets a belly laugh from Shumpeter, who calls it "positively cosmopolitan." I think he means it as a compliment.

By the time the mountains are swallowing the sun, we've got a stack of wood big enough to build a house. I give some feed to the horses and stow the saddles. When I get back to the center of the clearing, I'm expecting Shumpeter to be hard at work lighting the fire. Instead it's Reeves, grousing about his creaky back as he blows beneath a pile of kindling.

"Shumpeter?" I ask, looking around.

"The great hunter went to relieve himself."

"Oh," I murmur, wincing. I don't need the reminder of how my own body's feeling, especially since I haven't been stingy with my canteen. I stare at the tree line, foolishly hoping to spot a derelict outhouse or something.

"Our perimeter is clear," Shumpeter announces when he returns. Reeves sits up, blinking hard and looking unsteady. I hop to, kneeling and offering my arm.

"Thanks, Copper," he says, woozy. "Used up too much of my air."

"Let me," I reply, and I work at the fire until it's going strong. The boughs above us seem to close in and rustle, like old men warming their hands.

When he sees the fire, Shumpeter pats at the ground until he finds a dry spot. Then he reclines, propping himself on an elbow and pulling a block of cheese from his bag. He bites into it like it's an apple. I curl my arms around my knees.

"So your family's been in the Vale since the beginning," Shumpeter says.

"Yes?"

"You must be very proud."

"The Vale is home, sir," I reply.

"Oh, most certainly! Bet a boy like you would do just about anything for the Vale!"

It's dark enough now that I'm having trouble making out Shumpeter's face, especially with a hunk of cheese in the way. It almost sounds like he's poking fun at me, so I just say, "Sir?"

"Braving this adventure with me and grandpa . . ."

"I ain't your grandpa!"

"With the elder statesman here—it speaks highly of your upbringing, and I mean more than just Ma and Pa Inskeep. Why, I'll bet the whole town had a hand in raising you."

I think back on all the days I spent in the blacksmith's shop, or at the stables, or running wild along the Walk. "I guess that's so, sir."

"Yep. It'd take something powerful to shake your faith in Windydown Vale, of that I'm certain."

Reeves pauses halfway through a bite of bread, and I peer through the smoke. "I'm not afraid of seeing the Ghoul," I say.

Shumpeter laughs. "I can see that! It's one of the reasons I like you, Copper."

"You don't much know me, sir."

"I know your type. Good stock, hard worker, looks out for his own and others besides. Annabelle speaks very highly of you."

I'm hoping he thinks it's the fire glow that's ruddying my cheeks.

"I don't mean to tease, son," he continues. "All I'm saying is that, when the time comes, I'm sure you'll do what it takes to protect the Vale."

"Oh, you have no idea what we'd do to protect the Vale, Shumpeter," Reeves says softly.

Shumpeter finishes his last bite of cheese, sucks his fingertips, and smiles at me. "We'll see," he says, and he belches softly.

"I'll take first watch," Reeves offers, and Shumpeter agrees. Because I'm youngest, I offer to go second; I'm out at night half the time anyway. Not like this, of course, but I see good in the dark and hear better than Reeves. I guess the plan is fine with Shumpeter, because he rolls his pack under his head, curls his arms around his blunderbuss, and promptly falls asleep. Reeves tosses a few more logs on the fire, then hunkers down himself.

I try to get up enough courage to go pee.

Every few seconds, I tell myself to move, but every time, my body refuses. I try to clear my mind. I go through everything I know about the forest and swamps. I call myself every name I can think of.

Doesn't matter.

Weirdest thing is, I can't even tell if I'm scared. I shouldn't be—I survived a mud drowning. I've been shot at by tradefolk and chased by their dogs. I've haunted these woods hundreds of times, on nights darker than this, and I've never seen anything that shook me.

Well, 'cept Shumpeter's wagon the other night, right in this very spot.

And those deer carcasses.

Father always says that the easiest way to get stuck on the side of a mountain is to refuse to admit that you're climbing one. So I finally decide that I am, in fact, terrified. Every part of me feels cold, even my back—and it's just a few feet from the fire. The trees have all gone gray in the dark. The wind swirls around so thick that I can't tell what's the hiss of the fire or the grinding of Shumpeter's teeth as he sleeps. I look to Reeves for comfort, but he's nodded off, too, sucking softly on his beard.

It's when my bladder starts stabbing me that I finally move, and once I start, I can't stop. I sprint for the trees, thinking to get behind one, do what I have to, then get back before my legs lock up again. Trouble is, the longer you wait, the longer it takes . . .

And the longer it takes, the more scared I get. Soon as I finish, I button up and set to sprint back to the fire.

That's when I hear the cracking sound.

I freeze, head tilted toward a moonlit opening in the trees. With my bladder empty, a little courage sneaks back in, and I find myself able to creep forward. A fallen tree cuts across the path like a smear of paint, black on black. To the right, a huge, dark disk—the tree's roots, pulled up as it fell.

Whatever's making the noise is behind those roots.

Liza sometimes tells me I'm moment smart but life stupid, and I guess she's right. I can figure out how to stop a runaway horse once I'm on it, but can't see not to grab it in the first place. I can pick out the best branches to hook when I'm swinging over mirror mud, but it rarely occurs to me to go around. And now? I know just how to sneak up on whatever's behind those roots . . .

I bend down, untying my boots. I slip my feet out slowly, then creep toward the trunk of the fallen tree. I'm on it in one silent leap, and I crawl my way forward, no leaves or twigs or stones to kick. When I'm just a few paces from the root wall, I stop to listen. Sure enough, the cracking's still there, the sharp sound of brittle bone. There's more, though:

A wet, slurping noise.

And muttering.

I close my eyes and exhale.

Then I climb.

At the top of the mound of dirt, roots stick out like greedy hands, and I grab two, pulling myself to the lip just far enough to peek over.

Only then does it occur to me that I probably should've run away.

There are no flies this time, so it's easy to see the remains of the deer. It's been torn apart, insides haloed out in a ring of blood and viscera. At the center of that ring, hunched into a twitching, gibbering ball, is a creature. It reaches into the crimson pile in front of it, scraping around until it finds a sinewy, gore-streaked bone. It holds its prize aloft almost delicately, turning it about in the moonlight.

Inspecting it.

Appraising it.

Then snapping it in two.

The sound is what gets me—a knot forms in my throat, cutting my breath into a gagged strangle. The thing below me stiffens, cocking its head. It sets the bone down carefully. It sniffs the air.

And it looks right at me.

I gasp. Its head—too big and bulbous to be human—lolls,

twisting at an impossible angle. Most of what I see is pale, except the angry, wet streak of scarlet cutting from cheek to cheek. Its mouth opens, long tongue curling as it starts to gurgle.

In reply, I scream like a child.

Like a fool.

Like prey.

Chapter Twenty

I launch myself backward. The roots and dirt break apart under my hands, and I fall on the trunk hard. It blasts the wind out of me, cutting my hollering short. I've got no breath to run, so I roll to the ground and crawl beneath the trunk, wedging myself in.

The creature comes around.

I can see only its legs, spindly and pale. The moonlight reveals hundreds of little cuts across its skin, like it's been creeping through groundbriar. The stink of the deer corpse follows it, and I have to cover my mouth to keep from retching. At first I think it's going to shamble on by, but it stops, grimy, bloody feet kicking at the leaf cover as it hunts for me. There's a moment when a plan forms in my mind—I could burst free, tackle it at the knees, maybe get in a fist or two while it's down.

Of course, I don't know how strong it is.

Or how fast.

Or if it can even be hurt at all.

Still, it beats getting clawed to death just lying here.

So I get ready to attack.

"Copper! Copper, boy! Where are you?" Shumpeter's voice echoes through the trees, and I give up my plan. The creature's legs draw in like it's getting ready to spring, and I see Shumpeter storming toward us, blunderbuss in one hand and a fiery branch in the other. When he spots the thing, he squints through the dark, holding his makeshift torch up.

"Copper? Is that you?" he asks.

"That's not me!" I shout from my hiding place. The creature's feet pivot, its long, spidery toes curling and uncurling in the leaves. I can tell it's looking right at me, even though I can't see its face. Behind it, Shumpeter drops the torch and raises his blunderbuss.

The creature runs.

Shumpeter fires.

And the world turns to thunder and ash.

Chapter Twenty-One

By the time Reeves stumbles into our patch of woods, Shumpeter has me sitting up. He's rubbing my back while I hold a damp kerchief to my eyes. I think Reeves says something, but it's hard to hear him—my ears are still ringing. Hard to see, too, but I can tell the two men are pointing. Shumpeter looks angry. Reeves tries to calm him, and he kneels next to me.

"Important thing is that Copper's okay," I hear through the roar.

"Yeah!" I shout. "I'm all right!"

Reeves winces; I guess I'm being overloud. Truth be told, none of my senses seem to be working at peak. When Shumpeter fired his gun, there was a massive boom and an even bigger flash. I thought for a second that the blunderbuss had exploded, but Shumpeter has it over his shoulder, more intact than I am.

They give me a few more minutes to recover before helping me up. I look around, trying to see if there might be a trail of blood, a set of dragging footprints, or anything that'll let us track the creature, but there's nothing. As we make our way back to the clearing, Shumpeter and Reeves argue.

"Weapon like that, you could've torn Copper to shreds!"

"The boy is fine!"

"Only because he was under that tree!"

"Only because I know how to use my weapon!"

"If that's the case, why am I not looking down on the corpse of some diabolical fiend right now?"

"Otherworldly creatures follow their own rules, which don't always play well with ours. Might be that the kind of shot I used has no effect."

"Might be you're not a very good shot!"

Shumpeter stops, turning and shoving a thick finger right up in Reeves's face. "Oh, and what would you do with that little peashooter you brought along?"

I flinch. A musket's not an easy thing to aim, but I've seen Reeves hit a rabbit at two hundred paces. Anybody from the Vale knows not to question his shooting.

Of course, Shumpeter ain't from the Vale.

"If I were shooting, this'd all be over," Reeves warns. "No mess, no fuss. Just a little hole in the thing's skull, 'bout yea big . . ."

Reeves curls his index finger and thumb together, making a tight circle. He reaches up and presses it to Shumpeter's forehead. The bigger man slaps it away.

"Mighty talk for an old man who falls asleep during his watch. Can't even keep an eye on a boy, let alone the Ghoul of Windydown Vale! But don't worry, grandpa. I'm going to do you a kindness. Not going to mention that part when we get back to town. In return, you tell everyone what we saw. The Ghoul is real."

Shumpeter steps even closer to Reeves, who doesn't back down.

"And my fee just went up another three thousand."

For the rest of the night, nobody says a word. Nobody sleeps, either. We just huddle around the fire. Reeves keeps his musket trained on the tree line, and Shumpeter fiddles with his blunderbuss. Fortunately for me, both men are so mad at each other that neither bothers to ask what I was doing out in the woods in the first place.

Chapter Twenty-Two

There's no fanfare when we ride back into Windydown. Mostly, it's silent looks of concern. A crowd waits for us on the porch of the Sunken Inn: Mother, Father, Aunt Abigail, Stacy, Fran, the other two mayors, and Annabelle. She grips the railing with white knuckles. Her eyes are red and her face pale, like she stayed up all night worrying. She smiles when she sees me, but slumps when I shake my head. Then she runs inside.

We dismount, and Shumpeter goes to stow his gun and gear. He's surprised to find Laila sitting on the toeboard, his hat pulled low over her brow.

"Ain't nobody touched it this mornin'," she announces proudly. "Not sure about last night. *Somebody* made me go to bed."

She shoots her mom a withering look. Aunt Abigail ignores her.

"Good lass," Shumpeter says, and he fishes about for another coin. Laila snatches it and waves it at Stacy, who makes a gobliny face in reply. Shumpeter smiles, and then he strides up the porch steps. Reeves and I follow slowly; my head's still ringing, and I'm all-over sore.

When Shumpeter reaches the top step, he turns to face the crowd. It looks like he means to make another speech, especially when he raises both hands for attention. But all he says is, "We've encountered the Ghoul." Then he turns heel and marches into the taproom.

There's an explosion of chatter, too much for my still-tinny ears to follow. Instead, I fall into Mother's arms, letting her guide me inside. She plunks me into the fluffy chair in the corner, where I slump so far my backside almost slides right off the cushion. Aunt Abigail brings me a cup of tea, hot and honey-scented. She must have given me a double spoonful. I hold it under my chin and watch the room through the steam.

"Thirteen thousand?" Parsons squeals. "You know this is coming out of our pockets! It's not like we collect taxes!"

"Maybe it's time to start," Shumpeter retorts.

"Reeves! You saw the Ghoul?" my father asks.

Reeves hooks his thumbs in his belt and squares his shoulders. "I did not; this ogre scared the thing away with his—"

"The boy saw it," Shumpeter interrupts, and he points at me.

Father slides over, kneeling by my side. "Copper, is that true?"

"Come, boy," Shumpeter says, his voice deep. "Tell them of the threat the Vale faces."

It feels like all of Windydown is staring at me: Friends. Family. The mayors. A dozen tradefolk desperate for answers.

Annabelle.

I close my eyes. That bulby head and blood-smeared mouth are right there in my mind. But so is the clearing. Shumpeter's wagon.

And Reeves's words: *It's my job to look out for all of Windydown Vale . . . That includes its Ghoul.*

Way I figure it, that's my job, too.

So I decide to make it simple.

I tell the truth.

"I saw something," I concede.

Shumpeter leans in. "Go on."

"But I don't know what it was."

"Damn it!" Shumpeter screams, and he kicks a table with his steel-shod boot. The taproom erupts.

"See? There's something out there! If it's a threat, we should kill it!" a trademan declares.

"The Vale's not handing no bleedin' thirteen thousand over for the hide of a mangy bear!"

"Bear? I've seen that thing in the flesh more'n once. It's no bear!"

"Pay the man!"

"Show us the Ghoul! Then we pay him!"

"Enough!" Shumpeter growls, and a hush falls. "It

doesn't matter what the boy thought he saw. Your doom is out there, Windydown, and everyone knows it."

Doc Bunder leans over the table, hands flat on the wood, good eye trained on Shumpeter. "Ghoul's been about for decades. We've done all right."

"You have!" a voice near the bar calls. The room turns. Standing there is a gaunt man, his gray hair greasy, mustache long, and eyes haunted. I recognize him immediately.

It's Cutty's dad, Mr. Villers.

He staggers toward Doc, finger poking at the mayor's shoulder. "My family's not fared so well. If this man can end that miserable creature's existence, then I say it's worth every coin . . . including mine."

With a flourish, he rips a pouch from his belt, tossing it onto the table. A few pieces of silver spill out. One rolls all the way to Shumpeter, who slams a hand atop it.

"I go out again tonight," he says, the coin pressed between finger and thumb. "I hunt it. I kill it. You pay me."

Several Valers cheer, led by Mr. Villers. A good many tradefolk join 'em. Still others grumble uncertainly. A few have heard enough, tossing up their hands and storming off. Shumpeter makes a move toward the kitchen, but Parsons stands in his way.

"Beware the self-described saint, who speaks grandly of his miracles but performs none!" he says, good eye taking the measure of the room while the glass one roots Shumpeter to his spot. "What stops you from killing, as one of my wise constituents said, a mangy bear, then demanding we pay for a mussed-up hide? Hmm? Or prevents you from getting out there, deciding the task is too great, and leaving us to twist?"

"Oh, he won't," Reeves replies. "I'm going, too. You don't skedaddle, or see a ha'penny of our money, unless I confirm the kill."

Shumpeter scowls at him. Reeves crosses his arms.

Another of those unspoken conversations.

"Fine," Shumpeter grumbles. "You and the boy can—"

My father stands. "Copper isn't going."

"But—"

"That's final. Look at him."

I'll admit, right now? I ain't much to look at. Shumpeter snarls, but his stare softens when he sees me.

"No—you're right, Douglas. The boy has done his part. Mayor Reeves and I will go out alone. In the meantime, I suggest you do what you can to obtain my coin."

Doc Bunder inserts himself into their circle. "Reeves? You sure?"

"I'm going. Someone needs to take care of this problem," Reeves says, loud enough so Shumpeter can hear him. Doc glances at Parsons, who nods.

"Be safe," Doc murmurs, patting Reeves on the shoulder before heading out.

As folks settle in to talk business, I feel my head getting foggier and foggier. Sleep's been hard to come by of late, and even though I'm in for a whole mess of nightmares, I know I can't ward them off for long. With only one eye half-open, I watch Annabelle. She's skirting the group, hand raising every so often like she's trying to sneak in a word. Nobody notices her until Shumpeter snaps his fingers for silence. He beckons her over, wrapping an arm around her waist. I sit up a bit.

"Begging your pardon, Mr. Shumpeter," Annabelle says meekly. "The creature you faced . . . Could . . . Could it have attacked a man and dragged him off a horse?"

The tradefolk at the table lean in. Father and Reeves do, too. Shumpeter looks around, then stands and puts his hands on Annabelle's shoulders. She's trembling, fingers worrying at the lacy cuffs of her dress. With a kindly, sad smile, Shumpeter whispers something to her. A few moments pass, and then Annabelle murmurs, "I . . . I see . . ."

Shumpeter sighs and tries to pull her in for a hug. She squirms away, though, and hides her face in her hands. Before Shumpeter can stop her, she runs, disappearing down the hallway. I try to stand and chase after her, but my legs have beaten the rest of my body to sleep, and I get so wobbly I collapse into the chair again. A couple seconds later, we hear a door slam.

"I can—" Father begins, but Shumpeter shakes his head.

"Give the lass time."

A chill passes through me, and I shudder. Ghoul or no, if that creature got Annabelle's father, time is one thing we don't have.

Chapter Twenty-Three

I wake up muddled.

Not, you know, 'cause of where I am; I reckon most of the world wakes up in bed. But I can't remember how I got here, which is a mite troubling when you sleep on a roof.

I groan and sit up. There's enough crust in my eyes to salt a soup pot, and I rub until a little light manages to break through. With it comes the vision of Liza's face hanging just a few inches from mine.

"Gah!" I yelp, kicking myself back against the wall.

"You need to get up, Copper," she says. "It's almost nighttime!"

I blink and run my tongue along my teeth. It feels heavy and gross.

"What kind of sense does that make?" I mumble. It was midmorning when we got back to the Vale . . .

"It'll make sense when you hear what I'm about to

say!" Liza whispers, and she slips past the curtain into my space. I tug the blankets up around me so she can sit on the mattress. She kicks off her boots and plants herself, cross-legged, right next to me. "Last night, while you were out . . ."

"Oh!" I exclaim. "I've got news, too! Huge!"

"Not bigger than mine."

"I saw it," I say.

Liza's jaw drops. "It?"

"The Ghoul. Or some kind of creature, anyway."

"Is that why everyone's walking around all twitchy? They won't tell us anything!"

"That's why," I say, grinding my palms into my eyes again. My mouth still tastes like ash and sleep, and I make a face.

"Oh," Liza says, "I brought you this."

It's a lidded cup, warm and filled with tea. I flip the lid open, letting the blast of steam tickle my face. It's chicory and cream, and lots of both.

"Thanks," I sigh. "So what was your news?"

"Annabelle," Liza murmurs darkly.

I take a tiny sip of tea. It stings my lips, but I hold it on my tongue as long as I can. "I know about that, too. She was so upset when Shumpeter told her—"

"I don't care," Liza snaps. "That's not what I'm talking about."

I frown. "Then what? If this is about before, I think you owe her an apolo—"

"That's what I'm trying to tell you, Copper! I did! Or at

least I meant to. Yesterday, after I spent a few hours poundin' metal, I felt a little better. Realized I was harsh. So I ask myself, *What would Copper do?*, and silly me, I go to apologize, because you're so infuriatingly nice all the time."

"You're blaming me for . . . being nice?"

"Hush. And yes. If you weren't, maybe you'd've been a little more skeptical of Annabelle."

"Skeptical?"

"She's up to something!" Liza hisses. "I know!"

"How—"

"Drink your tea and let me talk."

I scowl, but I take another sip.

"So anyway, I'm going to apologize, right? And it's late—like, stars-out late. Annabelle should be at bedside sayin' prayers, or whatever they do in the south. But she's not."

"What *was* she doing?"

"Hell if I know! She wasn't there!"

"Wasn't . . ."

"In her room. Or the inn. Or anywhere. I looked!"

I set my tea down between us. "You sure? Maybe she was sleeping in another room? Father sometimes asks guests to move so that he can—"

"I'm not finished. This morning, I went back. The door wasn't even open yet; Mrs. Abigail had to let me in. I look for her again, and I find her . . . in the *bathroom* . . ." Liza's voice drops, her arms crossing like she's just unveiled the greatest scandal ever to rock Windydown Vale.

"Um . . . what *will* the neighbors think?" I joke. Liza ain't laughing, though.

"Copper, damn it . . . she was washing mud off her feet. She went into the swamps. Alone!"

That does get a jump out of me, so much so that a little tea sloshes onto my sheets.

"What do you think she was *doing* out there?" Liza asks grimly.

"Liza, her dad . . ."

"Ain't gonna get found! Not after more than a week, and not at night by a girl who doesn't know the swamps."

I square my shoulders. "She *kinda* knows 'em. I taught her!"

"Listen to me, Copper. My intuition cat's been spittin' in her direction ever since she showed up. I think—"

"Intuition cat?"

"Yeah. You know, when something feels off, the hairs on the back of your neck get prickly, and your ears feel like they want to pull back. Like an angry cat inside you."

I shake my head. "I . . . um . . . don't think I've got one of those."

"That's because your intuition stinks."

I roll my eyes. "What's there to *feel*, anyway? Annabelle's dad is missing; she wants him back. There. I'm a regular sage."

"You're a regular fool, Copper Inskeep! Haven't you been paying a lick of attention? The way she clings on you, won't talk to anyone but you when you're in the room. Betcha she's even held your hand. Has she kissed you yet?"

My cheeks go from a chicory tingle to outright burn. "Um . . . what? No?"

"Liar."

"She's just nice, is all!"

"She's playing you, is all! Trying to get you sweet on her so you won't notice what she's doing!"

"No she's not! Pretend or no, if someone was sweet on me, I'd know it!" I shout.

"Oh, you'd *know*, would you?"

"Course I would!"

Liza scowls so hard her eyebrows quiver. She grabs handfuls of sheets and twists. She takes a deep, growling breath.

And then she kisses me.

It's quick—a mush of her lips on mine, a little clack of teeth, and then me jerking back so fast my head thunks against the chimney. I accidentally kick the teacup, and it rolls out of the tent, down the roof, and off the edge. A split second later, we hear the sound of splintering ceramic and someone yelling in shock. I slap a hand over my mouth. When I pull my palm away, I see my lip is bleeding a little from where it caught her tooth.

All things considered, that couldn't have gone worse.

I close my eyes and pucker for another.

But Liza's already standing.

"What you don't know could fill a swamp, Copper," she murmurs, and then she runs. A second later, I hear the hatch clatter closed. I'm so gobsmacked that I can't even follow her. Instead, I lie down, ignoring the crumpled bedsheet bunched under my back. I slip my hands behind my head and stare up at the top of the awning. Thousands of thoughts burst into my brain, like a mess of squirming eels so slippery I can't hold one steady. Still, through it all, a single word cuts—one that sums it all up just about perfectly . . .

Huh.

Chapter Twenty-Four

It's well past nightfall by the time I sneak out of bed. I'm so hungry my belly is echoing off the rooftop, and the taste of tea in my mouth is just an angry reminder of what once was. I notice that Liza was in such a hurry to escape after she made her point that she left her boots. I grab them and tuck them under my arm. Before I head downstairs to the kitchen, I look out across the Vale. It's not too windy tonight, so the smoke from the forge is thick and lazy, a brushstroke of gray against the starry black. I smile, reaching up to touch the little sting on my lips.

Yep. Liza's going to need her boots back.

Better return them as soon as possible.

Right after I eat.

Somewhere between the third floor and the kitchen, I pick up a little tune, and I'm humming it as I root through the larder. I emerge with three cold sausages, a stack of rosemary shortbreads, and half a melon. I dump it all on the counter, right next to Liza's boots, and I tuck in.

Annabelle catches me in the middle of my third bite of sausage, melon, and shortbread sandwich. Her face is a mask of worry, but she manages a wince of disgust when she sees what I'm eating. I wrangle down one more bite and push the plate away.

"Sorry," I mutter through a crumble of melony sausage.

"It's . . . okay . . . ," she replies. "I was hoping we could talk."

I take a quick sip of water and nod. "Me too."

Annabelle smiles weakly, dabbing a few tears from her cheeks with the overlong sleeve of her shirt—one of mine that she borrowed. With a deep breath, she steps forward, closing the space between us.

"I'm terrified, Copper," she whimpers.

My chest tightens, and I feel the heat of tears in my own eyes to see her so hurt. "I know," I offer. "I was out there—"

"Then why?" she demands suddenly, voice raised and desperate.

"Wh . . . why?"

"Why tell them you didn't see it? Why deny the hunter his payment?"

My mouth is open, but I can't conjure words.

"That man . . . he's the best chance we have of finding my father! And now he's upset, and he left. Maybe never to return!"

"I . . . He . . . um . . ."

"All you had to do is say you saw the Ghoul, Copper! Why couldn't you do that? Windydown Vale respects you! They would have believed you!"

"Sh-Shumpeter," I stutter. "He'll . . . he'll be back. Reeves went with him so that—"

"Reeves is an old man! What good will he be against the Ghoul!"

"Annabelle," I say softly. "Truly—I'm not sure it was the Ghoul."

"Did it not look like the creature you described?"

The thing's horrible face flashes in my mind, and I close my eyes. "It did, but . . ."

"Then tell them! Go out there and testify! They will pay the hunter, he will kill the Ghoul, and we will find my father!"

I sigh, and I open my eyes. "Your father . . . ," I whisper. "It's . . . it's been too long, Annabelle. If he was attacked . . . if he's been out there all this time, then he's . . ."

"Don't!" she cries. "Don't you say it!"

There are times the truth is more heartless than lies.

This feels like one of them.

I say it anyway.

"He's gone."

"No!" she wails, and she turns, boots squeaking on the floor. She starts to run, and I reach for her. My fingertips catch nothing but air. As she storms into the taproom, I slump against the counter. My hunger's gone. I touch the cut on my lower lip, grimacing at the sting.

That's when I remember what Liza said.

Annabelle went out last night.

Out in the swamps, where that creature lurks.

I scramble after her. Because the way she just left?

I'd bet thirteen thousand coins she's fixing to go out again.

Chapter Twenty-Five

I find Annabelle in her room. She's sitting on the edge of her bed, kicking her boots off and rolling up her pant legs.

"Annabelle, you can't go out there," I say.

"You can't stop me."

"I could tell my parents."

"Yes, well. You have parents to tell, don't you?" she snaps. There's a fury in her eyes, just for a moment, but then it softens. "I . . . I'm sorry, Copper. I just . . . I just don't know what else to do!" Tears start flowing down her cheeks heavy and fast, like their path has been well-worn.

"If there was anything I could—"

"Tell them about the Ghoul!"

I shake my head. "It's too late. Shumpeter and Reeves must've left hours ago."

"It's not! It can't be!"

My shoulders slump. I wish I had more to offer her than a shrug, but I don't.

"Please, Copper . . . ," she sniffles. "Please . . . Without my father, I have no one . . ."

I muster the gentlest smile I can. "You've got me."

She meets my gaze, dark eyes aglitter with tears. Amid the sorrow, there's a flash of something else.

Hope, perhaps.

Which makes it all the more heartbreaking.

"I . . . I know, Copper," she says softly. "And I'm grateful. You've been my only comfort here, and I can't thank you—"

"No need," I say.

"Yes there is," she replies, and she stands up, gliding to me in two silent steps. She takes both my hands, lacing her fingers with mine. "We've a connection, Copper Inskeep. I know you feel it, same as me. When we were attacked . . . when my father disappeared . . . it tore a hole in my heart. And I would've died from it—I swear I would have, except for you. You bound that wound with your kindness, with your compassion. And I can think of only one way to show you my gratitude . . ."

Annabelle's fingers, slender and soft, tighten about mine, and her long, tear-tinged lashes flutter closed. Gently, she pulls herself toward me, head tilting and lips ready.

I squirm away about as fast as I can.

"Oh God," I mumble. "I . . . I'm dreadful sorry, Annabelle. I . . . You're . . . That is, we . . . I mean, you're right. Course you are. A connection, yeah. We connected. But not . . . not like *connected* connected. Or . . . or maybe we did, and I didn't know it? If I accidentally connected, well, that's my fault, and . . ."

She looks so shocked, so hurt. And I don't know if it's better to shut my mouth or try to explain my way out of this. So I keep going, even though I get less and less sensical the more I blather.

"You see, I've got another connection . . . had it already, you might say. Liza . . . you know Liza? Yeah, course you know Liza. Anyway, there's this thing . . . kinda funny, if you think about it . . . Earlier tonight, she . . . well, she and I? We kissed. I didn't expect it; it just sorta snuck up on me, but I feel like it was always right there, only my intuition cat was blind, or dead, or something, so I didn't see it but now I do and I think I finally get what an intuition cat is. You know?"

Quiet tears glide down her cheeks, and she clasps her hands over her heart like I just reached in and tried to tear it out of her. It takes my breath away, and I look to the floor. Her feet are cut and bruised, a lot like mine when I first got up to haunting. Clearing my throat, I fall to one knee, gathering her boots.

"Here, Annabelle. At least let me help you with—"

I freeze, voice petrified somewhere between throat and jaw.

Under her bed, pale and lifeless, is the face of the thing in the woods.

My head snaps up so fast my neck cracks. Annabelle is still standing there, only she's not weepy anymore. Or even sad. And she's got the water pitcher from her bedside table clenched in both hands. She rolls her eyes, lifts her arms . . .

And smashes it upside my skull.

Collapsed in a heap, world going blurry, the last thing I see are those deep, empty sockets beneath the bed, mirrors of the ones on my own mask.

Chapter Twenty-Six

He ain't dead! Just knocked loopy!"

"Poke him again, just to be sure . . ."

I feel a worminess at my earlobe, and I flap my arms about my head, kicking along the floor until I can prop my back against the wall. My vision is mussed, but I can see Stacy and Laila, hunched near the bed where I was just lying. I blink, trying to make sense of why there seems to be four of them.

"He don't look so good," Stacy murmurs, and she frog-hops over to me, peering into my eyes.

"I'm fine," I say slowly.

Then I twist to the side and get sick on the floor.

"Ew!" Stacy screeches.

"I can see melon in there!" Laila giggles.

"Get someone," I groan. "Mother, Aunt Abigail, Doc Bunder . . . I don't care. Go on now."

Laila scuttles out of the room, and Stacy tugs the sheets off the bed and covers up the mess. "I'd get you some water, too, but the pitcher's all busted."

"It's okay," I mumble, wincing.

"Hope Laila gets Doc. Your face is bloodified."

I run my hand through my hair. It's spiky with blood, and my fingers come back crimson-gooey.

That's good.

Means I wasn't out that long, since it hasn't had time to dry.

We hear a commotion in the hall, and Mother bursts in. She's wearing her nightgown and slippers, and her feet knock shards of porcelain under the bed as she runs to me.

"Copper! Copper, baby, what happened?"

"Annabelle clocked me," I say, shifting so her head blocks the lamplight. I feel better almost immediately.

"Whatever for?"

"Betcha Copper tried to get fresh 'n' she decked him. She's a proper lady, you know," Laila declares.

The line of blood down my face must intensify my glower, because it sets Laila back on her heels some.

"Or not," she murmurs.

"Copper?" Mother urges. I lean up, pressing my cheek to her shoulder. The soft fabric of her gown feels good, and it dulls the throbbing a bit, but I'm not there for comfort. Instead, so the girls can't hear, I whisper what I saw—both last night in the woods and just now with Annabelle and her ghoul mask. Mother pulls away, her eyes wide.

"Are you sure?" she says.

I nod, wincing at the effort.

Mother stands. "Girls, go get Doc Bunder. I don't care if he's rattling the rooftops with his snores. You rattle his door harder."

"Yes, Aunt Nettie!" they say in unison, and they scramble over themselves to comply. Mother fetches me a cup of fresh water and I drink, glad to have something to wash out the taste of my own sick. She helps me to the bed, and then ducks to check beneath it.

"No mask."

"She must've taken it," I say, leaning back against the headboard. Mother cranes over me and starts picking pieces of pottery out of my hair. There are sharp jags of pain, but I take 'em.

"Cut isn't as bad as the blood makes it look," she says after dabbing at my scalp with a wet cloth.

"That's good," I murmur, and I close my eyes, leaning back against her. She puts the cloth down and wraps me in a hug, holding me while the room spins.

When Doc Bunder arrives, he wastes no time, tossing his black bag onto the mattress. "Nettie, light this, if you please," he says, handing Mother a candle while he crouches in front of me.

"Hey, Doc," I manage.

He reaches up and tugs my left eyelid all the way open in response. "Candle, Nettie," he demands, and she puts the long taper into his hand, having lit it at the oil lamp. I hiss as he brings the flame up to my face and waves it before my eyes. It hurts and makes my head feel muddy, but Doc seems relieved.

"Got your bell rung, didn't you?" he says.

"Good and proper," I reply.

"Here. Sniff this." Doc holds a little vial up beneath my nose. I inhale.

And it feels like I get whacked with another pitcher.

"Holy God in a haversack!" I exclaim.

"Language!" Mother scolds.

My nostrils feel like they're on fire. Come to think of it, my whole body does, from footpads to fingernails, hairtips to heartbeat. The wooziness is gone instantly, replaced by a powerful desire never to smell anything like that again.

"What *was* that, Doc?" I beg, reaching up to feel whether or not my nose is, in fact, still there.

"Guntherwood extract. One hundred percent pure."

Mother stares at him. "That's straight poison, Doc!"

"You'll kindly note I didn't spoon-feed it to him," Doc replies. "Though to be honest, even inhaling the fumes for more than a few seconds is enough to provoke paralysis in weaker systems."

"Good thing my system ain't weak?" I chuckle nervously.

"I dare say," Doc replies. "And I apologize for the drastic measures, but I'm afraid you've no time to rest, Copper."

Mother scowls. "What do you mean, Bunder?"

"The girls told me Annabelle did this."

"Yeah, we told him everything!" Stacy confirms.

I catch Doc's eye. There's only one staring back, so I guess the guntherwood did its job.

Not everything, I mouth. Doc nods.

"Stacy, Laila, go find your ma. Tell her we've got a situation, and that she should prepare some good, strong tea. I've a feeling none of us will be sleeping much tonight."

When they're gone, I tell him what I told Mother. He's grim, but doesn't seem surprised.

"Doc?" I ask after a few moments.

"Girl's story never did quite add up," he admits.

I nod. "And I fell for it. Taught her everything about the swamps, about the Ghoul."

Now Doc's eyes do widen.

"'Cept that," I quickly amend. "She doesn't know about me . . . or, I don't see how she could . . ."

"There's a blessing," Doc sighs. "But it might be our only one."

"What're you thinking?" Mother asks.

Doc puts the guntherwood back in his satchel and stands. "I'm thinking we're being played. Ain't a coincidence that Annabelle knew where Shumpeter was camped last night."

Mother crosses her arms. "Those two? Working together? Why?"

Doc frowns. "I can think of ten thousand reasons."

"Thirteen," I reply. Doc nods.

"And they're out there again tonight," Mother says softly. "Shumpeter and Reeves."

"What happens if she gets to 'em?"

Doc shrugs. "That I can't figure. Reeves sees her, Shumpeter pretends to kill her, he brings the costume back as 'proof,' with Reeves's word as backup?"

Mother puts a hand on Doc's shoulder. "But then . . ."

"Then there's a major problem," Doc finishes.

"What?" I ask. I can feel their misgivings, crackling through the air like lightning.

"Might be that's their plan, and might be it works. Or it would've, 'cept now there's you . . ."

"Maybe Annabelle thought she killed me?"

"Doubt it. I don't think the girl's got it in her."

"So when they come back, I just tell folks what happened, and . . ." I trail off. A thought, dark and ugly, begins crawling its way through my mind. "You . . . you don't think they're coming back . . ."

Doc nods. "If Annabelle reaches Shumpeter and Reeves, I see things going only one way. They make a run for it, knowing their scheme is done for."

"They can't. Reeves won't let them. They'd have to . . ."

I don't even want to finish the thought. Doc does it for me.

"Girl might not be a killer. Not so sure about Shumpeter."

I gasp. "We need to get Annabelle back here. Now."

"Nettie, I'm sorry," Doc says, and he turns and clasps her hands. She stares past him.

Right at me.

"I understand," she whispers, and she breaks away,

collecting the soiled sheets and picking up pieces of the pitcher.

"What, Mother?" I ask, voice cracking.

Doc looks at me somberly. "Copper . . . ain't nobody in the Vale knows where the girl is going."

"'Cept me," I say.

He nods. "And she has a head start. You're the only one that can stop her."

"And if I do?"

"Bring her back here. We'll mind her while we figure out Shumpeter."

I grab the post of the bed and use it to pull myself up. I expect to swoon and fall right back down, but the guntherwood still has my fingertips tingling and toes twitching. When I realize I'm stable, I take a deep breath, glance once at Doc and Mother, and sprint out.

It's time Annabelle met the real Ghoul of Windydown Vale.

Chapter Twenty-Seven

The moon peaks right as I'm smearing the last of the larvae across my eyelids. It's petty, I know, but I figure I owe Annabelle a proper scare.

She did pitcher me upside the head, after all.

I check my reflection in a nearby puddle, decide I'm fearsome, and set out. Since I'm not trying to be sneaky, I can go full speed. I claw into branches so hard and fast that they crack above me, but I've already shot ahead before they have a chance to break. I don't even think my ankles taste mud— that's how fast I pick up and put down. I slash through low vines and twigs easy as mist, streaking like a musket ball toward the clearing.

I'm not even halfway there before I catch Annabelle.

Seems she had to make a costume stop, too.

The pale head of the creature I saw before is bobbing through the bushes about thirty paces away, twisting and dipping as she tries to navigate the dark. It looks so hideous and real that for a second I shrink, a worm of doubt wriggling into my mind. But then she steps on a sharp stick or stone and I hear her swear, loud and creative-like.

For some reason, that surprises me as much as her being out here.

I let her fight with the bushes for a bit, and then, right when she's in the thickest part, I dart around, using my pole-claws to shred through the lighter shrub. She freezes at the noise, and I hear her gasp.

Makes me smile, that does.

After a few seconds, her arms start flailing as she tries to fight her way out. I break through easily, looping into her path. I could just take the mask off, wait for her, and then warn her about the trouble ahead. That'd be the affable thing to do, I suppose.

But I'm not feeling affable.

Finding a thick, low limb, one gnarled and covered with moss, I leap up. My claws snag the wood satisfyingly, and I'm perched up there in no time, a hunkered vulture lording over Annabelle's path. When she finally wriggles her way free of the bushes, she takes the head off her costume, eyes darting to find what made all that noise. It lets me see the workmanship of her getup.

It's impressive.

But it ain't the Ghoul.

Building up a prodigious amount of phlegm, I gargle such a scream as to wake the dead. Her head snaps up, eyes wide, and she chucks her mask at me, wailing as she turns tail and runs. Within seconds, she's tangled up in the same bushes she just left, their sharp limbs grabbing at her costume and slowing her terribly.

I drop from my branch and skulk toward her. When I reach the place where her mask lies, I crouch like a beast catching a scent. It's a damn clever piece; all the stitching's on the inside, and there's little silver fibers woven in tight, helping it get that ghostly glint of moonlight. Painted across the mouth is a jagged line of crimson.

I start there, ripping the thing to shreds.

Annabelle must think her prop has bought her some time, because she renews her battle with the bushes. I can hear her cursing, pleading, and crying, then shouting triumphantly as she bursts free.

It takes me less than a five-count to catch up with her.

"No!" she screams, the mud gripping her feet. I claw a branch and leap alongside her, forcing her to veer left. She stumbles, her hands plunging into the mud. After that, she's slowed too much, and it's all she can do to pull herself onto firmer ground before she falls to her knees, weeping and desperate. She finds a stick and waves it in front of her like a spear, but it's woefully scrawny. Even if she caught me with it flush, it'd just break into bits.

Not that I mean to let her hit me again.

Gurgling and spitting, I circle her. My saliva coats the nails that serve as the Ghoul's teeth, a hungry monster's drool. I keep my claws raised so she can see those, too. Once

I'm close enough, I roar, lashing out and knocking that stick from her hands. In response, she raises her arms, covers her face, and yells in as vulnerable a voice as I've ever heard, "Daaaddy!"

I stop. I know she's done me harm, and lied to me, and played me for a fool. But the sound of that scream takes all my hard feelings and turns them to mud.

Because unlike everything else? Her terror? It's real.

And I somehow can't abide the notion that I'm the cause.

"Daddy!" Annabelle shouts again, her head turning as she desperately scans the trees. I lower my claws and back up a step. Seems like she doesn't even notice.

"Daddy?" I mutter, my glowing eyes blinking. The sound of my voice stuns Annabelle into silence. I can actually see her face twitch as she tries to square what she just heard with the creature before her.

Truth be told, I'm just as bewildered.

Why would she be calling out for her daddy now? Even if her story wasn't full of muck from the get-go, there's no way he's out here. Not in this part of the swamps. In fact, there's really only one man who might be close enough to . . .

Oh Lord . . .

"Shumpeter is your *daddy?*"

"C . . . Copper?" she whimpers, voice breaking like the dawn's own angel just appeared unto her. I let my claw-poles dangle and take the mask off, tucking it beneath an arm.

"Yeah. It's me," I say. "Is it true?"

"What . . . Why are you . . ." She trails off, squinting through the dark. Then she gasps. "You're the *Ghoul*?"

"My question first. Is Shumpeter your father?"

Annabelle scoots forward, hands coming up in a prayer-ish sort of way. "Copper, please . . . you have to help me find my father. I've . . . I've got no one—"

"Spare me," I say, lifting a claw. "Last time I opened an ear to your nonsense, I got a water jug upside the other one."

Her voice takes on a sharp, surly edge I've not heard before. She stands, clasping her hands behind her and thrusting out her chin defiantly. "Fine. Yeah. He's my father. You happy now?"

"Not remotely," I reply. "You've got a lot of explaining to—"

"You're rubes. Small-town yokels. We played you like always. End of story."

I frown. "Only you didn't."

"Well, yeah. This is a wrinkle," she scoffs, sweeping a hand up to indicate my costume.

I pull my shoulders back proudly, holding my claws wide. "Takes more than what you've got to fool the Vale."

Annabelle laughs. "You do that plenty enough for us."

I roll my eyes. "I don't see you carrying a sack of Windy-down gold, do I? And you're not getting away from me, either. I'm bringing you back to the inn so we can hold you to account, and so you and your daddy don't hurt Reeves."

I let a bit of spite trickle into my tone, and I add, "Who knows? Might even use you to lure Shumpeter in. Give him what-for, too."

Annabelle scowls deeply, and she spits at my feet. I know she's a viper, but it takes me aback a little, even so.

"We don't hurt people," she says, low and serious.

"My skull says otherwise."

"That was nothing," she counters. "You forced my hand, is all. You could've just let me go."

"So you can kidnap Mayor Reeves? Kill him, maybe?"

"We'd never!"

"And I'm about to believe you? Everything you've ever said is a lie!"

She sneers. "Look who's talking, Ghoul."

A flush of anger heats my skin. "This is different."

"Oh?"

"The legend of the Ghoul has been Windydown's for near a hundred years!"

"A legend's nothing but a lie that's had time to grow a beard!"

I raise a claw, but her words flummox me.

"It's all the same with you people," she sighs. "Ghosts? Dragons? Trolls? Doesn't matter. You plant your stories and let 'em grow like weeds, till they're so thick around your town that you can't rip 'em out without the whole thing crumbling."

"And that's what you're here to do? Bring the Vale down?"

She laughs. "No. We just want to pluck a few roses from the vines before they drag you under."

"I've got news!" I shout defiantly. "We've *been* down. We're sinking, even as we speak. But we've still got our pride. We're still the Vale. We keep the road open and the tradefolk fed. We're the bridge north and the path south. And, unlike you, we're good people."

She steps back, almost like I punched her. The moonlight catches the hurt in her eyes, and for a second I wish I could take back what I just said. With her lip quivering, she responds. "I . . . I guess you're right, Copper. Windydown Vale's full of *kindly* folk happy to charge you for a bowl of stew and a warm bed—right after they've scared you senseless. Totally different from my father and me."

I may be mad, but I'm not so hot that I can't see the sense she's making. I lower my claws and take a deep breath.

She uses the opportunity to hurl the handful of mud she's been hiding.

It hits me square in the face, blinding me and making me sputter. When I've cleared my eyes, she's gone.

"Dang it," I murmur, and I give chase.

Chapter Twenty-Eight

Doesn't take me but a minute to catch up with Annabelle; I know every tree, pit, and briar patch in these swamps.

She's running blind.

"Annabelle!" I shout. "It's over! Just . . . Would you . . . You're gonna run straight through—"

Her string of curses puts even Laila to shame. I hear the groundbriar thorns shredding her costume; doesn't take much to imagine what they're doing to her feet and legs. I skirt the patch of inky green easily, coming up beside her. She doesn't even look at me—just hurtles ahead, panting and swatting desperately at branches and swarms of flies while the mud and briars grab at her from below.

It occurs to me that I could stop her. I could lash out. A claw to the thigh would end this. Or I could tackle her, plant her facedown in the mud. As ragged as she's running, I doubt she'd get up.

I try to get furious. Try to tell myself it's righteous.

But I can't bring myself to do it.

So I let her run on. Heck, I even help her, darting in to scare her left or right when I know we're coming up on a nasty bit of bog. Way I figure it, she'll collapse before too long.

Only she doesn't.

It's just as I'm starting to marvel at Annabelle's grit that we break into the open. Her feet squelch in the mud as she wills herself up onto a little rise. There she slows, then stops, gawking at what she sees.

We're in Old Windydown. The moonlight is playing across the husks of what was, and in that pale glow, the ruin is clear.

"See?" I cough, leaning on my claws. "We sank before."

She swallows like she means to speak, but her body won't let her; she's run too hard and too long. Her breath bursts from her, only to be dragged back in desperate lungfuls. It's so sort of awful to watch—the gagging and gasping—that I find myself dropping a pole and reaching out, my hand gentle on her back, just to let her know I'm there.

Mistake.

With a ragged, defiant growl, she swats me away. Then, to my disbelief, she takes off again, making for the moonlit cross rising in the distance . . .

. . . the one with a sea of mirror mud around it.

"Annabelle, no!" I yell, my claws ripping at the measly patch of grass beneath me as I pursue. But her feet kick up the cloying ooze, forcing me to shield my face, and I veer right to get a better angle.

Just as she reaches the edge of the mirror mud, I slash at her. My claw catches the fluttering, torn fabric of her shirt and I heave, yanking her to a full stop.

She jerks back.

Her shirt rips.

And the swamp sucks her in, quick as that.

"Annabelle!" I scream, plunging a claw into the mud. I feel it catch on something, but it comes up empty. I try again.

Nothing.

I hiss in frustration and start raking both claws through the muck. Every second or third pass, I feel something, and I try to hook it, try to dig in and pull. But my claws won't stick.

And even though I'm on firmer stuff, I start sinking, too.

Tears in my eyes, I begin to back away, feet seeking purchase. It's instinct—my body telling me to save myself.

And I'm inclined to listen.

At least until a mud-slick hand bursts out of the bog, not more than a couple of paces from where I was fishing.

"Hang on!" I yell, and I turn about. I sprint for the Windydown Inn. When I get there, I attack my old home, claws slamming into the wood until I've got both stuck in good. Then I plant my bare feet against the splintery boards, and I heave. Every muscle in my body, every sinew and bone and joint, strains.

And with a catastrophic crack, the board comes free.

I don't even bother trying to pull my claws out. Instead, I use them to drag the board to the mirror mud, thrusting it at where I saw Annabelle's hand. Then, using the claws to balance, I walk myself out, pushing the other end down, down, down.

Until I hit something.

There's no way she'll hear me, but I holler for her to grab the thing anyway, and I back up, using my own weight to will the board upward. After a moment, I can feel it shuddering, and I whisper a little prayer.

It's answered a second later.

With a primal howl, Annabelle heaves herself up, retching and sputtering. In the moonlight, she looks like a phantom rising out of the mud. I start tugging, each of my steps driving my own legs knee-deep. I can feel my thighs burning and lungs protesting, but I don't stop. Not for anything.

Not until Annabelle loses her grip and sinks again.

"No!" I growl, and I wrench my claws free. Diving out as far as I dare, I plunge one straight into the mud. This time, I hit something solid, and I wince, hoping I haven't wounded Annabelle grievously.

Of course, it won't matter if I can't get her out.

I drop my other claw, letting it dangle from my arm by

the cord, and I grab on to the first with both hands. Leaning back, I pull until my backside is in the muck.

Then I twist myself out, straighten up, and drag some more.

When a head appears from beneath the mud, I whoop with elation. The arms and torso are next, and finally the legs. I pull until I've got her on the grassy patch, and then I drop the claw and lunge forward, turning her over so I can clear her nose and mouth, maybe give her a fighting chance.

Almost instantly, I realize there's no hope.

I'm staring at a corpse.

And it ain't Annabelle's.

Chapter Twenty-Nine

gawk at it, dumbfounded, for several seconds.

Then I hear Annabelle.

"C . . . Copp . . . Copp . . . ," she gurgles, fingernails scraping along the board as she battles for purchase. I throw myself at her headfirst, sliding through the mud until my fingertips meet hers. They twine, and I let her use my body as a lifeline, pulling at her as much as she pulls at me. It takes everything I've got, and likely more than Annabelle ever knew she had . . .

But we get her free.

For many minutes, it's us lying there—me trying to find my wind, Annabelle turning over to puke more mud every few seconds. And nearby?

That corpse.

When I can move, I crawl to Annabelle. I'm not sure what else to do, so I rub her back. Even through the thick coat of mud, I can feel her shaking. Gradually, though, she calms.

"I'll let you be," I mutter, and I start to scoot away.

"No," she coughs. "No. It's helping."

Warily, I reach out again, not entirely sure whether or not she's fixing to flip over and bite my fingers off. But she lies still, like she's re-educating her body on the basics of breathing.

"Um . . . ," I say, gaze flicking over to the muddy man-shaped mound to our left. "Got no easy way to ask this . . ."

Annabelle turns to look at me. Her face is completely coated, gobbets of mud slowly sliding from her hair, her cheeks, and her chin. Still, her eyes are big and bright.

"Wh . . . what, Copper?"

I can taste the swamp as I clear my throat. "If, uh, your daddy is Shumpeter, that means he didn't disappear, yeah?"

She blinks at me. I bite my lip.

"Yeah . . . ," she echoes skeptically.

I bring my legs up and curl my arms around them. "Right. Yup. I figured," I say.

"Why?" Annabelle asks, pulling herself to a kneel.

I tilt my head toward the body. Annabelle squints through the dark. Then she gasps.

Then she panics.

"Don't try to run!" I warn, but she stands up anyway. The dizziness hits her like a hammer, spinning her about and knocking her right back on her rear. Still, she kicks her feet, sliding as far as she dares from the lifeless lump. I stare at her across the body.

"Are you acting again?" I ask.

"No! What? No! Copper . . . that's *someone*! Someone *dead*!"

"It surely is," I say, trying to keep calm. Ain't easy, though—looking at the thing makes me wonder if that's what I was like when my father hauled me, breathless and bedraggled, from a hole not twenty paces away.

"Who is it?" Annabelle whispers.

"This is not your doing?" I respond, my voice gravelly.

"No!" Annabelle shouts. "I . . . We'd never! Never in . . . *never ever*!"

I do believe I've truly offended her; there might actually be tears mixing with all that mud. Still, I press. "Right. You 'n' old Shumpeter never blunderbussed someone who got in your way? Figured out your secret?"

She wobbles to her knees, fingers raking the mud from her face as she squares up. "I said never, Copper Inskeep. My father wouldn't hurt a soul."

"He shot at you!"

"I was out of range, and I made sure you were, too! That old gun is all for show! Just like everything else!"

I wipe my sleeve across my own cheek, spit, and wipe again. The anger's up in me, and it makes me forget about the body for the moment. "I know a few deer who would beg to differ."

"I promise, Copper! None of it's real! The claims, the

trophies, even that ugly old skull on top of the wagon. My dad's no killer. He's an artist!"

That one does throw me. "An artist?"

"He used to work for a crummy traveling theater company. Made costumes and props. We scraped by, traveling to little backwaters like yours—"

"Hey!"

"Like *yours*," she hisses, "and it was enough, until our manager decided to haul off with the lead actress, three weeks' worth of profit, and any hope we had of performing again. Left my dad, my uncle, and me with nothing 'cept a wagon full of junk."

"Your uncle?"

"It was Uncle's idea to sucker folks in the first place. Easy money, he said. And he was right! Either we build a stupid dragon out of felt and wood, *slay* it . . ."

She pauses, lifting up her drippy arms like she's holding an invisible blunderbuss. She pretends to fire it . . . right at me, of course.

"And gather the reward, or some old codger with a title and airs comes to us on the sly, offers us good bribing coin to leave town and let them keep playing their little goblin or ghost games. That was supposed to be the way of it here, too. After I told Daddy what you and the triplets said of the Ghoul, he made my costume like *that*," she says, snapping her fingers. "Left it for me beneath the wagon. I was to put it on, scare you some, and run, only . . ."

I cross my arms proudly. "Only we figured you out."

"Only things went sideways from the start! Uncle Reynard was supposed to tell my dad to come into town sooner, but he didn't show, so Daddy had to ride in and start without him. Dad always said he'd up and run off one day, just like . . . What? What are you doing, Copper? Don't . . . don't touch it!"

I'm only half listening. Soon as she said that name, I knew. Like, with my heart, I knew.

The size is right.

The shape is right.

All that's missing is the green hat.

With a groan, I flip the body onto its back. I've got to fight the urge to get sick, but I manage to wipe my fingers along its cold, bloated, claylike cheeks. Once I've cleared enough mud away, I can see his face, blue and veiny in the moonlight.

"That him?" I ask grimly.

Annabelle's curiosity overcomes her revulsion, and she crawls over. When she's close enough, she covers her mouth with her hand.

"Uncle . . . ," she whispers.

"I'm sorry, Annabelle. I really—"

"No!" she gasps. Her eyes dart around, like she's expecting the edges of the world to peel back and reveal a nightmare. I half crawl, half slip my way to her, and she collapses against me, pressing her face against my neck. I can't bring myself to hold her, but I let her grab me, and I can feel her tears hot against my throat. It takes her a long time to calm.

"H-how?" she asks once she's pulled away.

"How?" I echo, but then I see she's staring at Reynard's body again. "Oh," I murmur, and I rub the back of my neck. "Well, there's lots of things in the swamp. You could make a list. But I guess you know that. Like as not, he just fell in the mud and couldn't—"

"He didn't just fall into the mud, Copper. He'd have no reason to be anywhere near the mud. Least of all *this* mud," she says, sweeping her hand around.

I blink. "I suppose not," I offer, glancing at the body again. "But I'm no doc, and unless it was a bear or wolves or . . ."

I didn't see it before, but here, on Annabelle's side of the body, it's plain as day. In the middle of Reynard's muddy, matted hair, is a hole, puckered and oozing. I squint through the darkness, trying to see if there's any other marks on the side of his head.

There aren't. It's just that one hole, round and wicked and . . .

"What? What do you see, Copper?"

I don't answer her. Instead, I use my sleeve to dab the mud and strings of hair away from the wound. When I've got it as clean as I'm going to, I look at Annabelle. She slides forward in the mud, putting a hand on my shoulder as she peers down. Then, my knuckles cracking, I curl my finger up with my thumb, making a tight little circle. I put it up to Reynard's head.

A perfect match.

"I know what killed him," I murmur.

Chapter Thirty

ell me, Copper!"

Annabelle is in my face, mud crusted around her eyes, nostrils, and lips. Before I can ward her off, she's got me by the shoulders and is shaking me. I have to grab her wrists. As soon as I touch them, she pulls away like I've burned her.

"I . . . I don't believe it," I say. "Can't be."

"You start making sense right this second, or so help me, Copper . . ."

My whole face screws up. I look from Annabelle, to the mud, to the man. I mumble, trying to work my way through it, to figure some way that what I'm thinking might not be what is.

I'm coming up empty, though.

Annabelle senses my discomfort and retreats, knees slithering along the slick ground. "Was it the same thing that killed the others, do you think?" she asks quietly. Her eyes are locked on the mirror mud.

It takes me a few seconds. But then . . .

"Others?"

She nods, jaw trembling, and she points. "Down there . . . when I was sinking. I could feel them—arms and legs and everything . . . like they were dragging me under to join them."

I stare at her blankly.

"Copper . . . Uncle's body isn't the only one . . ."

I shake my head. "No. Tree limbs. Or pieces of busted building. Or—"

"I felt *fingers*, Copper."

I lean forward, planting my hands in the cold, shallow muck. My teeth grit as I try to fight off the logic of it all. But every excuse I growl seems weaker than the last. Eventually, I'm just punching the ground and spitting curses— mostly because I know what I have to do.

And because I'm scared to death of what I'll find.

Annabelle is watching me with mouth agape. When I suddenly stand, she gasps. I'm not sure if she thinks I'm going to attack her, or run off, or throw myself into the mud, but she stands up, too, reaching out with dirt-caked fingertips. To comfort me? To stop me?

No.

To help me.

"Your claws are there." She points.

Numbly, I nod, my feet squelching in the wet grass as I

retrieve the poles. I wrap the cords around my arms, so tight my hands tingle.

Then I get destructive.

Not sure where the energy comes from. I should be exhausted. I should collapse. Instead I rip board after board off the old inn, Annabelle takes each one and drags it toward the mirror mud, laying them out like a bridge to nowhere. A few times I see her wince, splinters digging deeply into her palms, but she doesn't stop. By the time we're done, I'm panting, Annabelle's hands are dripping blood, and the inn looks like the devil himself's taken a bite off the side. We share a wearied look.

Our work's only just begun.

What comes next is the most awful, most dangerous, most heart-wrenching thing I've done in my life. Annabelle squats on the back of each board, keeping it steady while I crawl out over the stinking mud. Blindly, I thrust my claws in, dredging them through until they catch on heavy things. The first time I snag something, I hold out hope, not even daring to breathe as Annabelle helps me wrangle my catch up the boards and onto firmer ground.

I can tell after just a couple of seconds it's no tree limb.

"Lord," I blurt. "Oh Lord . . ."

Annabelle makes like she's gonna be sick again, but she's empty. Still, it takes a long time before she stops shaking.

Grimly, we continue our work.

Horrified, we line them up—bodies, or parts thereof.

We pull out three before I start to weep.

Five before my heart goes cold.

It's the sixth that breaks it.

Annabelle watches me scuttle back, watches the claws drop from my hands and hears the wail of despair that bursts from me, one I wasn't even aware I had breathed deep enough to make. She peers down at the last body, confused and afraid. She can't see what would've caused me to react so. And how could she? The body's covered in mud, just like the others. It's in the same condition. In fact, there's nothing to distinguish it from the rest of the corpses in the line—no sign of age or gender, no peculiarity of form. Nothing the mud hasn't hidden or time hasn't erased.

Except, of course, for the smith's apron.

Chapter Thirty-One

Broken window.

Broken world.

Annabelle does me the kindness of letting me be. I think she busies herself saying words over the bodies. Or Reynard's, at any rate. I cleave to myself, eyes closed and head down. I'm vaguely aware of my own muttering, though not how long I've been at it. Enough for a chill to set in, I guess, because I'm shivering head to toe.

"I know Reeves," I whisper. "I *know* him."

"Copper?" Annabelle says softly. She sits down next to me, shoulder to shoulder.

I whimper. Can't help it. "He . . . he plays cards on our porch, and tells stories about Old Windydown. He keeps us safe. Annabelle . . . you've seen him. You've talked to him! You . . ."

I swallow hard.

You have no idea what we'd do to protect the Vale, Shumpeter.

Annabelle waits, but I'm silent. A night crow cackles from the spire of the church. Eventually, she takes a deep breath. "Reeves did this?"

"I don't know," I say.

But I do.

"We've . . . we've seen this before," Annabelle whispers. "Once. It was the third town we ever visited. Vampire of Culbarrow. A dozen orphan kids missing in a dozen years. Turns out it was the local constabulary. Sold the kids to the next town over, had 'em working in the basement of the town hall, sewing frocks and living off bread crusts. We put on our usual show, made our demand. They came in the dead of night with long guns and black masks. We were lucky to escape with our lives."

"That's not us! That's not Windydown!" I protest.

"I heard the stories, Copper. People disappearing. 'Eaten by the Ghoul.' It's what brought us here in the first place."

"There is no Ghoul!"

"But the people disappeared."

I drag both hands through my hair, tugging until it hurts.

"They left . . . ," I mutter. My voice cracks. "Went north, or . . . or south . . ."

Annabelle meets my gaze, then lets hers drift to the bodies.

To *that* body.

I bury my face in my hands, pressing my palms to my eyes. Even so, I can see most of the truth, shining through cold and clear. Only the *why* of it's still hidden, buried under broken glass and bloated bodies. I can tell it's there, like a sinkhole waiting to swallow me up. But there's nothing for it now, especially since . . .

"Your dad's in danger," I whisper.

"I know it," Annabelle says.

I turn to her. Her face is gentle and hopeful. It's not what I expect.

"Why are you still here, then?"

"Because that?" she murmurs, gesturing back at the bodies. "That might be Windydown. But it isn't you. And Copper . . . I need *you*. I can't get to him in time."

"It's probably too late," I say. It's a cruelty, but I only realize it when she winces.

"I . . . I hope otherwise," she replies.

I nod mutely. Annabelle, shaking with exhaustion her own self, helps me up. I fix my costume, getting myself ready for another run.

"It'll be dawn soon," I say.

"What should I do? Try to find my way back to town?"

"No!" I snap. It startles her. Startles me, too, especially when I hear myself explain. "Reeves might not . . . that is, I don't think . . ."

I can't bring myself to finish. Annabelle does it for me.

"He's not the only one in on it."

I grimace. That tells her everything she needs to know.

"Right. Okay. Town's dangerous. I'll . . . I'll hide here, I guess. Once you have my daddy safe, you come back to get me." She pauses, tapping at the ground with her foot until she finds a sticky spot. As I watch, she hunches down, scooping up a thick wad of mud. Solemnly, she spits into the center of it.

Then she holds out her hand. "Promise, Copper. Promise you'll come and get me, no matter what."

I stare. Her hand is dripping, and I can still see the blood from her splinters crusted along her long, slender fingers. I let my right claw dangle, and I grasp her palm tightly, squeezing until the mud oozes out—every last drop.

"Promise," I say, and then I'm gone.

• • •

With the dawn comes rain. The mask protects my eyes for the most part, but I'm not seeing much of what's in front of me anyway. I'm not feeling my arms or legs—if they're bruised, or I stumble, or they're screaming at me to rest, it's not getting through. Matter of fact, I probably lope most of the way to the clearing without even knowing I've done it. I mumble as I move, talking my way through things. Trying to figure a way around . . .

But there isn't. Reeves killed those folk.

I slow up. My face twists beneath the mask, and I duck under a leafy tree, back to trunk. The rain isn't so bad here, and there's a gentleness to the way it rolls off the leaves, pattering softly around me rather than driving against my shoulders. I close my eyes to listen. That's when the weakness takes me, like a blanket of bone-deep ache over my whole body. I sink to the ground, head between my knees.

If I was smart, I'd know what to do. I'd be able to see the why behind what Reeves did. I'd be able to weigh it all out and get the measure of things. *What we'd do to protect the Vale* . . . The inn, the stables, the tradefolk . . . our stories, our traditions, our people . . . Mother. Father. Liza. They're worth protecting.

Worth dying for, even.

Worth killing for?

Hissing, I shake the thoughts away. I draw a breath through clenched teeth and lash out with my left claw, burying it in the soil before me. Then I haul myself up. The effort hits me hard, and I think I actually sob. But I'm moving. "Gotta save Shumpeter," I growl. It's naught but words, but it's enough for the moment.

Chapter Thirty-Two

I stand in the middle of the clearing. Mist swirls and sinks in the steadily falling rain, shrouding the ground as I search. Bloodstains. Hoofprints. Food scraps. A half-dead ember still smoldering in a campfire—I look for all of it.

And find none.

The blackened remnants of our old fire are still there, soaked to the soil. And up the path, I can see the grim outline of the closest deer carcass, bones broken and stained. Maybe Reeves and Shumpeter were here briefly, but if that's so, then they left no trace . . . at least, nothing that wouldn't have been obliterated by a few hours' downpour.

I slip my mask off and let the rain hit me. It's cold but calming, and for a brief second, I imagine I'm back on the Long Walk running errands and dodging raindrops. I'm saying hello to folk, and they're waving back. I reach the steps of the inn . . .

Where Reeves is perched, gun across his lap.

I flinch. A sudden pain shoots up my right arm, and I realize I've been gripping my claws so hard my knuckles have gone white. I curse and shake out the stiffness.

Then I take off again.

I keep to the woods, though I'm never so far that I can't see the trail. I follow it as close to Windydown as I dare, hoping with everything I've got that I don't stumble on Shumpeter's body. Would Reeves have just pulled off the side of the trail and ended it? I can't reckon. Not on the fly, and not in any case.

Nothing's making sense, 'cept the branches above me and the mud below.

By the time I can see the plumes of chimney smoke battling the rain, I'm convinced there's nothing more I'm going to find. This close, folks in Windydown would've been able to hear a musket shot, even through the rain. And it wasn't raining last night. So I turn toward Old Windydown, thinking to give Annabelle the news about the clearing.

But I'm so close to home. To Mother and Father.

I could ditch my costume. I could slip in, tell Mother everything. She'd make tea and honey. There'd be bread, and the fire, and blankets. She'd have advice. I could rest, and get my bearings. I might even see Liza.

Liza . . .

I run my tongue along my bottom lip. It catches the little cut, and it stings. Sorrow hits me like a punch. Her dad, dead after all.

Murdered.

Just like Annabelle's?

I growl. With a burst, I snag a tree trunk, using it to whip sidelong. I follow the outskirts of the town until my feet find the familiar path toward Old Windydown.

. . .

Annabelle's hiding under the partially collapsed roof of Doc's old house. It's a meager spot at best; even curled up, chin to knees, she's shivering. I call out so as not to spook her, and she crawls from beneath the eaves. She wants to stand, but her legs won't let her, and she collapses into the nearest patch of grass. I hurry to her.

"Annabelle . . . ," I pant. She looks up, eyes wide. Her lips have gone purple. My instinct is to give her my old, ratty Ghoul shirt, but it's soaked through. Instead, I hunch down, dropping my poles and rubbing my hands together as hard and as fast as I can. Then I catch hers in mine and hold them. Or I try to. She pulls back, tucking them against her belly instead.

"Don't," she says, voice weak. "Don't try to comfort me."

"Huh?"

"Just tell me what you found. Is . . . is he . . ."

I sit. The cold seeps through my britches immediately, but it's just more of the same. "I didn't find anything," I mutter.

"You . . ."

"Found nothing. Not a damn thing. No Reeves, and no

Shumpeter. Whatever happened, it wasn't in the clearing. Or on the trail back."

"What does that mean?"

I shrug mightily and throw up my hands. "Mucked if I know," I spit. It's a bit of anger she doesn't expect, and truthfully, neither do I. But the heat of it feels right, smoldering in my chest on a kindling of shock and sorrow.

"Do you think he's still alive, then?"

My eyes flick toward the corpses. Annabelle hasn't moved them. Probably hasn't gone near them. Good thing—the rain has washed off most of the mud, and it's a gruesome sight.

"Maybe?" she continues, talking as much to herself as me. "Maybe they couldn't kill him? Daddy's twice Reeves's size. What would he do with . . ."

She can't bear to say it. I think it for her. *The body.*

"It'd be impossible," Annabelle reasons, her voice climbing higher. "Too dangerous to do it near Windydown. That's why he brings them here. Nobody comes here, and even if they did, they wouldn't be stupid enough to get close to the mirror mud . . ."

Now I do catch her gaze, just for a second. She swallows, but keeps going.

"But how does he manage it? Swamp's bad; a horse wouldn't do. And even with help, dragging . . . dragging *it* here would be exhausting. No . . . no . . . there's something wrong. Something that doesn't add up . . ."

She falls silent, catching a strand of sodden hair between

those purple lips as she thinks. She's rocking back and forth. It's kind of mesmerizing, and pretty soon, I'm swaying, too, getting angrier and sadder by the second. Feels like if I don't let some of it out, I'm gonna explode.

"Add up? None of this adds up," I mutter. "Being run over by a horse and lied to? That don't add up. Getting blunderbussed and brained with pottery? Hard to see the arithmetic there. Finding a mess of bodies stuck in the mud less than a stone's throw from where I used to sleep? Where I just about bit it my own self? Damn right that's not mathematic. So why not throw one more mystery into the pot? Hey, maybe old man Reeves doesn't even bother with bodies! Maybe he just invites folks down here! And if they say no, why, a musket in the back'll get you stepping light! 'Right this way, sir! How's your day going, and where do you want to be shot?'"

Annabelle is staring at me. I grumble and turn away.

She's still looking. I can sense it.

"What?" I snap.

"Copper . . . that was it."

"What was?"

"What you just said."

I scoff, flicking my hand toward the bodies. "Sure. He marched them down here while they were . . ."

I trail off, blinking. Annabelle finishes for me.

"Still alive."

My mind races.

Annabelle's too, from the look of her. She shoots up,

defying the tremble in her knees, and starts to pace. "He's still alive. My daddy's *still alive*. Has to be. Reeves'd bring him here at night . . . too risky during the day. But he wasn't here last night; we'd've seen him! Copper!"

She drops to her knees right in front of me. Rain ricochets off her brow and tickles my face, she's so close. "Take me back to Windydown," she whispers.

"What? No. Annabelle, they sent me out here to bring you in."

"Who did?"

The name sticks in my throat. I know it. Know what it means. But saying it's going to make it more real.

"Copper, *who*?"

"Doc."

She frowns, wrapping her arms around her rib cage. Her teeth are chattering.

Mine are, too.

"Any chance he's not in on it?"

I think back, recalling the way all three mayors acted when Reynard Finch did his grandstanding in the taproom. It was much the same as they did when Shumpeter showed up—all glancy and fidgetful. I crack my knuckles and sigh.

"Not much of one," I admit.

She nods somberly. "I'm a loose end."

"You're a scared kid."

"Does that matter?" she asks.

I want to say yes, to tell her about all the times Doc Bunder's taken care of me. Taken care of her. But it's hard to imagine Reeves doing something like this without Bunder and Parsons knowing. They're thick as . . . well, they're close. That row of bodies is powerful evidence, too—and they're just the ones we were able to drag out of the mud. No telling who else is in there. Maybe a child. Maybe Cutty, who Father said must be lighting up stages across the south. Maybe anyone who's ever disappeared from the Vale.

I lock eyes with Annabelle. Defeated, I shrug.

She catches the corner of her lower lip between her teeth. Ruefully, she says, "Looks like Windydown really does have ghouls."

"Maybe," I reply. "And you're asking me to take you into the middle of 'em."

"I am."

"Even if we don't know he's alive?"

"Copper, he's my daddy."

The way she says it? There's no arguing. I could knock her out, tie her up, and I'd still find her standing on a table in the taproom a few hours later, shouting for Shumpeter, fire in her eyes and chewed-through ropes dangling from her wrists.

"Fine," I mutter. "But you stay hidden. Don't do a darn thing without my say-so."

"I understand."

"Is that an 'I understand,' or an 'I understand that I need to wait until the right time to crack Copper upside the head and run off again'?"

"The former."

"All right then. Let's go find your dad."

Chapter Thirty-Three

We take it slow through the swamps, partially because we're exhausted, and partially because I don't fancy dropping by the inn during the supper rush. Annabelle's antsy—keeps looking at the sky, trying to figure out the time. There's too much rain, though. After she steps in her third patch of groundbriar, I convince her to pay more attention. Still, I share her nerves.

Every advantage nightfall gives us? The mayors have it, too.

It's dusk when we reach the shed behind the inn. I make sure nobody's peeking out a window or sitting on the back stoop before I pull the shed door closed. It's dark as pitch inside, but we're not getting rained on, and that's something.

"Do we really need to go through the inn?" Annabelle whispers.

"*We're* not. You stay here," I reply, shedding my costume and feeling around for a place to tuck it.

"Not on your life!" she hisses. "I'm not going to wait in some shack while your mayors haul my dad into the swamps!"

I drop my tone to near nothing, hoping it'll cue her to do the same. "It's just until I find out where he is. After, I'll come straightway to fetch you."

"How long will that take?"

I shrug, then realize she can't see it. "Not sure," I add.

"Can't you just waltz in there and ask? They're not trying to kill *you*."

"And raise all that suspicion? I'm supposed to be *hunting* you, remember? If they see me back without you, what do you think Reeves and the others'll do?"

"Give up?"

"Hunt you themselves. You said it—you're a loose end. Only thing between them and you is the notion that I'm tracking you down."

Annabelle is silent for a moment. At first, I think it's because she's decided to agree with my plan. But as I turn to leave, she grabs my shoulder.

"What?"

"You're not playing me, are you?"

I snort. "Like you did me?"

"That's my point. 'Oh, Annabelle . . . come back to the Vale! Wait in this shed! I promise I won't send Reeves out while you're locked in here!'"

"You're the one that wanted to come back. I said you should wait in Old Windydown!"

"I know!" she snaps. And then, softer: "I know. I'm just scared, Copper."

"You can trust me," I say.

"How do I know that?"

I crack the door, just enough so she can see. Then I hold up my hand, palm out. "Because I promised."

She sniffles, purses her lips, then nods. "Fine. I'll wait here."

I offer her a hopeful smile.

She tosses a rag at me.

I take it as a good sign.

There's not many who fancy a nighttime view of rainy swamps, so I'm able to scamper to our back door without much risk. I grip the knob with both hands and tug gently; on a good day, the darn thing squeaks like it's made of mice. In this weather?

I just have to pray nobody's in the kitchen.

Once I've guided the door closed behind me, I take a moment to let the warmth soak in. Steam rises from every part of me, like home is drawing vile toxins out of my clothes, my skin, and my heart. A sudden ache strikes, a desire to run right to Mother and Father so they can fix everything. They would, too. They'd march straight up, demand the mayors confess, and . . .

. . . and get shot for it, just like the others.

"No!" I whisper, shaking my head. I may not have a clue how I'm going to get Annabelle out of this mess, but I'm sure as sin not bringing my parents into it. Gritting my teeth, I tiptoe forward, feet tracking mud on the floorboards.

The kitchen is dark—a very good sign. Mother's shut down the stove for the night. I feel around for matches and a candle. When I've got it lit, I cup my left hand around the flame. I can hear voices from the taproom, so I sneak forward, navigating past the stools, counters, and hanging pots and pans. Knocking down even one of them would be disastrous.

The door opens inward, so I lean my shoulder against it—if anyone tries to come in, I'll feel it, and I can douse my candle and bolt out the back door before they know what's what. Pressing my ear to the wood, I try to listen.

No good. Whoever's in the taproom is speaking in a hush. I can't even tell how many there are, 'cept that there's more than a couple. A woman's voice, for sure, and several men.

One of whom sounds like Doc Bunder.

Frowning, I clasp the door handle. I figure if I can ease it open just a little, I'll be able to tell for sure. Wax drips down and stings my other hand, but I ignore it. Slowly, painstakingly, I begin to pull.

A sudden snap makes me freeze.

The noise is close.

Like, right-behind-me close.

Holding the candle forward like a knife, I spin.

Then I gasp.

And then I scowl.

There, standing on the counter, is Laila. Stacy's peeking out at me from the cupboard beneath, and Fran's tucked into the corner, her book in her lap and a sugar biscuit between her teeth. As the candlelight flickers over them, Laila slowly retracts her hand from the jar where Mother keeps the hard candies. Stacy tries to maneuver a loaf of bread behind her back.

Fran takes another loud bite of biscuit.

"Where in the devil's name did you three come from?" I whisper.

"I got hungry . . . ," Laila confesses. She drops her hands over the pockets of her nightgown. They're bulging.

"So did I," Stacy says.

I stare at Fran. She polishes off the biscuit and pulls another from beneath her book.

"Don't tell on us, Copper!" Laila begs, hopping down. Stacy clambers out of the cupboard, sneaking forward on her knees. She stops just in front of me, rising up with her hands clasped. I grit my teeth.

"I don't have time for this."

"Hey, yeah!" Laila says, a mischievous wrinkle appearing over her brow. "Weren't you supposed to be findin' Anna-belle?"

"How did you know about that?"

"Eavesdroppin'," Fran says.

My eyes go wide. "How much eavesdroppin'?" I ask suspiciously.

"Not much."

"Just a little?" Stacy adds.

"We heard it all!" Laila decrees. I press my finger to my lips, grab my cousin's wrist, and drag her behind the counter at the center of the kitchen. Stacy and Fran follow so they can hear, too.

"What *exactly* did you hear?"

"We were worried about you, I'll have you know," Laila says. "That's why we were listening to you and Doc outside Annabelle's door. Heard him say Reeves was in trouble, and Annabelle's the reason."

I let a bit of wax drip onto the floor, then stick the fat end of the candle into it. It illuminates three impish faces.

"Thanks for your concern," I mutter. "But there's nothing to worry about. Reeves is fine."

"Oh, we know," Fran says.

I arch an eyebrow. "How?"

"More eavesdroppin'."

I stare at them.

"What?" Fran says coolly. "Folks know I get up in the tree to read. Not my fault they forget I'm there."

"Reeves is fine *how*?" I insist.

"He came back last night. Had a drink with the mayors. It was the stinky stuff Mama keeps on the top shelf."

"It's nasty. Burn the tongue out of your face," Laila adds, grinning. "I tried some."

"I don't care if they drank mud straight from the swamp. What did they *say*?"

Fran shrugs, and I kneel in front of her. She shrinks against the wall.

"You smell as bad as the top-shelf stuff."

"I've been running around in the mire for over a day. No sleep. No food. Nothing to drink 'cept what rain I've sucked off my own lips. So when I tell you, I need to know what they said when Reeves came back, I mean it."

Laila crouches next to her sister, thrusting her freckly face right up to mine. I can smell the candy on her breath.

"Back off, Copper. You can't boss her."

I set my jaw, steely as I can. "I'm not bossing her. I'm begging her."

Laila squints at me in the half-light of the flickering candle. After a few moments, she says, "Oh," and she scoots away.

Stacy slides in, completing the line of identical faces. "Fran, you best tell."

"Fine," she says. "But it don't make much sense."

"Whatever you've got," I reply softly.

"It was weird. At first, they didn't say anything at all. Just drank that stuff and made faces. Then Parsons says, 'So it's done?' and Reeves shakes his head. That made Doc Bunder and Parsons mad, or scared, or maybe both. They got really whispery after that."

"That's all?"

"Heck no. Folks think I don't hear nothing, but I do. I listen lots."

"She does," Stacy confirms. "Even with her nose so deep in a book you think it's gonna poke out the binding."

Fran nods proudly.

"So?" I press.

"So Reeves said it couldn't be done—not with the girl still out there. Said he's the only one might know where she's hiding. 'Gotta wait for Copper,' they said. And here you are. But you don't got Annabelle."

"Yes, he does."

My heart stops for a second. The girls' eyes go wide, and I reach out quick, slapping my hands over Laila's and Stacy's mouths. I try to get a foot up there for Fran, but I'm too late.

"Annabelle!" she gasps.

"Shh, Fran! Please! Please, just listen!" Annabelle whispers urgently.

"You were supposed to wait outside!"

"I couldn't, Copper, and you know it. That's my father they've got."

Laila bites me. I stifle a scream and yank my hand away. I expect the girl to holler, but she leans in, voice soft and conspiratorial. "Your father?"

Annabelle joins us on the floor.

"Mr. Shumpeter," I say, hoping I don't regret it.

"Whoa," all three triplets reply at once.

"Is that why you clobbered Copper?" Fran asks.

Annabelle nods. I shoot her a glance. She mutters, "Kind of? I . . . I made a mistake—one I'm hoping Copper can forgive in time."

Laila, Stacy, and Fran lock eyes on me.

"Not now," I say. "More important things. Immediate things. Like, do you know where Shumpeter might be?"

"Why would I know that?" Fran asks.

"'He's the only one might know where she's hiding,'" I repeat.

"Oh! The 'he' is Mr. Shumpeter?"

I nod.

"Prolly at Reeves's place."

Annabelle clasps her hands. "Are you sure?"

"Pretty sure," Fran says. "Reeves didn't come in with his gun, so he musta stowed it. Dunno where else he'd do that but at home."

"Yeah, he won't let me touch it. And I've asked." Laila pouts.

"So he might've locked my dad up there, too!" Annabelle exclaims.

I sit back, plucking the candle off the floor. The wax breaks with a soft snap. "I reckon that might be so. But it means we've got a mountain to climb to get you two out of here."

Stacy crosses her arms. "Why, though? She did you dirty, Copper. Don't see how she deserves helping."

"'Cause Mr. Shumpeter has lots of coin, that's why," Laila says, her fingertips curling greedily.

"That's not why," I retort. "And we're not for telling the reason. But if they're waiting for Annabelle and me, then we won't be able to get out of the inn, much less to Reeves's place, without a heap of trouble."

"I still don't get it," Stacy says.

Fran smiles. "It's secret stuff."

"Yeah! Secret stuff!" Laila adds.

Stacy crosses her arms. Can't say I blame her, and I'm not coming up with anything I can say to convince her not to march into the taproom and declare our presence.

Heck, if it were me, I'd've probably already done it.

"It was a trick," Annabelle says after a moment. "I lied about my father disappearing. Shumpeter isn't a monster hunter. We wanted to fool your town into giving us money. But not anymore. Now we just want to leave and never bother you again. Is . . . is that okay?"

Stacy frowns. Fran yawns. Laila asks, "His gun is real, though, right?"

Annabelle smiles. "Yes."

"Knew it!" Laila murmurs.

"Stacy, trust me. Annabelle is more sorry than you can imagine. Shumpeter, too. They've paid the price," I say. In my mind, I see the body of Reynard Finch, and I shiver.

"Stacy, please?" Annabelle whispers.

Her lips still pursed and ginger brow knotted, Stacy thinks.

Then she nods.

"Okay," I say, exhaling sharply. Annabelle leans in to

hug Stacy, but she squirms away. I hold up a hand to still them. "I've gotta think . . . Gotta think . . ."

"That ain't his strong suit," Laila mumbles.

"And that's not helping," I snap.

"Annabelle could hide out here," Fran offers.

"No," we reply in unison. I continue, "She's gotta get the horses from the stables, be ready to run as soon as I have Shumpeter out."

"Not a chance, Copper. I'm going with you to find my dad."

"And get . . ." I stop myself, glancing at the triplets. They're leaning in like baby birds watching a worm dangle off a leaf. I cup a hand to my face, mouth, *Get shot!?* Then I say aloud, "Because that's what'll happen as soon as they see you. If it's just me, I can figure something out."

"Okay," Annabelle agrees. "I get the horses."

"You got the key?" Stacy asks.

"Key?"

"Stables are locked up at night. Big ol' padlock. Size of my head. And more on each stall, besides. Keeps the horses from wandering off and drowning in the mud."

Fran nods. "And keeps horse thieves out."

Laila adds, "Or kids wantin' to feed the horses a midnight snack. We know."

Annabelle looks crestfallen, but she says, "I suppose we could try on foot . . ."

"You wouldn't even make it to the end of the Long Walk before they caught you."

"So that's it, then?" Laila asks. Stacy and Fran shrug, and Annabelle winces, struggling to hold back tears.

I draw my lips in against my teeth and click my tongue. "No," I say slowly. "That's not it. You just need to break the locks."

"They're metal," Fran says.

"'N' thick as my arm," Laila adds.

"I can't break them," Annabelle concedes.

"Maybe not," I reply. "But I know someone who can."

Chapter Thirty-Four

oesn't she hate me?"

"Oh, I'm fairly certain of it."

"Then why on earth would she help?"

"Because it's me asking."

Annabelle sighs, and I shush her. Then I tease open the taproom door again.

No luck. There's still folk out there.

Annabelle leans over me, trying to spy for herself. I scowl and brush her back.

"What's taking them so long?"

"They only just left. And they have to go all the way up the back stairs, past the guest rooms on the third floor, then down again."

"What if they can't pull it off?"

I smirk. "The triplets? Trust me. They were born a diversion."

As if on cue, a commotion breaks out in the taproom. A girl's voice screams, "Ma! Come quick! There's a big hole, and rain's gettin' everywhere! Fran tried to plug it with her pillow, but she fell, and Stacy dropped the lamp! I think we got the fire out . . ."

There's a half-second pause, and then:

"Mostly!"

It's the sound of chairs tumbling over that makes me bold. I shove the door open, grabbing Annabelle by the hand.

Then we bolt.

Sure enough, the taproom's clear. I think I spot Father's silhouette in the hallway, but I don't stop to see if he turns around. Instead, we burst onto the porch. The rain lashes, wind-driven and heavy, and I drop Annabelle's hand to shield my eyes. There's no time to let them adjust, so I squint, trying to make out lights in windows. I can see a few, but their glow's not enough to tell us whether anyone else is on the Walk between us and Liza's house.

We're going to have to risk it.

"Go!" I shout, nudging Annabelle's shoulder and pointing. She nods and takes off, bare feet slapping against the boards. I wish we'd had time to grab boots, but they'd already be soaked, and my toes are numb anyways.

Even in the rain, even in the blackness of night, the smoke rising from the forge chimney is a beacon, and it doesn't take long to come into view. Soon, I'm outpacing Annabelle—my heart has the distance to the smithy memorized, and I'm sprinting. Within moments, Liza's porch is in sight.

And I stumble to a dead stop.

Annabelle barrels into me, knocking me on my hands and knees. She barely catches herself.

"Copper!" she cries through the rain. "What? Why have we . . ."

She sees it, too. Just a bit past the smithy, on the other side of the Walk, is a broad, squat house, a sturdy two-story built on a big, jagged boulder sunk partway into the mud.

It's Reeves's house.

And the front door just opened.

Light flows down the stairs to the Long Walk, cutting through the rain and framing a shadow. Stepping out is Reeves himself, a pipe between his lips and musket slung over his shoulder. I scramble backward, pulling myself up and dragging Annabelle with me.

"Where?" she asks.

"Back to the inn!" I growl, and we turn heel . . .

Just in time to see Doc Bunder and Parsons coming down the steps. They're deep in conversation, Parsons gesturing wildly while Doc holds a coat over his head to block the rain. I tug Annabelle down, hoping it keeps them from spotting us for a few seconds longer.

"The wagon?" Annabelle whispers.

I shake my head.

It's too far away.

"Can we crawl?"

I twist to look at Reeves. He puffs on his pipe a few times, letting the smoke pour from his lips in a long, even stream. He glances back inside, says something to someone.

And then stares in our direction.

"Oh God!" Annabelle gasps. I tap the board in front of her and point. Reeves is waving—but not at us. He's seen the other two mayors. It's a relief, but only momentary.

Especially when he sets his pipe on the railing, tucks his gun beneath his arm, and strides down the steps.

He's coming to meet Doc and Parsons.

They're hurrying to join him.

We're trapped.

Chapter Thirty-Five

thought I didn't recall much from the day Old Windy-down fell.

I was wrong. I remember this now.

The dying part.

There's a moment when what used to work together—arms and legs and guts and heart—decides it's every part for itself. Hands and feet quit. Belly rejects its own contents. Mind panics, and lungs get selfish. They demand to open, force your lips wide and nostrils broad, even though what's outside is as far from air as you can get.

And that's when the mud rushes in.

I take a great mouthful, but before I swallow, I feel a wrenching at my head, a yank that pulls my face free. It's naught but a second, but it's enough, and I spit out the vile muck, gasping in the good stuff. It gives me the strength to reach up, and my grime-slick fingers catch the tiny crack above me. I feel the top of the board and curl my fingers over it, then hang on for dear life.

What little of it's probably left, anyway.

When I catch my breath, I take stock. We're in a bad way, and in a worse spot. The stench of rot is everywhere, and a sickly, glistening mold covers the underside of every plank, like a blight beneath the skin of the Vale. Annabelle's left arm is wrapped tight about the central support pole holding up this stretch of the Long Walk. The rain drips onto her face through the slats, accompanied by just enough light to make out the look of terror in her eyes. Every few seconds, she slips, and she has to fight her way up again. Still, she's reaching out to me. I lace the fingers of my free hand with hers, giving them a silent squeeze of thanks.

It was my smart-dumb mind that got us into this mess. As soon as I realized we were boxed in, I grabbed Annabelle and rolled, not stopping until we landed with a sucking splat in the mud. I pushed her into the little opening beneath the Walk, shoving her while the mud eagerly sought to drag us under. It took every last bit of air and strength I had to churn, to force Annabelle forward until she was completely hidden by the boards. Last thing I saw was her arms wrapping around that pole.

"Are they . . . ," I start to whisper, but Annabelle shakes her head rapidly, eyes darting up. I follow her gaze through that crack, past my own aching fingers and through the storm. Not much is visible . . .

Except Doc Bunder's heavy boots to either side of my hand.

"The boy back yet?" I hear Reeves say. Doc shifts a bit, a hairbreadth from stepping on my fingers.

I close my eyes and pray.

"Not yet," Parsons grumbles. "And what about you? Shumpeter talking?"

"I do believe we've found the one way to shut that man up," Reeves quips. "Ask him to tell us where his girl is."

"His?" Doc Bunder asks slowly.

"Annabelle's his daughter."

Parsons sputters. Doc shifts again. The boards above us creak.

"He told you that?"

"Guessed it, and the look on his face revealed the truth. There's not much a man can hide when it's a musket staring him down." Reeves chuckles, but it turns into a throaty cough.

"And the swamps?"

"He's clueless. A two-bit profiteer, nothing more."

Parsons sniffles. "Still, man like that? Stirs up trouble and secrets. I'll feel better when he's sunk with the others."

"Remind me why we aren't feet-up in front of the hearth at the inn?" Reeves says. "Stay out here any longer and we'll catch our own deaths before we have time to bring it to Shumpeter and his girl."

Annabelle's hand spasms in mine. I open my eyes and

strengthen my grip—both on her and on the board above me. Not sure if either helps.

"It was those triplets," Parsons whines. "Causing an uproar. Couldn't risk them snooping around. Can we meet at your place?"

"And have Shumpeter listen in?"

"My shop's free. Might even have a match or two left for the fire," Bunder says. He sounds as gentle and friendly as ever.

That may be what scares me the most.

"Don't have to ask me twice," Reeves declares. Parsons agrees, and there's a shuffle of feet above us. Just before Doc's heel crushes my fingers, I drop my hand. Annabelle tugs me toward her, and I kick myself to the pole, joining her in clinging on for dear life. When we're sure the mayors are gone, she lets out a furious sob.

"Well, now we know for sure," I say. I mean it as a comfort. It's anything but.

"I can't do this, Copper," Annabelle replies miserably. Like she's fixing to make a prophet of herself, her arms slip toward the mud, which seems to surge up to her chin.

"You can," I reply.

"All of Windydown wants us dead!"

"Not all of it," I say grimly, and I give her arm a squeeze. I sink just a little farther as a result, and it sends a jolt of panic through me. "C'mon. We know Reeves isn't at home. If we can get you to Liza, we might still pull this off."

Before she can respond, I swing my arm up, grabbing

the board above me again. The mud drags at me fiercely, but it can't dislodge me, and soon I manage to work my other hand next to it. Still kicking and fighting, I walk my hands along that plank until I've dragged myself to the edge, and then I haul myself out from beneath. The mud lets me go with a thick, syrupy belch, and I lie flat on the Walk, panting and cold. Annabelle joins me a moment later. Someone could come along at any minute. A late-driving trademan could run us over with his cart. Lightning could strike between us. It doesn't matter. Neither one of us has the strength to move—not for a long time.

A lull in the rain prods us; I think we both sense that any letup in the weather might be folks' cue to move about, no matter how late. Joints cracking and sore, limbs still heavy with mud, fingers and toes numb, we clamber to our feet. Leaning on each other is the only way we can move, so we do, leaving a sticky trail all the way to Liza's door. Somehow, I find the strength to knock.

"Who in the world could that be at this—" Liza's mom says as she teases the door open. We see her face—pink and clean and concerned—appear in that crack, and she gasps. A moment later, we're dragged in, the heat of the forge rolling over us like an avalanche. It seems to steal all the breath from our chests and together we collapse, two muddy, sorry heaps staining Liza's floor. I try to get up, to find Liza so I can tell her. But my body's done, and the room starts to shift, then to spin.

And then it fades away entirely.

Chapter Thirty-Six

I feel before I see—gentle hands guiding me up. Strong arms easing me forward. Warm water on my face. Cold clothes peeled away from colder skin, and me not even having the sense to blush ... or maybe not having the strength to. It might be a few moments. It might be half the night. I do know that I sleep, because the dreams come dark and hard. Screams. Bodies.

Drowning.

My eyes snap open, and I thrash at the cloth tangling my arms and legs. Only takes me a second to realize it's a blanket, but it's enough to scare everyone else to jumping. I'm on a mattress on the floor near the forge, which has gone as dark as they let it. I push up against the bricks, breathing hard.

"Copper! Copper, it's okay!" Liza's mom says, dropping a wet shirt and a handful of clothespins as she hurries to my side. Annabelle, who was looking fretfully out the front window, practically leaps out of her chair to get to me.

For all that, it's Liza who reaches me first. Might've been by my side the whole time.

As soon as I see her, I'm done for.

Tears I didn't know I was keeping burst forth—great, rib-rattling sobs that I can't fight. She wraps me up, stubbornly hugging while I let whatever monster's in me claw its way free. And once it's done, once I'm nothing but hollow and ragged, she leans over me, whispering, "It's okay, Copper. Annabelle told us. We know."

I look up. Liza's eyes are red, like she's been crying, too. I press my palm to her cheek, and she covers my fingers with her own. "I'm . . . I'm so sorry. I can't . . ."

"Shhh. It was none of your doing. And . . . and I'm glad. Not about . . . but . . . but the knowing. He didn't leave us."

"He'd never," Mrs. Smith says. "Knew it in my bones."

"Mom . . . ," Liza whispers, leaning her head on Mrs. Smith's shoulder. She closes her eyes tight, but she keeps my hand in hers.

"It's okay, my girl. Just hate that I never figured it out. My husband went to the mayors. He said it was his duty, on account of all they'd done for us over the years! Told them we were for the north. Disappeared two days later. And I . . . I guess I was so devastated . . . I couldn't see it. Didn't want to. I . . . Lord, I thought it had to be the Ghoul. Didn't know it was you, Copper."

I feel a throb in my chest, and I sit up. Mrs. Smith

smiles softly. "Girls told me that, too. And it's okay. Your secret is safe."

"Thank you," I murmur. Mrs. Smith reaches behind her, where a cup of water is sitting at the edge of the forge. She hands it to me, and I drink—sips at first, then greedy swallows. When I'm finished, she takes the cup. Liza asks if I want more.

"I'd like to sleep for a million years, then wake up and find out I was dreaming," I admit. "But I can't. Annabelle and I . . . we're not here just to bring you news. We've gotta—"

"I told them," Annabelle says.

I scratch my head, fingers feeling bits of dried mud. "How long was I out?"

"Going on four hours," Liza says softly, and she glances at Annabelle. "Enough time for us to hash some things out."

I arch an eyebrow.

Annabelle nods. "Yes. Trust me. It's hashed. All the hashing's been done. Queens of hash, we are."

Something about the way she says it makes me think I'm not likely to be fending Annabelle off anymore. I bump lightly against Liza, and she surprises me by pressing a kiss against my hair. Blushing, I mouth a heartfelt *thank you* to Annabelle. She smirks.

Mrs. Smith stands up, smoothing her apron and thrusting a big, calloused hand toward me. "Think you can stand? We're a couple hours from dawn, and if what Annabelle says is true, we don't have much time."

I accept her help, and just about every joint in my body

pops as I stand. But I'm steady enough on my feet, and my stomach even rumbles. Mrs. Smith tosses me an apple from a wooden crate in the corner. I tear off half of it in one bite.

"Once it's done, we're going to meet by the wagon," Annabelle tells me.

"You're taking the—"

She cuts me off with a heavy sigh. "No. Too slow. And I'm only getting Bree and Perdy. They're the youngest and fastest, and we're going to need to ride hard. But we can hide behind the wagon until you get back, and I can grab a few supplies."

I nod, making a mental vow to look after Courageous Nellie. Annabelle's first horse, too.

"Liza's mom's taking me to the stablemaster's house herself," Annabelle says. "Going to wake him and demand he give us the horses."

"Good," I say, but then: "You're helping us? With our plan?"

Mrs. Smith's brow furrows, and she stares out the window toward Reeves's house. "Best of a bunch of bad ideas. Ms. Annabelle here is as sharp as they come, though. If 'twere just me, I'd've already marched over there, confronted that murderer, and made his skull my new anvil. But I do that, they know I know. Like as not, I'd end up dead as my husband. Then they'd come after Liza."

Despite what I've seen, her words still sting me. "But . . . but you're *Windydown* . . . Reeves and Doc and Parsons, they . . ."

246

"Would do it in a heartbeat," Mrs. Smith declares. "Best we just get Annabelle and her daddy out of here and far away. Then we figure out what comes next."

"How do we get Shumpeter, though?"

Annabelle throws one of Liza's cloaks over her shoulders. "That part hasn't changed. They trust you. You're the only one who can get in there without making 'em twitchy."

I nod. Then I look at Liza.

"I'll be watching. Anything goes askew, I'm at Reeves's door with a hammer in each hand."

The way she says it—back straight, jaw set, eyes dark as coal—bolsters me. I've seen her bend a cold iron bar with nothing more than spit in her hands and her own two arms. I don't imagine Reeves's door would give her much trouble.

"Okay," I say, steeling myself. "If we only have a couple hours till dawn, we need to move. Even in this rain, the Walk won't stay empty once light breaks."

"And we aim to be gone long before that," Annabelle adds.

Liza's mom hands me a cloak of my own—another of her husband's from the chest of his things. I fasten it about my neck reverently, and Mrs. Smith reaches up to touch the clasp, offering me a little smile. Then she tugs open the front door. A gust of wind blows through, the chill battling the forge heat. Annabelle and Mrs. Smith dart out into the darkness. I make to follow them, but then turn. True to her word, Liza's already hefting two wood-handled smithing hammers, her fingers curled tight near the base of each. It reminds me of the Ghoul's claws. With the rain biting at my back, I stride forward, step between those hammers, and kiss her.

"You taste like apple," she whispers, and she smiles.

I grin, too. After a moment, she pushes one of her hammers into my hand. "In case you need to break in," she says. I nod, tucking the tool into my belt. With a deep breath, one that fills my lungs with the warmth of the smithy and the smell of the forge, I slip out into the storm. When the door shuts behind me, I glance back. Liza's watching through the window. She's not smiling anymore.

And neither am I.

Chapter Thirty-Seven

Reeves's house squats on a craggy piece of black granite, one made from the same stuff as the mountains that loom behind. Instead of a wooden porch and stairs like the rest of the buildings in Windydown, the stoop is carved right into the rock itself. The windows are all dark, save one: There's a flicker of candlelight coming from the second floor, right-hand side. Might be that Shumpeter is up there. Might be that Reeves is asleep, or still at Doc's place.

Or it might be that while I was at Liza's, Reeves and the other mayors decided to march Annabelle's dad into the swamps and get it over with.

I creep up the stone steps, rain beading along the hood of my cloak. A quick jiggle of the knob at the front door reveals it's locked, so I skirt the house. There are enough footholds and flat spots on the rock that it's not too difficult, even with the little waterfalls that cascade into the mud. A back window, shaded and small, seems my best bet; I'm hoping the curtain and rain muffle the sound of what I'm about to do. With one guilty glance over my shoulder, I grit my teeth, pull back Liza's hammer . . .

And realize I haven't even tried to open the window yet.

Moment smart. Life dumb.

Sure enough, it's unlocked, and I manage to bully the window open using just my hands. From there, it's an easy climb in.

My eyes adjust quick, but I'm only seeing in shades of gray. It's still enough to reveal a tidy little kitchen. A table with two chairs is tucked into the corner. A single place setting—cup, plate, napkin, fork, knife, and spoon—has been arranged just so. Jars of different sizes sit on the shelves. Each one is labeled. It strikes me how much it looks like Mother's pantry.

Or the inside of Shumpeter's wagon.

There are two doors out of the kitchen. I choose the one in the direction of the front of the house. After a few steps, I pause. The boots I borrowed from Liza are the clomping kind, and no mistake. I try tiptoeing, heel-to-toeing, and walking sideways.

Clomp. Clomp. And *clomp.*

With as silent a sigh as I can muster, I leave them behind; I'm going to owe Liza a lot of footwear. My feet are sweaty in the heavy wool socks they loaned me, and I wiggle my slippery toes, reminding myself that it's worlds better than being barefoot and knee-deep in the mud.

There is no hallway; room just leads to room. Each one is as prim and spare as the kitchen. The only exception is the living room. Two plush chairs sit in front of a bear-skin rug, backs to the wider world. They face the fireplace, a thick-manteled square of the same black stone the house sits on. It's surrounded by trophies and baubles of one kind or another: A set of moose antlers. An old military uniform on a hanging dummy. A deep-burnished box of pipeleaf. Three half-empty bottles of liquor, wax-stoppered and lined along the top of the mantel, next to two upturned glasses. A rack of muskets, each polished to a mirror shine and displayed one above the other. A portrait, paint chipped and frame weathered, of five familiar faces: Reeves, Parsons, Doc Bunder, Liza's grandma.

And my grandpa.

The founders of Windydown Vale.

I shake my head, wondering what Grandpa'd think of me now: breaking into a mayor's house, trying to spring the man who came to fleece Windydown for all we're worth. Unable to help it, my mind bounces right down the family tree, settling square on my own parents' faces. No matter what, I'm going to have a lot of explaining to do. It's almost overwhelming, almost makes me drop the hammer and walk out the front door.

Almost.

But then I remember pullin' those bodies from the muck, and I realize I can't turn back.

I take the stairs three at a time, mindful of the dwindling

darkness outside. At the top of the steps, there are only three doors. The one to my right lets a smidgen of candle-light dance along the jamb. I lick my lips, set my feet, raise the hammer . . .

And freeze, just long enough for my thoughts to catch up with me.

Glad I did, too. The first one is: *What happens if you startle a man with a loaded musket?*

I stow the hammer and rub my damp palms against my britches. Then, brave as I can, I say, "Anybody there?"

My voice cracks right on the *body*.

"Copper? Copper, boy? Is that you?" I hear in response. It's Shumpeter.

"I'm coming in!" I reply, and I swing open the door.

It looks like Shumpeter's had a bad go of it. He's bound, arms tugged back and ankles tethered to the legs of the chair beneath him. A generous slick of dried blood cakes the left side of his face, and his once-fine clothes are all torn up. Wig's long gone, too, revealing a nest of dirty curls framing a shiny bald spot. My nose crinkles at the smell of the place: sharp and heavy, like sweat and pee and fear. The candle is on a table just beside him, along with a cup and a water jug.

"I'm here to get you," I say as I rush over. I fall to my knees to tackle the foot knots first, and I see that Shum-peter's soiled himself. Explains the smell. "How long have they had you tied—"

"Stop!" I hear. "Stop . . . Stop right there, please!" My

eyes flick up to Shumpeter, who tilts his head forward. I turn slowly.

The bed is tucked into the corner of the room. It's small, meant for a child, perhaps.

Or someone sickly.

"Copper Inskeep? Is that you?" Reeves's grandson says. He speaks slowly, voice rasping.

"Nestor," I reply, my hands raised. In his bony arms is one of his grandpa's muskets. The butt is nestled into the pillows that prop him up.

The muzzle's aimed at my chest.

"Been a while," he mumbles.

He's right. I haven't seen him in months, not since the spring. He used to sit by the window, and he'd wave down at Liza and me while we ran errands. Looks like he's taken a turn for the worse since. His cheeks are drawn, face pale and glistening. A brass pot sits on the mattress near his elbow.

"I . . . I wasn't expecting you," Nestor admits, swallowing nervously.

"I s'pose I could say the same," I reply.

Nestor rubs his cheek against his shoulder, scratching at a bit of patchy stubble. The tip of the gun waves about unsteadily. After a few moments, Nestor says, "So . . . um . . . what brings you by?"

I glance at Shumpeter. "You been watching him long?" I ask.

Nestor nods and tries to shift positions, but it sends him into a coughing fit, one that shakes his whole body.

"I need water," Nestor says weakly, "but I can't get it 'n' hold the gun."

"You could put the musket down," I offer.

"Can't. Grandpa told me that villain is the snakiest we've seen."

I point at the pitcher at Nestor's bedside. There's a wooden cup there, too. "May I?"

"S'pose so. But I've gotta keep him down the barrel, if you don't mind."

I shake my head. Then, moving slowly as I can, I fill the cup. Nestor hacks dryly a few more times but quiets as I bring the glass to his lips. He sips at it for a long while—time enough for me to consider grabbing the musket. My gaze flicks down to the trigger. Nestor's got it half squeezed already.

So no heroics for me.

When I pull the water away, some escapes to trickle into the folds of his neck. He swallows with effort, and his grip on the gun eases. I take a deep breath.

"Thank you," Nestor whispers. "Now, about why you're here . . ."

"I know about him," I say, jerking my head toward Shumpeter.

"Grandpa told me. Girl's in on it, too, yeah?" Nestor says eagerly. His front hand twists along the metalwork of the gun.

"Girl?" I ask, calm as I can.

"Annalise? Annabelle? Something southern like that."

"There's an Annabelle just came to town, yeah," I reply.

"That's the one. Grandpa's out looking for you, actually. Says you might have a bead on her whereabouts."

Shumpeter, who was quietly shifting behind me, goes still. I shrug. "I sadly don't. Came looking to see if there was anything I could do to help."

Nestor peers at me, teeth clacking as he thinks.

"Now maybe you did, 'n' maybe you didn't. That's for Grandpa to sort out," he says after a bit. I notice him looking at the hammer tucked in my belt. "And don't worry . . . he won't be long. I'm expecting him back round dawn. Meantimes, you can have a seat." Nestor swings the business end of the musket toward a chair near the window. I trudge over, setting the hammer before me. Then I sit and wait, an awkward silence settling over the room. Looking out the window, I can see the mountains at the opposite end of the Vale. They've caught the beginning of dawn on their pale faces. Annabelle and Liza's mom must have the horses by now . . .

"The . . . the young man . . . ," Shumpeter sputters suddenly. It startles me, and I'm half out of my seat before Nestor looks me back down. ". . . young man in the bed was just telling this old monster hunter about his grandfather. Good fellow, he says. Backbone of the town."

"Tell 'im, Copper. Grandpa's only doin' what's best for the Vale."

My lips part, but I have trouble with the words that're supposed to come next. Instead, I shrug.

"Nestor, was it?" Shumpeter asks. I peer at him. He's talking to Nestor, but he's looking right at me. There's a spark in his eye.

"Yeah, that's it. Was my pa's name, too."

Shumpeter nods. "Don't worry, Nestor. I don't think your grandfather's a monster."

Nestor seems much relieved. He even smiles.

"He's just people," Shumpeter continues, his voice grave. "And that's worse."

I shift, watching Nestor carefully. He's sweating more now. Musket's getting shaky, too. He blinks quickly, then clears his throat and spits a wad of brown phlegm into the pot near his pillow. Voice still thick and gummy, he asks, "Is that so?"

"It's so."

"How you figure?"

"Because," Shumpeter replies, locking eyes with Nestor, "there ain't a monster in the world that wasn't born in the mind of a man."

At first I think Shumpeter has gone mad, baiting Nestor like this. But then I get it. I can see the wheels of Nestor's mind clicking along, thready eyebrows twitching and dry lips parted. He starts to respond, but he's so flustered that another coughing jag grabs him. Shumpeter murmurs, "Copper . . ."

I hold my breath.

The tip of the gun swings wide as Nestor leans for his pot.

I leap. Just as I do, Shumpeter wrenches against his bonds, dropping, chair and all, to the floor. Nestor screams, but before he can fire, I rip the musket from his hands. He's even weaker than I expected, and I nearly fling the gun across the room, it comes away so easily. My instincts tell me to thump Nestor upside the head to knock him out, but I see I needn't bother. His lungs have betrayed him; it's all he can do to gurgle a breath at a time, hands clenched around his brass pot and eyes closed tight. He's twisted all awkward, too, and I realize I'm kneeling on his legs. Slowly, I back off, holding the musket well clear.

Nestor keeps hacking, spitting up more of that rot. Shumpeter groans. I'm not sure who to help first, so I slide off the bed, lean the musket against the wall . . .

And hear a telltale click behind me.

"You'll want to turn around slowly." It's Reeves's voice, and no mistake.

I obey.

Wish I hadn't.

Reeves stands in the doorway, gun at his hip, muzzle pointing at my belly. He's dripping rain, a broad hat casting shadows across his face. What once were friendly eyes, narrowed like he just finished laughing at a pleasant memory, now seem suspicious. His beard has gone from grandfatherly to ungainly, yellowed teeth from amusingly crooked to sharply canine. The stoop of his posture, one I always thought of as wise and settled, is predatory, like a buzzard leaning over a meal. I've known Reeves my whole life, and he's never looked like this.

Even though it's the same as he's always looked.

"G . . . Grandpa . . . ," Nestor sputters.

"You'll be all right, boy," Reeves says. Then, to me: "Sit."

I do, right on the floor. My hands are shaking, and I tuck them into my armpits. Reeves uses his foot to drag a chair in front of the door, and he parks himself there. He rests his musket across his lap, just like he'd do on our porch. And though he's old, I've got no illusions about being able to wrest that gun from him like I did from Nestor.

"Got ourselves a conundrum here," Reeves observes. Shumpeter groans from next to the bed. Nestor hacks a couple more times, wipes a corner of his quilt across his mouth, and says, "Sorry, Grandpa. He jumped me."

"It's none of your fault, Nestor. I'm proud of you."

I glance up at Nestor. He's grinning. When I look back, Reeves is staring right at me.

"Proud of you, too, Copper."

It takes every last bit of me not to smile just like Nestor, but I manage. I even conjure a fine, bittery scowl. "That don't mean much coming from a murderer," I say.

Reeves purses his lips, then sucks his teeth. "Reckon you found a thing or two in the swamps, then."

"Maybe," I reply.

"Find Annabelle, too?"

"Wouldn't tell you if I did."

"That's unfortunate. I always thought the Vale could rely on you, Copper."

My nostrils flare, but I don't respond. Shumpeter, though? He has a few words.

"Leave the boy to go, Reeves. And my girl, too. They're naught but bystanders to this."

"Wish I could," Reeves replies. "But I'm sworn to protect Windydown."

"By killing Liza's dad?" I blurt. My eyes go wide, and I clamp my hands over my mouth. But damage has been done.

"It's an oath you swore, too, Copper, when you took up the mask. We're on the same side here."

I shake my head. "That ain't so! Mother and Father taught me ghoulin'. They'd never—"

"They always!" Reeves growls. I flinch. Reeves looks up at the ceiling. "Told 'em they should spill it all to you years ago. Rip the bandage off quick and clean. But no. They wanted to shelter you. And look where that's got us."

"Spill . . . spill what?" I whisper.

"Windydown lives on a razor's edge, Copper. Always has. Between the mountains and the mud? Our survival's been no sure thing."

A sharp, metal tang reaches my tongue, and I grit my teeth to keep from getting sick. Part of me already knows where this is going.

Most of me doesn't want it to get there.

"We protect our secrets, any way we can," Reeves

continues. "All of us. And that includes your parents. Who was it, do you think, that told me about Cutty? About her finding the Ghoul costume while she was cleaning? She threatened to tell all and sundry about your mom. Demanded gold. Did you know that? Hmm?"

"Shut up," I hiss. Like a little kid, I cover my ears with my palms. Reeves just leans in, speaks louder.

"How many blackmailers would you have us bow to, Copper? How many fortune-seekers, scouring our swamps?"

I'm all over shaking, and it makes mouse squeaks of my voice. "The Ghoul stops . . ."

"Ghoul's a parlor trick! Always has been."

"Has not . . . ," I mumble. "Scared away highwaymen . . . bandits . . ."

Reeves slaps his hand sharply against his knee. "Lord almighty . . . Copper . . . *we're* the bandits!"

I can't make heads or tails of what he's saying, so I tell him to shut up again. He glowers at me a moment, scratches his nose, sucks on a bit of his beard, and nods. "Yup. It's time," he says.

And then he leaves.

I daren't move for the first few seconds. His feet fall heavy on the stairs, and I can hear him grumbling the entire way. Once he reaches the first floor, things get quiet. I crawl forward until I can see Shumpeter. His face is scrunched as he flexes and strains against the ropes. I scramble over and attack the knots at his ankles.

"Where'd he go?" Shumpeter whispers.

"Dunno," I respond.

"What did he mean about—"

"I don't know!" I shout. It's too loud; Reeves definitely heard. I don't care. Tears sting my eyes as I attack the ropes. But they're wound tight as iron. I twist and tug at them, rip at them with too-short fingernails. All I end up doing, though, is hurting Shumpeter. He lets me know it, too.

"Confound it, boy!"

"Confound you!" I snarl back. "Confound all this!"

Shumpeter blows sharply through his teeth, but then sighs. "He might be lying," he says softly, like he's cooing to a baby. "Trying to get in your head. Don't let him."

"My grandpa doesn't lie," we hear from above. I sit up sharp, shooting Nestor such a glare that he grabs his spit pot and holds it in front of his face. In its glint, I can see my own, warped and dim.

Almost ghoulish, in fact.

"No," I whisper, and I dig into those knots again.

I don't even manage to free a leg before I hear bootsteps on the stairs.

"Copper, that's enough," Shumpeter murmurs.

"Suck mud," I reply. "He wants to shoot me? Let 'im shoot me."

Reeves doesn't shoot me. In fact, he kneels down, groaning with the effort. Both of his hips crack, bone on bone, and he exhales slowly through pursed lips. Once settled, he rests his musket on the floor. Shumpeter cringes; the barrel's so close to his face he could kiss it.

I keep working at those ropes, trying my damnedest to pretend Reeves isn't there. I expect him to rip me away, or to punch me, or to embrace me and tell me it's all a bad dream. But he does none of that. Instead, he drops something, which lands with a single, deep thud. Startles me so bad I fall away from Shumpeter. I huddle against the foot of the bed, and that's when I spot what Reeves thought it was time to show me. Guess Shumpeter spies it at the same time I do, because he whistles sharp through his cracked and bruised lips. Have to say, I'm inclined to do the same. Because what Reeves brought? What he tossed, casual-like, to the floor?

It's a bar of pure gold.

Chapter Thirty-Eight

I stare at the thing as it gleams in the lamplight. How can I not? It's more wealth than I've seen in my life. Makes the little slugs Mother gives me seem like spit in a rainstorm.

"Perfect, ain't it?" Reeves asks.

I nod.

'Cept it isn't.

On the top, closest to me, is a symbol, pressed right into the metal: four long guns, crossed to double *X*s. Seal of the Great Northern Army, it is. Reeves reaches down, running his fingertips along the grooves.

"'Twas sixty years ago we met," Reeves says. "Your granddaddy. Liza's grandma. Doc. Parsons. Me. Raggediest bunch of greenhorns the army ever saw, I reckon. Gold was our first assignment. Ten wagons' full—half the war budget of the entire north, by all accounts. They wanted it moved through the hinterlands on the quiet."

"You were meant to guard it?" I whisper.

"Parsons had a different idea. Always schemin', that one. By the time we hit Jandy Ford, the whole regiment was in on it. We'd split up, five per wagon. Drive hard in every direction. Figured that by the time the army caught on, we'd be so scattered that they'd just give up."

Shumpeter snorts, drawing a daggery look from Reeves. I catch the meaning well enough. "You figured wrong," I mutter.

Reeves nods solemnly. "They hunted us like the devil, our souls come due. And there wasn't a haven to be had. 'Cept here. 'Cept the Vale."

"Never was any panning gold, was there?" I say bitterly.

Reeves smiles, like he's proud I'm catching on. "Never none but what we brought on that wagon, and that was a fool mistake. Weren't but a day's ride in when we sank. Lord, you should've seen your granddaddy fight the mud. But it was a lost cause. Swamp took the wagon whole, along with enough gold to make each of us kings a dozen times over."

I glance at the bar. Reeves picks it up, cradling it to his chest like a runt pup.

"Doc says it was that folly that saved us," he continues. "Northern army caught every other wagon. Hanged the thieves what took 'em. When they came sniffin' in the Vale, though, there wasn't a sign of the gold. Just the huts we'd managed to cobble together to keep the rain off. They left us to our misery. And it *was* miserable . . . least until Liza's grandma found a way to get at the gold. Ropes and pulleys and prayers netted us a bar at a time, two if we were lucky. What we fished out, we melted to nuggets. It was enough to turn legitimate. Build something to be proud of. Even took new names, according to our lot. Reeves, Parsons, Smith, Doc . . ."

"Inskeep," Shumpeter says softly. "Oh, Copper . . ."

"Shut your mouth," Reeves warns, and he reaches for his musket.

Shumpeter presses on, voice throaty and raw. "But it *wasn't* enough, was it? Gold like that, even a little, brings attention. Prospectors. Treasure hunters. You needed a way to keep folk out of the swamp, keep 'em from finding what you stole. You needed . . ."

"A . . . a ghoul," I mutter. "You . . . used me?"

"We used the Ghoul."

"You used *me*!" I shout, my voice cracking. "To trick people! Terrify 'em!"

"To protect 'em!" Reeves insists. "Me 'n' Parsons 'n' Doc 'n' anyone else who knew. Nestor. Wendell . . ."

He leans in.

"Your parents."

I gasp. The truth, the horrible *why* of it all, is coming clear, a looming mountain through a jagged windowpane. Makes it so I can barely breathe, like someone punched me right in the rib cage. "Mother . . . Father. They're—"

"*Good people*," Reeves insists. "And yeah, to protect the good, we've done bad. Had to! Lord, Copper . . . what do you think'd happen if Liza's daddy took our secret north? Or Cutty to the south? What happens to Windydown if word gets out that the Ghoul ain't real? If schemers and cutthroats learn we've got twenty crates of gold buried in the swamp?"

"I . . . I don't . . ." I wheeze. Reeves rubs at my back, but I smack his arm away. His nostrils flare, and I can hear his jagged teeth gritting behind his lips. Then, faster than I'd guess was possible, he stands, ignoring the angry clack of his hips.

"It'd end us—the inn and the Walk and every good thing we've built these sixty years past! So we made hard choices, like you're gonna have to. Like your mother and father've done. Like your grandpappy and me and anyone who has a stake in Windydown."

I reach out, grabbing the base of the bed. The wood, at least, is solid. Unmoving. Unlike the rest of the room seems to be.

"This man," Reeves says, pointing at Shumpeter, "and his spawn are a threat to us. They get free, it'll only be a matter of time before holy hell rolls through here, borne on the backs of the greedy and vengeful. Now, I ain't asking you to pull no triggers. All you've got to do is get the girl. Tell her you've found her daddy. Tell her he's hurt and needs her. I don't care. Just get her here. Then you go back to your inn. You hug your mother and father, and you sleep well, knowing you've done your part for the Vale. After that, things'll be normal again."

"N . . . normal?" I whisper.

"That's right."

I blink back more tears, and I rub a shivering hand beneath my nose. It comes away slick. Seems like it takes every bit of strength I have to move my head, but I do, swinging my gaze over to Shumpeter. He looks as miserable as I feel—jaw slack, eyes dark, hair filthy and wild. Still, he manages to lock eyes with me. And he mouths something.

Something I don't expect.

It's okay, son, he says.

My reply is equally silent.

Liar.

He smiles sadly and offers me a little nod. I look away. Then I feel Reeves's hand on me, guiding me up and to the door.

"Sooner she's here, the sooner it's done," he says sternly. "And the sooner we're all safe."

Without looking back, I trudge down the stairs. I'm dimly aware that Reeves is behind me. When we reach the first floor, he stomps ahead and swings the door open. A sharp swirl of wind eagerly rushes in, carrying the scent of mud stink and forge smoke. I shiver.

"You're the Ghoul, Copper. Nobody more important to Windydown. I know you'll do right by us," Reeves says. Then he pushes me out the door.

And I walk, weeping, into the rain.

Chapter Thirty-Nine

Liza rushes out into the storm to meet me, hammers swinging in her hands. When she sees my face, she pulls up.

"Shumpeter?" she asks softly. The rain strips the soot from her face, leaving deep, dark lines. She doesn't wipe them away. "Is he . . ."

"Alive," I reply. Should be a happy word, but it echoes about in my chest, bouncing against my heart and threatening to smash it to bits. Liza looks around.

"But not with you . . . ," she observes, slipping the hammers into the big pocket of her apron.

"Couldn't get him. Nestor stopped me. Then Reeves."

Liza nods. "I saw him go inside."

"Yep. He caught me before I could untie a single knot."

Liza starts to fret, but I think she can see that I've done

all the worrying that's to be done, so instead she hugs me. I let her, though I don't have the courage to hug her back.

Not now that I know what I'm supposed to do.

She lets go when she feels my limp arms, and she holds me at length. "Do we have a plan? Anything?"

"Reeves has one," I reply. "Wants me to do what's right for Windydown."

"Which is?"

"Bring him Annabelle. Let him end this quietly."

Liza's lips press tight. "Are you gonna?"

I stand there for a long time. I look up and down the Long Walk, at the rain-shrouded silhouettes of houses that Valers built out of nothing. In the distance, a determined trademan has set up shop, a tattered awning fluttering against the wind. A young woman stands opposite. I can't hear what they're saying, but after a few moments, they shake hands. Closing my eyes, I picture the same spot, midday and in the shining sun. The triplets are playing games. Mayors are on the porch, cracking jokes and spilling tea. Mother's calling folk in for lunch—chicken and dumplings, with molasses thick-cake for dessert. And when I open my eyes?

Liza's right there, nervous and shaking and strong.

"What's right for Windydown . . . ," I whisper.

"Copper?" she asks. "What's in that head of yours?"

Too much.

More than I can handle.

So many thoughts that I can't keep hold of any of 'em.
'Cept maybe one.

"Something stupid, I guess."

She reaches up to brush the rain off my cheek. "That's my Copper," she says, and then: "What kind are we talking? Jump-in-front-of-a-horse stupid?"

"Worse," I reply.

Her brow furrows, but not on account of me. She tilts her head toward Reeves's house. "He's watching through the upstairs window."

"Then I better talk quick," I say, and I tell her what I'm thinking.

Doesn't take long at all.

"You're sure there's no other way?" Liza asks.

"Gotta get Reeves away from Shumpeter if we're gonna do anything. And his guard is every which kind of up. If you've got a better plan, I'm for it."

She pulls out her hammers, bringing the heads together to clink softly. "I surely don't."

"Then wish me luck," I whisper.

"Good luck, Ghoul," she replies, and I'm gone.

Chapter Forty

There's no sign of Annabelle, though Brimstone's and Perdy's reins are tied loosely to the hitching post next to Shumpeter's wagon. I know she can't have gone far; my quick guess is she's either behind the wagon or somehow in it. I lean against one of the massive wheels, acting like I'm catching my breath, which ain't too far from true. Across from me, the Sunken Inn looms, rain sloshing out of over-full gutters and wind whistling around the eaves.

"Don't say anything," I murmur, loud as I dare. "But there's been a complication."

I hear what might be a gasp.

Might also be a trick of the storm.

"Got a plan. It ain't a good one, but it's a plan. Starts with you being ready to run, daddy or no. Pretty much ends there, too. Things go sideways, you get out. That's all."

I leave it at that. Part of me regrets not being able to tell her more, but the truth is I've got no clue what's about to happen, 'cept what I'm going to do.

Assuming I can make it past my parents first.

I rush up the steps of the inn and burst through the door. I don't even bother wiping my feet. Aunt Abigail's setting up for breakfast, lining mismatched mugs along the bar. Stacy, Laila, and Fran clean the tables—probably punishment for last night's mischief.

"Copper's back!" Stacy declares. I'm making a beeline for the kitchen, but Aunt Abigail steps in front of me. I think to muscle past, but her hug's not to be denied.

"Lord, Copper! We were worried! Where've you been?"

I sneak a peek at the triplets. Laila winks, and I nod in reply.

"You're crushing my ribs, Aunt Abigail," I mutter.

"If that's what it takes to keep you from running off again, so be it!" she says firmly. Then she cranes her neck and hollers, "Nettie! Copper's back!"

I'm instantly aware of how hard my heart is pounding. It only gets worse when both Mother and Father fling open the kitchen door. They take turns wrapping me up, tugging at my collar, pressing their palms to my forehead, and making fitful appraisals of my well-being. I withstand the storm, then say, "I don't got long."

I don't need to pretend to be nervous or upset.

It's all right there, plain to see.

"Son, should we talk in the kitchen?" Mother asks softly. I nod, and Father leads the way.

272

As soon as the door closes behind us, Mother's pouring me a mug of tea from the kettle, and Father's rummaging in a drawer for a towel. I take a moment to breathe.

This is not what I expected.

Reeves? He changed, like someone yanked his mask off to expose the monster underneath. I thought it'd be the same for my parents. That's why I was hell-bent on getting through the inn as fast as possible.

I didn't want to see what they'd become.

But here, in our kitchen? Like this? It seems so normal, a big ol' invitation to sit down, close my eyes, and pretend like all's well. Mother and Father are as they've always been. They haven't changed a lick, and that's the most terrifying part. Because that can mean only one thing.

The one that's changed is me.

"I . . . I can't stay here," I say, and I shoot toward the back door. Father intercepts me, though.

"Whoa, son! Where you going?"

"Got no time," I say truthfully. "Reeves . . ."

"You spoke to the mayor?" Mother asks, setting a steaming cup of honey-laced tea down on the table, handle toward me.

"Yes," I reply. "I saw him."

"Good. And you found the girl?" Father says.

I nod, determined not to lie for as long as I can.

"Is she with Reeves now?" Mother prods.

"Not yet," I reply weakly. "But that's why I have to hurry."

Father glances at Mother. They can tell something's wrong.

Probably because I've turned green as a pear.

"Copper, I think you should rest," Mother says after a moment. "Wherever the girl is, we can get her. Then we'll take her to Reeves so she can talk to him. He'll clear all this up, no doubt."

"No!" I insist. "It's . . . it's gotta be me."

"You've done enough."

Images of Reynard Finch, of Cutty, and of Liza's dad flash in my mind, clashing hard with what I see before me. A scream starts brewing in my belly, but I swallow it like the bitterest tea and I whisper, "Not nearly."

Mother blinks. Father's lips purse.

"Copper . . . is there something you're not telling us?"

I look down. My hands are clenched into fists. I'm shaking all over.

"Yeah," I admit.

They step toward me, nothing but concern in their eyes.

"Whatever it is, son, you can say it."

I turn around, picking up the steaming mug on the table. I hold its warmth between my fingers, and I inhale the scent of sweet mint. Mother smiles comfortingly. Father reaches out to offer me the towel for my dripping hair.

"I'm sorry," I whisper.

Then I slam the mug down at their feet.

"Copper! What in the—" Mother screeches, hopping back just before the tea can scald her. Father tries to twist away, too, but his knee buckles, and he cries out as shards of ceramic cut his legs. I leap through the middle, darting for the back door. I wrench it open, throw myself outside, and sprint for the shed.

Time for Windydown Vale to meet its Ghoul.

Chapter Forty-One

I put on the costume as I race through the swamp, shedding the clothes Liza loaned me even as I tug the tattered shirt, torn britches, and macabre mask into place. I do it at full stride—it's that much a part of me. I only slow once I've got the old tree husk in sight. Reverently, I use my claws to rip away a wide piece of bark.

My mask is illuminated by a familiar green glow.

"Last time, guys," I whisper. "I promise."

Two quick smears of gnat larvae later, and I'm Windy-down's hero. Or nightmare, I guess.

Assuming there's a difference.

As the trees start to thin on the way back to town, I can see the forge smoke, thick and dark, roiling up from Liza's house. It's my beacon, and I pick my way toward it. Gets to a point that if I wasn't wearing my gear, I wouldn't be able to avoid the mud.

Then I'm in it anyway.

I let loose that scream I've been cultivating since back at the inn, and I slash my way forward, claw over claw when I have to. The wind seems to push me, and before the mud can even reach my belt, I'm diving for the back of Liza's house. The tips of my claws dig into the lowermost boards, and I drag myself up, heaving until I'm clear.

Right on cue, Liza slides open her window.

"It better be Copper Inskeep under all that muck," she says as she grabs one of my poles and hauls me up. When I'm inside, she backs away slowly, a hand over her mouth.

"Hey, Liza," I say, cheerfully as I can, and I wave a claw.

"This is what you wear when you're . . ."

"Haunting," I supply.

She nods, and I step away from the window. It backs Liza up, and she nearly knocks her hammers off the table behind her.

"What, no kiss?" I ask. A thick rivulet of mud oozes off of the chaos of nails that pass for the Ghoul's teeth.

"I'll pass," she says, grimacing. "Let's get you cleaned up, then—"

"No," I insist quickly. "Leave it."

"It's gross," she retorts, and she reaches up to poke a finger at my glowing-green eye socket. I swat her hand away.

"Kind of the point."

"Well, if there's anything that can scare Reeves out of his fortress over there, it'd be you."

I pick my way through the room to the front door, trying not to track mud anywhere I don't have to. Liza grabs a sheet of scrap iron from the corner near the forge, a heavy piece that she has to half lift, half drag behind her. Her eyebrows knot with concentration, she clenches her jaw, and the tendons in her neck bulge, but she manages to wrestle the thing to the door, where she leans it against the wall. Then she retrieves her hammers.

"Give me about thirty seconds," I say.

"Yep," she replies, forearms flexing as she grips those steel-headed mallets.

I tug the door open, letting the weather in. Liza pulls a faded red-and-blue kerchief from her apron pocket and ties it round her head. Then she reaches out with one of the hammers, tapping it against my right claw.

"Be safe, Copper," she whispers.

"You too," I say, and I jump off her porch . . .

Right into the middle of Windydown Vale on a rainy morning.

I get my first scream straight off; I nearly barrel into a mule drawing a little cart. The tradewoman holding the reins tugs so hard the poor creature bucks, and I skitter to the side just as its hooves crash down. The woman curls into a ball, arms shielding her face as she trembles. I snag the lip of her cart with my claws, plant my foot on the wheel, and leap up next to her.

Then I scream, too—long, loud, and from my gut.

The woman faints; I have to hook her arm to keep her

from keeling over. When I've got her steady, I arrange her as safely as I can on the wagon seat.

As I do, a thunderous clang splits the air.

Liza's lugged that massive metal plate onto her porch and propped it against the railing. With a fierce two-handed chop, she pounds it, metal on metal. It's so loud and powerful, Liza's so strong and imposing and perfect, that I stare. She catches me and shoots me a scowl. "Go!" she shouts, pointing up the Walk. I do, hurtling away from the wagon and toward the next house down—Casey Milliner's place. Following me is another great, deep *gong*, along with Liza's piercing alarm:

"Ghoul! The Ghoul is come!"

Old Mrs. Milliner is already on her porch by the time I'm scrambling up her stairs. She's got a frying pan in one hand and her cane in the other, and she's beating them together furiously.

"Away! Away, fiend!" she spits.

I oblige.

All through Windydown Vale, I make myself known. The Mighty Ruckus builds quickly, just like it does on a full moon. Prayers and curses are hurled in equal measure. Doors are flung open or locked tight. Either way, though, people are watching. They're making noise.

They're seeing the Ghoul.

When I reach the steps of the Sunken Inn, I'm greeted by chaos. A dozen tradefolk are straining at the rails to glimpse what's causing the commotion, and when they get a look at me, they fall over themselves to retreat, chase me down, or get a better view. In the tumult I spot Aunt Abigail, panicking as she grabs at the triplets. They're jammed at a window, nearly spilling out. Stacy's screaming her head off. Fran's gawking harder than she ever has at any book. Laila's grinning from ear to ear. "It's real, Mama! Lookit!" she squeals. "I think it's gonna eat someone!"

In response, I rear up, claws raised, and I yowl to curdle blood. I get a hearty chorus of screams right back at me ... along with a volley of fruit, cookware, porch chairs, and anything else folk think to throw. My bare feet slip on the wet boards and a spoon pings noisily off my mask, but I manage to turn tail and retreat.

Or at least I try.

People have packed the Walk behind me. Some are empty-handed. Most are armed.

And all are shouting the warning.

"Ghoul! Ghoul!" they holler. Behind them, the deep, brassy boom of Liza's hammering rings through the Vale like the tolling of a funeral bell. I squint through the eye slits of the mask, looking at that house upon the rock.

Reeves is on his porch, musket in hand.

He peers over the crowd.

He sees me.

And he pulls the trigger.

The gunshot silences everything else but the rain. No more screams. No more pounding. Stunned, the mob turns to look at the man who just fired into the sky. They stay mute when he trudges down to the Long Walk, hunched over his musket, trying to keep the powder dry. There isn't but a sliver of room on the Walk, but everyone makes way for the mayor.

I wait until he's right in the middle of the crowd.

Wait until I can see Reeves's eyes.

Then I charge.

I doubt any of these poor folk have ever seen anything on two legs move as fast as I can. Even though I'm trying to avoid them, some dive out of the way, throwing themselves into the mud to escape. A few brave souls heft poles, pans, or other tools—one man has an ax—and they try to stop me. But I'm not fixin' to fight, so I skitter out of the way, leaping, dodging, and shielding myself with my claws as I go. I still take a pretty nasty shot to the shoulder as I try to skirt Wendell Fishmonger, but my body's too busy to feel the pain, and my mind can only hold one thought right now:

Get to Reeves before he reloads.

And I do, just.

Ducking low, I come up with both claws crossed, pushing the barrel of his gun high. Steel screeches on steel as we lock weapons. The rain pelts us both, like it's driving us together. I press in, the green glow of my eyes reflected in his.

"Damn it, Copper!" he demands. "What is this?"

"*What's best for Windydown*," I hiss, my words curling from the mask as steam.

Reeves snarls and heaves me back, swinging the musket into the space between us. He's panting, teeth bared. "I'm not letting you get Shumpeter, boy," he growls.

"Don't aim to," I retort. "That's Liza's job. I'm just the ruckus."

Reeves's jaw drops, and he whips around to look at his house.

I pounce.

My claws snag the musket. At the same time, I shove my shoulder into his chest. The gun goes flying, spinning through the rain to land in the mud just off the Walk. Reeves bellows with rage and makes to dive for it, but I block him, my mask a finger's breadth from his face, two rows of rusty and dripping nails one quick twitch from taking out his eyes.

"It's over, Mayor," I whisper.

"Not quite," he replies.

And then the mob's on me.

A dozen hands drag me down the Walk. A heavy stick, maybe a broom handle, slashes across my arm, buckling it. I try to cover my head, but my claw-poles get tangled, and my bell gets rung proper. Frying pan to the face, I think it is. I go down in a heap.

Moments later, I'm covered . . . but not by mob or mud. Whoever's atop me is shrieking, lashing out with a claw I dropped in the tumult. Through the broken lines of my mask, I see that the crowd has formed a circle around me.

And above me, fierce and furious, is Annabelle.

And Aunt Abigail.

And my mom.

"Nettie!" Wendell shouts. "What're you doing? Get away from that monster!"

"You'll back off, Fishmonger!" Mother insists, thrusting at him with a poker from our fireplace. Aunt Abigail's armed with two jagged, broken-off wine bottles, and Annabelle's holding the claw-pole like a sword. The wind whips about, cold and soaking. The mob presses in.

The three don't budge.

"I want my father!" Annabelle shouts. I push up to my elbows. Even though my world's spinning, I can still see the faces of folk. They're confused. They're angry.

Mostly, though, they're afraid.

Reeves slips through the crowd. Next to him are Doc Bunder and Mayor Parsons. Shoulder to shoulder, they confront the three women standing over me.

"My father!" Annabelle repeats.

Parsons inches forward. "Look to the fiend at your feet, girl!" he says, thrusting a finger at me. "You said it yourself—the Ghoul took your—"

"Lies!" Annabelle screams. "All of it. Ours and yours. Where is he?"

A screech from the back: Granny Erskine, I think. "This is Windydown Vale, young miss! If a man is gone, it's the Ghoul. If a man is dead, it's the Ghoul!"

A murmur of agreement twines its way through the mob, joining the drubbing of the rain on the Walk in a madcap chorus. Doc Bunder raises his hands like he's the conductor, and the gasps and grumbles die away.

"Good folk! I know the power of curiosity! But I implore you—go back to your wagons and homes. Find shelter from this storm. These brave women have subdued the creature for now, but the danger has not passed. If we—"

"Annabelle!" someone shouts, loud and deep and desperate. It cuts Doc Bunder off. Startles him, too, by the look of things. The crowd pivots, boots shuffling against the boards, and I smile weakly as another voice, familiar and comforting and strong, yells, "Y'all want this hammer upside your heads? Move!"

As the crowd obeys, Shumpeter and Liza come into view. He's leaning on her, but she's up to the task. She even has an arm free to wield her mallet, which she points at the mayors like she's warding off evil spirits. As soon as Shumpeter's close, Annabelle drops the claw and runs to her father. Liza trades him off, then comes to me.

"Nestor give you trouble?" I whisper.

"I'm persuasive," she says, setting her hammer down with a thunk. "Can you stand?"

Gritting my teeth, I use my remaining claw to steady myself, and then I push up.

Just in time to see someone press a fresh musket into Reeves's hands.

"You see before you two false dealers!" Reeves shouts, gun leveled at Shumpeter. "Cheats. Frauds! By their own words, they've admitted it. This is the girl's father!"

Despite Doc Bunder's earlier plea, not a soul has left. If anything, the bizarre spectacle before them has only brought more.

"He's no monster hunter, either!" Reeves continues.

The crowd picks up Reeves's refrain, slinging all manner of insults and worse at Annabelle and her daddy. I wince as a hurled stone catches Shumpeter in the chest, knocking him to his knees. Annabelle's screaming, and she drapes herself over him just in time to be pelted with a half-dozen rotten apples.

"Copper," Liza whispers.

"I know," I reply, and I heave up, ready to fight.

But I can't. Mother's grabbed me. "Run," she pleads, dragging me toward the inn. "While folks' fury is on Shumpeter. Then we'll worry about—"

"No!" I snap, shaking free.

She lets go of the poker, which clatters on the Walk. Taking me by both arms, she whispers, "Why?"

"I *know*, Mother," I reply. "About all of it. The thieving. The gold. The bodies. And I can't let Annabelle and her daddy be next. I just can't."

Her lips tremble, tears mixing with the cold rain. "Don't, Copper. Don't do this."

She almost breaks me. I glance past her at the inn, where the triplets gawk and Father stands wringing his hands at the porch rail. A powerful ache, the guilt of all I'm about to betray, rolls over me like a mudslide, threatening to bury my courage and make me silent.

But I know what that's like.

And I won't be buried again.

"They ain't the only liars!" I cry, twisting away from Mother and limping forward. The crowd goes quiet, shocked to hear a boy's voice comin' from a beast's body, though with my legs wobbling and one claw halfway down the Walk, I think it's pretty clear I'm no otherworldly demon. Parsons lifts his hands, good eye wide and fearful. Reeves's nostrils flare. Doc shakes his head desperately.

And I pull off my mask.

Chapter Forty-Two

o!" Doc Bunder shouts. Parsons clutches his heart and collapses, forcing Wendell to catch him. Reeves curses my name. The crowd, packed ten deep and eight across in either direction, seems to bubble and seethe. The ones up front brandish weapons. Just behind them are a hundred heads, all bobbing and weaving to catch a glimpse, whether over hats, around shoulders, or between elbows. And in the back? That's where the whispers live, people grasping at gossip like mudjays tugging on stubborn worms.

"There's no Ghoul!" I call, raising the mask skyward. It's creased, cracked, and uglier than ever. With a deep breath, I huck it as far off the Walk as I can. "Never was! Just a trick to keep folk from finding the truth!"

"Which is what, exactly?" demands Mr. Villers, stepping into our standoff. His scraggly hair is matted down his forehead, and rain drips from his sunken cheeks. He drags a heavy pickax behind him, metal grinding on wood. "My daughter's gone! Others, too. And they didn't just vanish."

An angry buzz of agreement ripples through the mob, like a nest of biteflies fixin' to swarm. Villers hikes his pickax to his shoulder and takes another stride toward us.

"That's close enough," Aunt Abigail warns, the jagged edges of her broken bottles gleaming. Villers ignores her.

"Well, boy? If you know something, you best say. Where's my girl?"

I wipe my sleeve along my brow. Then, calm as I can, I look at Reeves. "You want to tell 'em, or should I?"

Reeves's lips purse tight, and he doesn't respond—not for a long time. He looks at his house. He peers through the mist at the inn. He tamps the butt of his musket on the sturdy boards of the Walk, ones he might've laid with his own two hands. He scans the soaked and scared faces of our people, goodly folk who have seen too much of the truth in the Ghoul, in the battered body of Barl Shumpeter, and in Reeves's own fury to swallow another lie. Then he locks eyes with me. I match him, steady as I can. For a moment, I think he's going to rush me, try to tear me apart with his bare hands. But then his face softens, a spark of sadness melting his anger. There, in his gaze, I see the kindly old man I thought I knew, one who realizes he's sinking, and all that's left is to decide whether or not to drag the rest of the Vale down with him.

I offer him the slightest of nods, and he sighs.

Then he speaks.

"Windydown! Listen to me, and listen close!" Reeves cries hoarsely. To a one, they do. I've heard the tellin' already, so I mostly focus on the crowd, watching as they cling to one another, hands trembling and tears flowing as he lists the names. Finch. Villers. Smith. A dozen more.

Broken windows.

Broken worlds.

When Reeves is finished, he leans heavy on his rifle, like an old soldier tired of the march. Villers grips the handle of his pickax, knuckles white and face red with fury. He stalks toward Reeves, arms raised.

And Liza's mom stops him.

"No," she says, voice soft. "Vale's had enough of killin'."

He turns on her, and for a half second I think he's gonna end her, so wrathful he seems. But when he sees who it is, and realizes what she's lost, that pickax slips through his hands. It tumbles to the Walk between them as she wraps him up. When they're done, she's the one to turn on the mayors.

"We know what you did for the Vale. How you led us. How you built for us, and rebuilt. How you healed our wounds and shielded our souls and shared your wealth. But now we know who you *are*. And for that, there needs atonin'."

"Justice!" someone yells.

"Revenge!" adds another. A stone, much like the one that hit Shumpeter, sails past Doc Bunder's head. He ducks, huddling over the still-prone form of Parsons.

"Enough!" Reeves demands, slamming his rifle onto the Walk and backing the mob up a step. "I know you want recompense. But not like this! There ain't a body in those swamps that wasn't my doin'. *Me.* Not another soul in Windydown can say the same. And yes, some knew. Most didn't, and I'm not for tellin' which is which. So the way I see it, you want to bring justice down? You bring it here."

Doc Bunder and my mother share a glance. Villers sniffles, then spits into the mud. "And how you propose we do that?" he shouts.

"You could kill me where I stand," Reeves replies, holding his arms out. They're bony thin, his gray shirt and trousers clinging to him wetly. We can see the shadows of his ribs, the odd tilt of his hips, the splay of his feet. "But I'm a seventy-nine-year-old man. And maybe Emeline's right. Maybe there's a better way."

The mob churns nervously for a moment. Reeves waits for them to settle, then continues.

"What's left of the gold'll be melted down and paid to those who lost. Blood money for a blood price. 'N' after that, I'm gone. No more secrets, no more lies."

"What of your grandson?" Wendell calls.

"I'll look after him," Mother replies. Four other Valers say the same. Reeves nods at each in turn.

Villers crosses his arms. "Where'll you go?"

"Head south. Turn myself in to the first lawman I meet."

"And we're supposed to trust you to do that?" a shrill

voice calls. It's Granny Erskine, who hobbles her way through the mob to confront Reeves herself.

"I can take him," Shumpeter says, rising slowly. "I . . . I've a cage in the wagon. We can—"

"Don't trust you, either," Granny snaps. Villers nods, his hands sliding slowly back down to his pickax. Reeves's fingers fidget round the barrel of his musket. The rain softens, like it knows something's about to happen.

I know it, too.

"Do you trust me?" I call. They turn as one, mayors and Valers and tradefolk, to stare.

Granny cups a hand to her ear like she didn't hear me right.

I walk up and repeat the question.

Granny takes my hand. "You're a good lad, Copper, ghoulin' aside. Course we trust you."

"Good," I say. "Because I'm going, too."

Chapter Forty-Three

'm terrible at thinking ahead. I try to picture life in Windydown after all this, and I see nothing. But I know what's past, what I thought my home was and what it turned out to be, and I know what I see in front of me: two sides, fixing to lay into one another. Shumpeter wounded, Parsons breathing ragged on the boards, and none getting any better lying here in the cold and rain. I see friends, and neighbors, and mentors. I see my mother, the one who taught me to look after Windydown.

I see this moment, no more, no less.

And I see my choice.

Villers squints at me through the fog. I'm stooped over my claw, more soaked swamp rat than Ghoul. He blows sharply, sending a mist of raindrops from his mustache. "You sure?" he asks.

I nod.

"Then it's done," Villers says. "The Ghoul and Shumpeter will take the mayor for his reckoning, and good riddance to all three!"

Reeves holds up a hand, maybe to protest my goin'. But before he can utter a word, Parsons cries out in pain, grabbing his left shoulder and gasping for air.

"You heard him! It's done!" Doc Bunder hollers. "Help me get Parsons and any other wounded to the inn, then go home!"

And, just like that, it's ended. Villers and Granny Erskine lead Reeves to his house, probably to gather the gold, maybe let him say goodbye to Nestor. Many, tradefolk and Valer alike, cast a baleful eye at me as they trickle away. I can tell they're not satisfied with the verdict, and I can't say I blame 'em: Ghoul was more than just a thorn in their side. I offer as many apologies as I can, but most folk shun me. I slump to the Walk, watching 'em go. As I do, Mother rushes to me. Father's joined her, limping to keep up.

"Copper?" Mother sobs desperately, falling to her knees before me and grabbing my collar. Father eases down next to her. "Copper, what did you *do*?"

"Kept a promise," I mutter.

"Well, break it. You're not leaving," she demands.

I reach up, hooking my fingers over her arm. Her skin's cold. "I got to," I say. And then: "I want to."

"You're the future of this town!" Mother cries.

"But it ain't mine," I reply gently. "Not anymore."

She reels like I've slapped her. Slumping against Father,

she presses her hands to her face and weeps. He holds her tight, and as he does, we share a glance. No words pass 'twixt us, but I know he can see it: My hurt. My guilt.

He can see I'm done.

"Nettie?" Father says. "Nettie, it'll be okay."

"Yeah, it will," a soft voice adds. "We'll make sure of it."

We look up. Liza and her mother stand next to Annabelle and Shumpeter.

"Windydown's no good," Mrs. Smith sighs. "And we've no stomach for it anymore. Mr. Shumpeter, my daughter and I are fair handy with a hammer, and we'll earn our passage south, or north, or wherever you decide to go, if you'll have us."

"We'll find the room," Annabelle says, and she offers Liza a smile. Liza returns it, then slips down, joining me in comforting my mother. I take her hand, and she squeezes tight. Mrs. Smith kneels as well.

"Nettie, we'll look after Copper. God knows we will."

Wordlessly, Mother embraces Mrs. Smith. Together, we help Mother up, and we lead her back to the inn. Shumpeter and Annabelle go to retrieve the other horses and prepare the wagon. As the others head inside, I linger on the porch. A wicked wind whips around the oak, setting its boughs to swaying and the mist to swirling like ghosts. Shivering, I turn. It's only then that I realize Father's there, waiting for me. His leg is bandaged, and he's leaning heavily on the doorframe.

I try to apologize.

He silences me with a hug.

After many moments, he murmurs, "C'mon. Let's get you warm."

"Okay," I say, and I step into the Sunken Inn for the last time.

Chapter Forty-Four

After we unload Reeves, it's open road and plenty of it. Shumpeter's wagon is more than big enough for the five of us, especially when we jettison all of his fake monster knickknackery. We even toss the dragon skull. Turns out there's a hatch under there, one that lets me climb right onto the roof from inside. I use it whenever I'm feeling twitchy, or stifled, or mournsome.

I'm up there a lot.

Sometimes Liza joins me, our legs hanging off the back while we lie there. She'll rest her head on my shoulder, or mine on hers, the wagon bumping and jostling beneath us. We'll get to talking if we've a mind to. About little things, mostly; there are windows neither of us is ready to break—at least not at first.

"Think anyone's taken the forge?" Liza wonders, reaching up to snap a twig off a passing branch. We're a week out from Windydown, two days from Prosperity Notch. Shumpeter claims he vanquished a hellhound there. Annabelle says it was an overfed raccoon.

I sigh and close my eyes. I try to imagine anyone else leaning over a red-hot iron bar, hammer pounding so hard that sparks rain. "Doubt it," I say. "Their horses'll have to bring their own shoes."

Liza tosses the stick and scoops up my hand, lacing her fingers with mine. She extends her arm, using our hands to block the brightness of the setting sun as it streams through the boughs. "Inn's probably up and running," she murmurs.

"Hope so."

"Did Parsons . . ."

I spread my fingers, and she shifts hers to match.

"No . . . least not before we left. Doc didn't sleep a wink that whole night."

"Did you?"

I turn to look at her. "I surely didn't. Helped Mother in the kitchen. Cried a lot. Said my goodbyes. It was hard."

"Must've been. How did the triplets take it?"

I grin—it's my first real smile in days.

"Stacy was inconsolable. Fran ran and hid. Laila asked if she could have my room."

"And . . . and your parents?"

My smile fades. "Made me promise to come back someday."

Liza nods, shifting so her forehead touches mine. "You tend to keep those, as I recall."

"Not all of them," I murmur. "And anyway, I'm not sure there'll be a Windydown to go back to. Between the mountains and the mud? Wouldn't be surprised if the whole of it gets swallowed up, good as gone."

"Now that'd be a shame," we hear. It's Annabelle, head popping through the hatch. Liza and I sit up, crimson leaves reaching to tousle our hair. Annabelle climbs all the way out to join us.

"Didn't think you'd speak fondly of the place you and your pa nearly died," Liza says.

Annabelle shrugs. "There were a few good things about Windydown Vale."

"Oh? And what were those?" Liza asks.

"I'm looking at 'em."

Liza and I match each other, blush for blush. Annabelle winks, then flips open the hatch again. "Gonna stop soon. You two coming to help set up camp?"

I nod. After Annabelle disappears, Liza and I stay a few moments more. Together, we stare through the trees at the distant range of white-tipped mountains, each one slowly turning scarlet in the setting sun.

Acknowledgments

I grew up on fantasy literature. My dad read *The Hobbit* out loud to my brothers and me, complete with troll voices and all the Gandalf-gravitas he could muster. That hooked me, and once I discovered Rose Estes and Roald Dahl, there was no turning back. I still own my old copies of Joe Dever's Lone Wolf books, as well as three shelves' worth of R. A. Salvatore novels. Thus, the first round of thanks for Copper's story has to go to Dad, to Josh and Jon, and to all those authors who poured their creative spirits into the tales I read when I was a kid.

More recently, I've drawn no small amount of inspiration from those good friends with whom I'm blessed to share stories and adventures, whether it's Travis, Jenny, Matt, Joe, Cormac, Brian, and Amanda at the game table or the fine poets, playwrights, and memoirists of the Wallingford Writer's Group.

On the craft side, *Ghoul* benefited from the critical expertise of Liz Szabla at Feiwel and Friends, who valiantly sacrificed countless afternoons to video conferences with me as I wrangled my way through the groundbriar of Windydown's politics. She remains the world's foremost expert on getting me to clarify characters and up a story's stakes, and I'm forever in her debt as a result. Faye Bender, my wonder-agent at The Book Group, keeps us on the right path (and she's more than handy with a red pen in her own right!). Brian Edward Miller once again provided gorgeous cover art, and the team at Macmillan, especially Morgan and Melissa, continues to support my books in ways big and small.

Rebecca Stead and Jenn Bishop, two authors whose work I admire and whose friendship I treasure, read and reflected on early manuscripts, and their valuable input doubtlessly saved readers a fair number of headaches; be sure to thank them if you get a chance. I also received critical advice from Adam Solomon, Jim Adams, Jennifer Friedman, Theodore and Ruthann Gill, the Simon/Huber family, and Lauriann Burt, who is the best captive audience ever.

Speaking of Lauriann: Tell your mom I love her.